THE ANCIENT ENEMY RETURNS...

IT WAS IMPOSSIBLE. Chiun had killed the man. Yet he stood before Remo now, blood drooling from his grinning mouth. The professor's eyes had changed. They were totally white, staring at the world with milky malevolence.

The professor now possessed a fully formed *gyonshi* fingernail, which he brandished above his head like a blade. The Master of Sinanju stood with his back to Kovaks, his concern for Remo making him oblivious to the sudden danger.

"Look out, Chiun!" Remo yelled.

Too late. The zombie professor slashed down. His sharp nail pierced the old Korean's spine, severing it at the midpoint. Chiun's mouth dropped open in silent pain. Not a sound escaped his lips as his hazel eyes locked onto those of his adopted son. The Master of Sinanju had never looked so frail to Remo as he did in his dying moment.

The Destroyer #154:
BLOOD BROTHERHOOD

James Mullaney
Series created by
Warren Murphy and Richard Sapir

DESTROYER BOOKS
WARREN MURPHY MEDIA LLC

This is a work of fiction. All the characters and events portrayed in this book are fictional, and any resemblance to real people or real incidents is purely coincidental.

THE DESTROYER #154: Blood Brotherhood

COPYRIGHT © 2021 Warren Murphy Media, LLC

All rights reserved, including the right to reproduce this book or any portion thereof, in any form or in any manner, except for reviews or commentary.

This edition published in 2021 by Destroyer Books/Warren Murphy Media LLC.

ISBN-13: 978-1-955850-31-5

ISBN-10: 1-955850-31-3

Requests for reproduction or interviews should be directed to DestroyerBooks@gmail.com.

Front cover art and ebook edition by Gere Tactical

A NOTE FROM THE AUTHOR ON "LOST" DESTROYERS

About twenty (or was it 200?) years ago, Warren Murphy and I were discussing what could be done to save the *Destroyer* series.

I'd recently left a five-year run on the books, during which I'd produced twenty-one novels. My work was well-received by fans, reviews were great, the books were completely selling out in nine months, and by the end I had dragged the Amazon rankings up to around 120 for each newly released book. To put that last one in perspective, the books at that point were about 119 Amazon spots away from *Harry Potter*. It can't be overstated how remarkable that was for a thirty year old paperback series. The *Destroyer* was back, baby, and the future for Remo and Chiun was bright.

The publisher at the time — being a publisher and thus, also, stupid — had to find a way to torpedo all that, and they managed to do precisely that by opening up the Remo Williams All-You-Can-Eat Calamari Bar and Grill. Remo spent sixteen books punching a squid in the nose, with results predictable to everyone but a baffled publisher.

Warren in his most recent contract had gotten the rights to publish ebook spinoffs, and so he and I were discussing what we might do on the electronic book side of things while the paperback publisher north of the border was using the main series to reenact *A Night to Remember* with tentacles.

One of the ideas we discussed was doing "lost" Destroyers. These would have been stories that took place between the stories we all know. So, for instance, books #20 and #21 would still take place as they always had, but we'd have slipped in between them book #20 1/2 that readers never knew existed. They would have been period pieces, so the references to events and places would have been set back in the nineties, eighties, or even the swingin' seventies. It was a good idea which we never got around to doing. Until now.

This book you're holding is a "lost" Destroyer, although I knew where it was all along. I'd written the first version of *Blood*

Brotherhood many years ago, and it sat on my shelf ever since. I'm not obsessive compulsive, as the dust under my sofa will verify, but I do admit that unfinished business irritates me. I finally got so sick of this book's spine taunting me that I decided enough was enough. So I took it down and rewrote it. Lord, did I ever rewrote it. And here it is. After twenty years. The very first "lost" Destroyer. Don't pin me down on exactly when the story takes place. Let's just say 2002-ish and leave it at that.

There's a second "lost" Remo/Chiun adventure in the pipeline. Same thing. Another book that sat on my shelf for years. That book and this one are the realization of a conversation with Warren from two decades ago. That's a long time, but we got there in the end. Good on us, pardner.

—Jim Mullaney

A NOTE FROM CHIUN ON SCRIBBLERS
WHO SHOULD HAVE REMAINED LOST

When first I saw the name on the cover of this book I assumed my eyes were playing tricks on me. Not the title, which is as terrible as I have come to expect from this so-called "Destroyer" series, but the name of the cretin who was alleged to have written it.

Hastened I to my pupil, Remo Williams, for elucidation.

"Many years ago I asked a simple favor," I said.

"I am *not* setting up a basement love dungeon for you and Barbra Streisand," replied Remo, my son (adopted), who is sometimes nice but is never reliable. "What if we need the furnace worked on? The furnace guy would think we had a horse down there. I don't need PETA kicking down the front door."

"Not that," I said. "More recent than that."

"Same goes for Cheeta Ching, Judge Ruth, or whoever tickles your itch this week."

"You are gross, Remo. No, I asked you to address the trifling matter of a scribbler of words who offended me. You vowed you would take care of it."

"Did I? Someone's always offending you, Little Father. We can't start stacking up all your offenses on the front lawn. It'd look like London during the Black Death."

"So you are saying that this solemn promise you made to me, your father in spirit, to remove this writer creature went unfulfilled, and has joined the lengthy list of every other one of your promises to a kindly old man who never asks for anything?"

"I don't know what the hell you're talking about, but yeah, probably. Now down in front. You're blocking *Get Smart*."

I left Remo to gripe about the smoking hole in the TV screen. That boy is always kvetching about something.

So it turns out that the front cover of this book is accurate. This friend of original scribbler Murphy has returned, no doubt due to a feeling that he had insufficiently libeled the Master during his previous appalling runs on a series that simply refuses to die. I have been assured that this is only a brief visit for a book or two. We will see.

As for this being a "lost" Destroyer, there have been many adventures of the Master and his pupil throughout the years that have gone unrecorded. The simple explanation is that I have deemed you unworthy to hear them. I do not know if this is one that should have been kept secret. I have not yet perused the contents. It is like having a baby with a full diaper. The whiff is sufficiently awful. For the time being the Master chooses not break open the cover and sniff around inside.

If it turns out that this is one of those stories that I did not want to become public, this time it will be I, not Remo, who visits this scribbler. With, naturally, a clothespin on my nose to block out the stench of his talent. Consider yourself warned, defamer.

I am, with moderate tolerance for you,

Chiun.

Chiun,
Reigning Master of Sinanju

PROLOGUE

His spirit was old but it would not permit him to die.

All who had been young when he was a youth had long since turned to dust. They had joyfully gone to dwell with their ancestors. With *his* ancestors. Alas, that was a gift he would never share. For the Leader, the joy of the Final Death was never to be.

His time had long since passed, but his consciousness lived.

It was a waking nightmare, this life of bone and sinew and decaying flesh. It was said by the Creed that death was the only time that his kind truly lived. Life, therefore, was as death to the Creed's adherents. A living death. The one known only as the Leader had suffered a mortal existence longer than any of the others in his cult's long history.

Because of Sinanju.

Sinanju.

The word was like a curse to the Leader. It appeared in tiny print on many maps, but the world did not understand its significance. It belonged to a Korean fishing village, born in the vaguest mists of ancient history.

That lowly village's name meant much more than a collection of peasant huts, tattered fishing nets, and mud streets. The village on the West Korean Bay had deceived the larger world into believing that "Sinanju" was a patch of ground no different from any other. The greater meaning was hidden from prying eyes.

Sinanju was also a discipline, a philosophy, a way of life.

The chief practitioner of the art of Sinanju was called the Master of Sinanju, and he was at once both master of his village and of an esoteric craft.

The Master of Sinanju. It was this Korean master who had damned the Leader.

Sinanju was rich in its history and in its legends. One such legend included the Leader's own Creed. But just as one drop of water could not reveal the ocean from which Sinanju had come, neither could a single legend reveal all of the secrets of the Creed whose history was as old as that of the Masters of Sinanju.

The slitting of the throat.

The release of the life-force.

The stripping of the carcass.

The destruction of the Holy House.

The Final Death.

This was what had propelled the Leader forward in his infirmity. It drove him blindly onward. The Final Death was meant to be one last, massive slaughter of the meat-eaters that would feed his god and his ancestors for eternity in the afterlife.

But he had failed. Sinanju had stopped him.

The Master of Sinanju and his protégé. Years later, he had thought to seek revenge on the Master of Sinanju for the old Korean's role in the failure of the Final Death. It had been a mistake fueled by his decrepit state of mind. The Master of Sinanju and his heir had vanquished the Leader once more. Seemingly forever, or so the Sinanju masters would have thought. Would still think to this day.

Their ignorance of the ancient knowledge of his Creed was the Leader's saving grace. His spirit had persevered. It had found a host. He was reawakened to a new life. And in that rebirth came an epiphany. The words of the old scrolls he had committed to memory in his long-ago youth, only to lose them from his aging mind over the great span of his lifetime, appeared before him as if in a vision.

In that day, the Leader of the ancient Creed will twice fall in battle with the hated enemy. He will yearn to surrender his soul to the other world for the life which follows that of the living death, yet he shall not succumb. Only then shall vengeance be his. Only then shall he succeed. And in that time, the Creed shall be born anew...

Vengeance would be his. So it was foretold, so it would be.

CHAPTER 1

HER SKIN WAS A SPLOTCHY MÉLANGE of off-white and gray. An ugly blend of colors from the last sick winter snowfall as it swirls to slush down a storm drain. Yet she passed into the heart of twenty-first century communist China unmolested.

"This is exciting, isn't it, Ellie?" the woman sitting beside her on the bus insisted. "Well, not to *you*, I suppose. You've been here dozens of times, haven't you? Before now, the farthest I ever got other than Silicon Valley was Vancouver. *Once*."

Ellie McGlone's seatmate had been far too thrilled with what was supposed to be a simple business trip. The two women worked for Ranch Micro Industries, an international company based in San Francisco that produced semiconductor components. Ellie was a cog in motherboard accounting, her chattering workmate Peg was one of three assistants to one of four vice presidents who oversaw the graphics processing units department.

"So *this* is China," Peg Sampson announced.

China at the moment was a smog-choked traffic jam on an eight-lane highway. Previously it had been the airport, a hotel room decked out in plastic communist modern furniture, the RMI microchip factory, and the bus station.

"Isn't it wonderful?" Peg asked Ellie.

At another time in her life Ellie might have asked what was so wonderful about being surrounded by hundreds of unmoving cars in a traffic jam on a highway so thick with the pall of exhaust fumes that one could not see a hundred yards distant. This day, however, was different for Ellie.

The echo of the distant voice was calling to her. For many years she had not understood it. It was finally clear to her now. Or, rather, it was becoming clear.

A thick hand suddenly waved in Ellie's face, snapping pudgy fingers.

"Hello? Ellie? Penny for your thoughts?"

The voice that was always whispering in Ellie's mind these days grew silent. The presence remained, lurking in the back of her consciousness.

"You were far away there, weren't you?" Peg asked, flashing an insincere smile that was the best someone so shallow could manage.

Peg had taken the phrase "ugly American" as a challenge to be vigorously accepted. She wore a pair of too-tight jeans for which Levi's had been forced to add an extra shift in order to supply a sufficient quantity of denim. The mouth of the cartoon cat on her sweatshirt was meant to be grinning, but was stretched into a painful grimace across her chest. A pair of cameras on straps were slung around her bulging neck, and repeatedly smacked the unhappy feline in the face with every bump in the road.

Ellie had told Peg not to bother to bring the cameras, but nobody told Peg what to do. Just as Ellie warned, a Chinese soldier had confiscated her film the minute the women had exited the hotel. Instead of returning the useless cameras to her room, Peg had insisted on bringing them along for what was supposed to be a sightseeing tour.

Peg fondled one of the cameras now.

"I wish that chucklehead hadn't taken all my film. I'd have loved to snap a shot of you just then. You know, Ellie, you're as white as rice, but for a minute as you stared out that window you looked kind of different. Kind of, I don't know, Chinese almost. Weird, huh? Oh, well. Maybe I can pick up some film in the country."

The bus chose that moment to lurch forward, so Peg did not see that her words had given her workmate an involuntary shudder.

"*Finally*," Peg said, turning her wide face forward.

The strange Asian aspect that had passed like a shadow across the blotchy Caucasian face of Ellie McGlone surfaced briefly once more, and the sixty-something Ellie appeared much, much older than her actual age.

Traffic began to slowly move. It thinned considerably over the next half-hour as overworked Chinese citizens who toiled in the nearest sprawling, city-like factories turned off the road and headed for towering black apartment complexes that loomed like titans from a bygone age within the veil of choking smog.

There were many workers crammed onto the bus, yet some instinct within the mass of people forced them from the seats immediately around the two Americans. Peg had assumed politeness, and did not think it strange at all when the other passengers fled the bus as quickly as possible, stepping down in several large clusters at the next few stops. It wasn't long before Ellie and Peg were alone on the bus.

The factory cities and their smog-draped towers soon fell away behind them. A vast slum of rural Chinese poverty opened up ahead.

The bus drove deeper into the wild countryside.

With no bodies but their own to warm the interior, the bus grew cold. The women pulled on the winter coats that they had shoved to the sides of their seats.

There was a time when this sort of unsupervised travel for Western civilians in China was unheard of.

In addition to the more famous Great Wall that was the only manmade object that could be viewed with the naked eye from space, the communist government in Beijing had built a less visible but far more effective wall around the entire country. No one got in or out of China without the permission of the government.

The Great Wall had been built to keep invaders out. This new wall of tanks and trenches, satellites and soldiers, worked both ways. It kept out the world, while also containing within it the teeming mass of more than a billion prisoners who toiled under the watchful gaze of the world's only ascendant communist power.

But times were changing. America was rapidly becoming more reliant on China for everything from cheap box-store merchandise to medicines and electronics. As the business climate changed, the homogeneity of the faces one encountered was no longer the hundred percent it had been even a generation before. And so it was that the white faces of two female tourists were not shocking to the locals even in rural Manchuria, where Ellie and Peg's bus eventually rolled to a rattling stop.

The bus had stopped at the edge of some kind of open air bazaar. To Peg it looked kind of like the flea market that used to set up each weekend in the parking lot of the old Bradlees department store in her hometown of Stratford, New Jersey. Instead of Stratford's folding tables — made in China, of course — the booths here appeared to be assembled from whatever scrap wood the locals could find. Vendors were peddling cheap colorful clothes, cheap plastic items, and dead animals that looked as if they'd been run over on the road and crawled up into the booths to die.

"Oh, I wish I could take a picture," Peg lamented. "Maybe I can buy some film from one of these adorable little rustic kiosks. Oh, dear."

The last words were due to the fact that she had just slipped on a gooey puddle of blood that had run down the side of the nearest booth from something that Peg was pretty sure had been a living animal at one point but which was now a mound of matted fur with a mouthful of fangs and a crushed skull.

Peg scuffed her shoe on the frozen ground in an attempt to scrape the blood off.

"I'm not sure anybody here sells film, Ellie," she observed.

When the only answer she received was the excited chattering from the locals buying and selling items at the pathetic fair, Peg glanced around. She found Ellie already far away from the booths. Peg's workmate was heading across a vacant space of dead winter weeds toward some very dark woods.

"Ellie? Ellie, where are you going?"

Peg looked to some nearby faces for assistance, but found only a gibbering vendor thrusting the bleeding body of the unknown mammal at her.

She looked around for the bus. To her shock, she found that it was driving off without them. A cloud of filthy exhaust rose from the rear of the rusted old rattletrap.

Ellie was the one that had suggested they take that bus. It was Peg's first trip to China. She had happily latched onto the more experienced Ellie and had enlisted her casual workplace acquaintance to be her tour guide. But the guide she had trusted had led her into the middle of nowhere on a bus that had abandoned them, and Peg suddenly realized that she was in a foreign land with no understanding of the local customs, a phrase book left back on the dresser in her hotel room, a dead wombat or something being shoved in her face, and the only person she knew within a hundred miles currently disappearing into a forest that looked like something out of Grimm's Fairy Tales.

"Ellie!" Peg yelled, panic raising her voice above the excited chatter of the outdoor market as she watched her coworker vanish amongst the trees.

Peg abandoned the fair and hurried after her companion.

Some of the locals shouted after the pale, overweight woman as she ran into the thick patch of weeds through which there was no path save the one recently forged by Ellie's determined feet. Peg didn't understand a word of what was being shouted at the back of her heavy coat. Had she spoken Mandarin, she would have stopped dead in her tracks. She would have doubled back to the bumpy road down which Ellie had directed their bus at the very end of their trip. She would have flagged down the first vehicle she found. She would have fled the region in horror and flown back to the United States.

Instead, she ignored the shouting behind her. She found it easy to do since the narrow band of dead weeds at the forest's edge seemed to dull all sounds of the outside world as soon as she passed into it. There was still yelling going on behind her, but it was muffled, like when her ears sometimes clogged up with water in the shower.

As she approached the very first trees even the dulled shouts seemed to get swallowed up by a primordial stillness that smothered all sound.

Peg passed between the blackened trunks of a pair of ancient, gnarled trees and entered a silent, dark forest of such prehistoric menace that it would have frozen the marrow of even the brothers Grimm.

Peg spotted Ellie weaving through some trees fifty yards ahead. She called to her workmate, but the weird dampening of sound kept her voice from traveling.

Peg hurried after Ellie as quickly as she could.

The winter trees had lost their leaves, yet the high gnarled branches intertwined to create a forest canopy that kept the woods in perpetual twilight. Here and there was a break that allowed Peg to glimpse a sickly gray sky.

She began to worry that they would encounter some kind of Chinese military patrol, and feared what they might do. But the deeper she walked, tripping over exposed roots and fallen branches, the more it became evident that the government in Beijing had no interest in this place. Here one would find no tanks or soldiers.

In these woods there were no fences, mines, or motion detectors. No military planes flew overhead to keep watch on this forgotten forest. The sophisticated web created by the communist regime that would have prevented a pair of white American females from wandering off like this anywhere else in the country would have been a comfort to Peg Sampson right now, even if it meant landing them in a Chinese prison.

"Darn you, Ellie, stop!" Peg shouted.

She had kept a keen eye on her workmate ever since they had entered the forest. She had no idea what Ellie thought she was doing, but at least she hadn't lost sight of her companion. Ellie was always the same distance ahead, and seemed to walk with much more confidence than she should have in what had to be an unfamiliar place.

After only a few minutes, Peg had resolved to turn around and go back to the outdoor market. Unfortunately when she glanced back she realized that she was already hopelessly lost. She thought of fairy tales and bread crumbs, and how frightening those old stories from her childhood suddenly were. The only thing she could think to do was stick with Ellie and hope that the peasants would alert the authorities about the two foreign women who'd been foolish enough to wander into the forest alone.

One thing was certain. When she at last caught up to Ellie, Peg was going to give her crazy workmate a piece of her mind.

Peg Sampson turned up the collar of her coat and pulled the zipper up as high as it would go in a vain attempt to ward off the cold. Panting at the exertion, she hurried as fast as her stumbling, bumbling legs would permit after Ellie McGlone.

The forest had called to Ellie McGlone.

Somehow the siren song of the ancient twisted trees seemed to have always been flickering at the sleeping edge of her conscious mind.

How could she know about this place? How could such an alien environment possibly be so familiar to her?

Ellie strode through the great forest in the heart of Manchuria as if she were returning home, for that was precisely what she was doing.

It was cold. Fortunately no heavy wind could force its way through the thick old growth forest. Even so, the slight breeze that curled between the huge black trees created knives of ice that sliced through her parka. It was Ellie who felt the cold, but the thing that coiled like a serpent within her commanded his vessel to ignore it.

It was fate that kept her body alive.

Enough of Ellie remained inside her own brain that she could still be surprised by the fact that though she had never set foot in these woods before, she found the place nearly exactly as she remembered it. A thought impossible to reconcile. Dual thoughts competing for a single mind. A split personality.

"Ellie! Stop, Ellie!"

The pleading shout came from behind her.

Peg Sampson had followed Ellie into the woods. The woman was irritating, but it was good that she had insisted on attaching herself to Ellie. The assistant to the vice president of graphics processing at Ranch Micro Industries would come in handy.

The path before Ellie was exactly as it should be, barely discernable to strangers, threading nearly invisibly through the great wood. When she turned here, there was a rock she had seen before in many dreams. Over there was a towering, hundred year-old tree that the visions remembered as barely more than a sapling. Yet it was all familiar. Even the sweet, rotting metallic scent on the wind.

She walked on, impervious to the cold that sunk deep beneath her flesh or to the panting shouts that came from behind.

The visions that had nudged her along a heretofore unseen path in life, the same visions that had ultimately brought her to this place, had lurked just beyond conscious thought for years. Ever since that time back in New York. That awful, evil time when everyone she had worked with had either died or vanished. She was the sole survivor.

Ellie had tried to piece her life back together. It had taken many years to do so. The psychiatrists she'd seen had different names for it. Mostly it was attributed to PTSD and survivor's guilt. One doctor to whom she had been a little too forthcoming had suggested Ellie might be schizophrenic, and had wanted to have her committed.

Ellie always knew she wasn't crazy. The thoughts were real. The person who shared a corner of her mind existed, just not corporeally. Not yet.

He would come to her at night, whispering in her ear. She should have felt fear when she first experienced the dream, but he had prepared her for it.

She dreamed of a body. The psychiatrist who wanted to have her institutionalized had told her this was perfectly normal.

"It's a dead body," Ellie had said during their first session after her waking mind had finally been able to grab hold of and bring into waking memory the inchoate thought that had for weeks been flitting through her sleeping mind.

"That makes sense," Dr. Klein said, in his irritating soothing voice. "You experienced a great trauma. Tell me about the body."

"It's there every night," Ellie said. "It doesn't do anything. It just hangs there, like a side of beef in a slaughterhouse."

"What else can you remember?"

"There isn't anything else to remember. Nothing else happened in the dream. It's just the body. It just hangs there, all night long."

She saw it so frequently that she had it memorized every square inch of it.

"The abdomen is split open from the sternum down to the pubic bone. The organs are scooped out of the stomach and chest cavity. The carcass is stripped of skin, and the organs are tied up like my mother used to wrap Christmas presents. But it's wrapping paper of human flesh. The bundled-up organs are on the ground just below the dangling toes of the corpse that's suspended above it. The body is dripping blood. It's like from a leaky faucet. It sort of trickles from the end of one big toe onto that flesh bundle that's knotted up on the ground underneath the body."

Doctor Klein had tried not to show it, but he'd been rattled by not only the vivid description, but by the dispassion with which his patient had delivered the information.

What Ellie hadn't mentioned was that the corpse had a name: Ruth Angus.

The dream was no simple nightmare. The body was real. Ellie had dreamed of a real person who had died in a very real, very gruesome way. She didn't know how she knew it to be true. She had never heard of anyone by that name in her life. But she was certain that this dream individual had existed at one time in the real world.

This nightly image persisted in her dreams, joined by others. Many more faces, many more disemboweled bodies, stretching back years, centuries.

When psychiatry, psychology, hypno- and regression-therapy failed to explain her dreams, she'd turned to the spiritual realm. When organized religion offered no hope, she tried New Age solutions. When purifying incense, magic crystals, astral projecting and magic mushrooms failed her, she finally embraced the recurring dreams of an army of dangling murdered corpses as a normal part of her life.

On the day she accepted the normalcy of the dead who visited her nightly, the dreams changed.

Ellie wasn't sure at first what she had seen. It seemed to be someone speaking inside her head, as if she was wired up like some kind of ham radio.

One of the hanging corpses she'd come to know by name had been dangling in front of her. The voice spoke from behind the body's eyes. There was something soothing about it, as if it belonged to an old friend who'd been there all along and was at last making its presence known. A man stepped out from behind the body.

The difference was so abrupt that she awoke, startled.

And in the long midnight shadows of her bedroom, the same man stood.

He was a shrunken figure, seemingly as old as time itself. His eyes were an opaque film of white. His skin was a weathered yellowish-brown that appeared as dry as dust from years of exposure to harsh weather. It looked as if a stiff breeze would blow the frail skin away, leaving nothing behind but a shrunken skeleton.

His robes were a brilliant purple. When he raised his arms like a magician preparing for a trick, the sleeves rolled back to reveal two dark caverns that appeared to burrow deep into the apparition's black soul.

The ancient man pointed at her with a slender, accusing finger. The nail was long and gleamed in the amber glow of the streetlight outside her bedroom window. When he spoke, the words were in a foreign tongue yet somehow deep in her mind she understood.

"You have imprisoned me, woman."

"Um…excuse me?" Ellie asked.

She had no previous experience talking to dreams that had somehow managed to manifest in the real world, so she wasn't sure what the polite thing was to say.

"What is the year?" the vision demanded.

Ellie told him. The blind old man's weathered face puckered unhappily.

"Much time has been wasted since Three-G."

Ellie's thoughts raced back to a time years before when she and her coworkers had been infected with some kind of toxin. She'd been working at Three-G, Incorporated at the time, which had become infamous due to a series of murders. As the lone survivor, her alleged PTSD had been assumed to be the cause of her dreams. Yet this was not a dream. Her mind was clear. Down the street, a horn honked. Somewhere a dog was barking. And here in the bedroom of her apartment stood an old man who her waking brain had forgotten, but who she now remembered from that terrible time years before.

This couldn't be the same old man. He had died back then. And even if he'd survived, he would surely have succumbed to old age by now.

The old man leaned close to Ellie, who had sat up in her bed. The man's face drew inches away from hers. If he was a hallucination, it was a good one. She could smell his hot, reeking breath. The wrinkled lids of his fierce eyes blinked over sightless white orbs.

Ellie closed her eyes. Despite the fact that she screwed her eyes tight, she could still see the old man standing before her. And now she saw even more. Behind the vision, one of the rotting corpses from her dreams hung from a lone tree that stood in a vast limitless plain of desolate gray.

She opened her eyes. The hanging corpse vanished, but the old man remained. He was pointing at her chest. For the first time she noticed how wickedly sharp and long was the curving nail of his index finger. At its tip glistened a fresh drop of blood. The droplet dropped off the razor-sharp end of the fingernail.

"You will assist me," the old man insisted.

Ellie blinked her eyes, and swallowed. When she opened her eyes once more, the vision of the old man was gone. She felt something crawling around the back of her skull, like a lazy cat settling into a warm spot to nap.

Ellie snaked out a hand to the lamp on her nightstand. When the light came on, she found a single dot of red staining a spot on her white quilt. The lounging cat in the back of her brain stirred. Ellie smiled.

"I will do all that you wish, my Leader."

Unlocked from the prison that free will had placed on her mind, the vision was unbound from that night forward. As it gathered strength, the length of its visitations grew. It expanded beyond night and into her waking hours. Eventually it was as if she had a partner sharing all her thoughts. Ellie didn't even know when the image had taken complete control, she only knew that by the time she found herself walking through the familiar

Manchurian forest she was a spectator to the events of her own life.

Ellie saw a bend in the narrow path at the top of a small hillock. A cluster of boulders marked a fork in the narrow lane. In the pit of her stomach she felt a stir of recognition that was not her own. It was not far now.

"Ellie, slow down!" a desperate voice called behind her.

Ellie hurried up the slight incline, taking the left fork. Her nose drew in scents of a youth that was not her own, her eyes welcomed sights that should not be familiar, but somehow were. She raced down the hill.

At the base of the far side of the knoll she followed the path where it ran parallel to a partially frozen brook. She hurried across a stone bridge that was worn smooth with years of foot traffic. It was just ahead. The City of the Dead. She was returning home to a place she had never before set eyes on.

Cold air tore at her lungs. Tree branches lashed her face.

She ran into a clearing and nearly collided with a shocked woman carrying a basket made of reeds and filled with laundry washed in the stream. The washerwoman's gaunt, pasty face was not alone.

There were many more people in the vast clearing. There were huts, fires, pots for cooking. The faces were familiar in general appearance, although none belonged to anyone she had ever met. How could she know any of them after so many years?

It was a peasant village, but no settlement belonged here.

Many faces similar to the pale, emaciated washerwoman's glanced over from around the clearing.

They moved in quickly on gliding feet invisible beneath the hems of their long black robes. Like pack animals, they formed a circle around the white intruder.

Their eyes were black and dead. The skin of their faces was drawn thin over the protruding bones of their cheeks. All were dressed in the same black robes. Not one — male or female, young or old — wore another color.

"Welcome to the Forest of the Dead, wanderer," one man, taller than the rest, intoned in a language that was not Standard Chinese, nor Mandarin, Mongolian, Tibetan, Uyghur or any of the hundreds of other languages spoken throughout the country, "where you will soon crave the end of life, and the joyful beginning of death."

The language was music to the ancient soul within Ellie McGlone. The pale American woman's reply shocked the faces around the encampment.

"You shame your birthright living in squalor amongst the rotting trees," she replied in the same language. "This shanty village disgraces your ancestors, for it is not the gloriously decadent home of long ago. It is not the City of the Dead."

The thing that would not die, and which only out of necessity wore the skin and bones of Ellie McGlone, pointed beyond the simple huts and smoking fires of the makeshift village. Her confident finger extended to the nearby trees, to a place in the even darker depths of the forest through which she'd just traveled.

"That is the true ancient City of the Dead," Ellie said, "which your ancestors left when their Leader left on his quest to execute the Final Death years ago. It is the lost city, the city of pain and beautiful pestilence; the city to which you have all sworn an oath in blood never to return to until the old one either succeeded in his mission or returned."

At the words of the stranger, spoken in their own ancient tongue, the displaced villagers felt a stirring in their icy blood. But it was not the words that transfixed the skeletal faces of the men and women of the Forest of the Dead.

Although the intruder still pointed in the direction of the ancient city, no eyes looked in that direction. All stared at the stranger's hand.

The extended index finger of the right hand ended in a long, sharpened fingernail. It was cut at an angle like a guillotine blade, and polished to a great luster.

The fingernail was identical to the single deadly fingernails on the hands of every villager who surrounded their guest, and at once all in the clearing understood.

As one, the villagers dropped to their knees.

"With my return you will reclaim your birthright," Ellie McGlone proclaimed.

She commanded the tallest villager, the man who had first greeted her, to rise.

"You will be the honored vessel. The time our ancestors foretold is come."

Ellie stretched her arms out wide. A fine orange mist began to seep from every pore of Ellie McGlone. She was quickly consumed by a vaporous cloud that obscured her features and left her a shuddering, amorphous shadow encased in orange fog.

The swirling fog collected into a tight ball, and when the force that had been animating Ellie McGlone for years rose above her head, the body of the girl, who had been long dead without realizing it, collapsed like a puppet whose strings had been cut.

The life force did not wait for its previous host to hit the ground. Even while Ellie's lifeless body was falling, the orange ball of energy rocketed from the cold air and exploded with cannon force against the chest of the chosen villager.

The man jolted at the impact, but remained on his feet.

When the chosen one opened his eyes, the dead black orbs of the villagers had transformed. His eyes were now a milky, sightless white. Although blind once more, the animating source of energy that lived within the dead man's body smiled. His ears still functioned perfectly well, and he heard the stumbling footfalls emanating from the forest.

There was a great crunching and snapping of brittle branches, and a familiar voice, desperately out of breath, intruded on the momentous scene.

"Ellie? Who are you people? Have you seen...? *Ellie!* Oh, my God! What have you done to her?"

The blind man could not see Peg Sampson, but his thrilled senses were attuned to the song of the air and the trees and the dirt of his ancient home. He could not see a thing, but he could hear the blood pounding in Peg's heart; coursing through her veins.

When he pointed his finger with the guillotine nail, he knew it was aimed at the computer company secretary's panicked, heaving chest.

"Feed on that one, and grow strong," said the Leader. "For the time of death is here, and supreme sustenance will come in the slaughter of our greatest enemy."

The screams of Peg Sampson would have sent birds flying from the treetops in the ancient forest, if not for the fact that nothing warm blooded lived there.

A moment later, that included the late Peg Sampson.

CHAPTER 2

HIS NAME WAS REMO and he was a sucker for the classics.

"Are you sure it's heavy enough?" Remo asked. "I don't want to tell you how to do your job or anything, but you want to make sure it's heavy enough to pull me all the way to the bottom, plus keep me there. How would it look on your curriculum vitae if one of your victims bobs to the surface in front of a Coast Guard cutter?"

Remo's concerned words were directed at the sweating bald patch on the back of one of the three heads that belonged to the trio of men who were currently fussing around the stainless steel tub in which they'd sunk Remo's feet.

"Clam up, youse," Bald Patch replied.

Bald Patch and his friends — whom Remo had dubbed Unibrow and Imminent Heart Attack, respectively — continued to inspect the contents of the steel tub.

The men had picked up the stainless steel container from a local Lowe's, along with several sacks of quick-drying cement. Remo had no idea how they'd managed that feat without setting off alarm bells for every clerk in the store. Their beady, twitching eyes, perpetual five o'clock shadow, ill-fitting suits, and gangster patois straight out of a 1930s Jimmy Cagney movie should have screamed ill intent as soon as they dropped the bags of cement down in front of the garden center cashier. Yet here they all were, three miles off the coast of Rhode Island, and not a cop in sight.

When Remo got back to shore he intended to write a stern letter of complaint to Lowe's on the poor observational skills of their employees.

"Dis seems hard enough," Imminent Heart Attack observed. He had a set of car keys in his hairy hand and was tapping at the solid cement.

When they'd been discussing how to rid themselves of the skinny snoop in the black T-shirt and chinos who'd interrupted their perfectly innocent illegal drug inventory back on shore, it was their captive who had suggested the cement.

"Concrete galoshes," Remo insisted, with a knowing wink. "It's got a long and storied history with you people. Not to mention it gets us away from prying eyes."

Remo decided that the suggestible trio couldn't have scraped up a single brain cell between them, since they had quickly embraced their victim's suggestion of the traditional, if clichéd, form of execution. The hundred pounds of dried concrete currently around Remo's ankles was supposed to drag him to the ocean floor. At least that was what the mobsters said. But who could trust mobsters these days?

"I'm still not sure it's heavy enough," Remo said.

The salty wind tousled his short brown hair. The November air chilled the Mafia men to the bone, yet Remo appeared unaffected by the late autumn cold.

When the three men looked up at him, their victim was glancing down with an expression of deep concern.

"Didn't Joey here tell youse to shut your trap?" Unibrow snarled.

"Yes, but I let his rudeness slide because he appears to be under a great deal of pressure," Remo said. "Possibly pulmonary."

"Zip it, faggot," Imminent Heart Attack snapped.

Remo shrugged a "just trying to be helpful" shrug and stared out at the nearly complete blackness of sea and sky. The night was moonless and starless. It was a night seemingly designed for Remo's purpose, although his skills were such that he could have performed his assignment in broad daylight in Times Square without attracting attention.

Remo was an assassin. He was, in point of fact, one of the two premier assassins on the planet. He was currently in the secret employ of the United States government, even though his boss wasn't terribly happy with his job performance. In fact, Remo had been sent to Rhode Island to right a recent wrong.

A few months back, Remo had been dispatched to the Ocean State to convince a member of the Patriccone crime syndicate to turn state's evidence against his brutish capo, Don Raymond Patriccone. Unfortunately, in a *Prince and the Pauper*-like mix-up that still embarrassed Remo, he had recruited the wrong man.

"How was I supposed to tell the difference between Pauley 'Cadillac' Petricco and Pauley 'Lincoln' Patracci?" Remo groused when his screw-up was discovered. "These mooks should have to wear numbered jerseys so the fans can tell them apart."

It turned out the Mafia thug he'd surreptitiously slipped into FBI custody had known very little of the crime family's business. To add insult to injury, two days ago the man had fallen victim to a barrage of bullets en route to a Providence courthouse.

It had originally been the wish of Remo's employer to use the court system to go after the Patriccone Family, but it seemed that the Rhode Island Mob was still too powerful to just sit back and let normal justice handle things. Remo's boss had decided that it would take a little pruning of the crime family's ranks before it would be weak enough to attack through legal channels.

This hope of thinning the herd was why Remo had returned to Rhode Island, and why he was currently on a borrowed fishing boat that was slowly chugging around the dark waters of the Atlantic.

The group of three Patriccone foot soldiers waited impatiently on the deck around him, their hair blowing wildly in the cold, post-midnight wind.

"Guy might got a point," Unibrow reluctantly admitted.

"You listenin' to this asshole now?" Imminent Heart Attack asked.

Unibrow silenced his partner in crime with an angry raised palm.

"How much you weigh?" Unibrow asked Remo.

"How much I weigh what?" Remo replied. "Myself? Not often. I don't really have to, since my weight hasn't changed an ounce in years."

"Forget him," Bald Spot said. "Dis is more than heavy enough. When he goes down, he ain't comin' back up."

Bald Spot's joints creaked in protest as he stood up. His two companions made similar Rice Krispies rackets on their huffing way to their feet.

"Care to place a wager on that?" Remo asked.

"Yeah, right," Bald Spot mocked. "I don't know what you thought you was doin' at that warehouse, spoutin' that bullshit about workin' with the Feds or whatever. But you ain't coming back up. That's 'cause you's an amateur, and we is pros."

"Exactly when did your high school English teacher commit suicide?" Remo asked. "As for who around here is the amateur and who is a professional, I joined the pro circuit a long time ago."

The three gangsters snorted amusement. It was as much for the stupid arrogance of such a boast under these circumstances as it was for their skinny captive's bravado. He was going to die and yet their victim was acting like this was some big game.

"A pro don't allow a bunch of wiseguys to get the drop on him," Imminent Heart Attack pointed out.

"Says who?" Remo asked. "You? You three assholes aren't pros. You're jokes. Real pros like me don't get ourselves killed like you're all about to."

Unibrow smiled. Stained yellow teeth flashed in a fat face of dark stubble.

"And yet we mixed the cement you is ankle deep in, didn't we?"

"So what? Professional masons do that every day," Remo said. "We're talking killers here. You three clowns may have killed, but so does a kid stepping on an ant. Although that analogy doesn't quite hold up, because in this scenario you are the ants."

Unibrow looked to his companions.

"He's kiddin', right?"

Bald Spot and Imminent Heart Attack were no longer interested.

Up front in the cabin, the fourth member of their group had just cut the motor. The hitherto steady engine rumble spluttered to silence. Suddenly the only sound was that of the waves lapping against the sides of the rocking fishing boat.

Before they'd left shore, the thugs had ordered Remo to cart a wooden chair from the office of the drug warehouse. They had lashed him to the chair before sticking his loafers in the gooey fast-drying cement. Now that the boat was stopped, two of the thugs cut the ropes and grabbed Remo by the arms. They hauled him up from the chair.

Imminent Heart Attack kicked the chair away. The three men got back down on their hands and knees and, by aid of grunts and curses, began nudging the cement-filled tub to a gap in the railing. The mafioso who'd piloted the ship — a squat, surly-faced killer who Remo had dubbed Captain Schnook — came aft to assist the others.

"I hope I didn't hurt your feelings calling you a bunch of cement mixers," Remo said as the quartet inched him to his watery grave.

"Hey, no sweat," Bald Patch grunted. "It don't hurt us half as much as we's about to hurt you."

"Be that as it may, I'm sorry," Remo told them. "No one should leave this life feeling like he's a failure. It's just that where I'm from, being a killer means a little more than tearing open a bag and figuring out how much water to add."

"Yeah," Imminent Heart Attack huffed, "and where's that?"

Remo smiled wistfully. "Ah, now that's a subtly complex question. "The short answer is Newark. Originally, that is."

This brought a spark of interest from the group. Back at the Patriccone-owned warehouse where this nutjob had marched out from behind some crates while the four men were counting cocaine bundles and announced he was there to kill them, their victim had remained weirdly silent as they'd pulled out their guns.

They had attempted to knock him around to get some useful information out of him, but the weirdo's body seemed somehow able to accept their blows without injury. Punching him was like punching a feather pillow.

When they'd attempted to tie him up inside the warehouse, he had broken every cord they'd used to bind his abnormally thick wrists. Only once they'd set him in the chair on the deck of the fishing boat were they able to successfully tie his hands behind him, and even then they had a feeling it was only because he'd permitted them to do so.

There was something definitely off about the stranger. Now he was admitting he was from Newark. Maybe only to buy time. But the big boss would be pissed if they didn't find out everything they could. Ten feet from the edge of the deck, they stopped shoving the cement-filled container.

"Don Viscotti send you up here?" Bald Spot demanded, sweating and panting. He knelt on the deck as he attempted to get his second wind.

"Who?" Remo asked.

"Don Viscotti. He owns Newark. He send you here?"

"Ah, you misunderstand," Remo said "I only grew up in Newark. That was a million years ago. I don't have any Mafia connections. Unless you count all the greaseballs like you I've killed over the years."

There was laughter from the gathered mobsters, but this time it had an uneasy edge. There was something about the icy certainly of their prisoner's tone, which was far colder than the salty spray coming off the Atlantic.

"You kill anybody I know?" Bald Spot asked.

"Does the name Don Scubisci ring a bell?" Remo asked, smiling coldly.

There was no more laughter from the group. Cold mist sprayed on the deeply shadowed faces of the men arranged around Remo on the fishing boat's deck.

"You. You're sayin' *you* kacked old Don Scubisci?" Unibrow asked.

"You bet," Remo said, smiling.

"What's he talkin' about?" asked Captain Schnook, who was late to the party. He glanced around at his companions for elucidation.

Unibrow, Imminent Heart Attack, and Bald Spot were all staring at Remo.

"Oh, there was Scambia, too," Remo said. "You might have heard of that."

"The summit?" Bald Spot asked, clearly dubious of the claim.

The Scambia Mafia summit was legendary in the underworld community. Dozens of Mob leaders from around the world had been slaughtered on that African island. It had taken ages to recover from that bloody day.

"That was years ago," Bald Spot said. "You ain't much more than thirty."

"Clean living," Remo said. While the others were squinting against the mist, his deepset eyes were open wide, seemingly staring off into depths of time and space that only he could see. "I try to get at least eight hours sleep between knocking off bastards like you. I can't say it hasn't been gratifying. See a scumbag, knock off said scumbag. Wash, rinse, repeat. I confess it'd be nicer if there wasn't always another one springing up to take the last one's place. It's like pulling up dandelions with you guys."

The nervous men had heard enough. There was something about the stranger's tone; as if he believed every one of his own crazy words. The four goons resumed nudging Remo's heavy cement bucket to the edge of the deck.

"Take your boss Don Patriccone for instance," Remo said, as he was inched ever closer to his looming burial at sea. "The Mob is dying all around the country and he's still chugging along like it's the bootlegger days. He's like that bunny in the battery ad. He just keeps going and going."

"If you was thinkin' you was stoppin' Don Patriccone, you failed." Bald Spot puffed, not even looking up at their victim.

"Oh, I'll stop him," Remo assured the group with cold and absolute certainty. "It's just a matter of time."

"Are you some kinda psycho?" Imminent Heart Attack asked. He mopped at the heavy sweat on his forehead with the dangling end of his tie. "In case you hasn't noticed, you is standing in a tub of cement about to get tossed in the ocean."

"About that," Remo said, crossing his arms. "I guess you're all just softies for the traditional. You jumped right on this when I suggested it. I happen to know all about tradition. I was trained as an assassin by a man who believes in tradition more than anything else."

"Assassin? You? Maybe he should've been more worried about making sure you didn't get your dumb ass killed."

All the men on the deck joined in the laughter. All but Remo.

"That's part of the tradition," Remo explained. "Masters of Sinanju don't get killed. At least not by ordinary jerks like you. It's kind of a family legacy."

"Masters of whatsit?" Bald Spot asked.

"Sinanju," Remo said. "The greatest assassins in the history of mankind. The man who trained me is one, too. Except lately he's more of a Master of Kvetching. There was a news report on one of those honor killings you hear about sometimes. I made the mistake of saying that I didn't think there was anything honorable about killing. I might as well have lit a stick of dynamite and shoved it down my pants."

The fishing boat continued to bob on the black waves. The ambient light of a full moon hidden somewhere behind swollen clouds revealed few whitecaps.

The lights from Newport had long ago faded into the suffocating blackness of Rhode Island Sound. Remo stared in the direction of the shore, as if dreading a return to dry land. Bald Spot saw the look on their prisoner's face and shook his head. Crazy as a goddamn loon.

The men had dragged Remo and the tub of concrete in which he was planted to the edge of the deck. Sweating and cursing, they hefted him up over a final lip of damp wood at the gap in the rail.

"Nothing is ever easy for me," Remo groused.

"You got that right," Bald Spot agreed.

The men shoved once, hard. Cement bucket and all, Remo toppled into the cold Atlantic swells, disappearing with a mighty splash beneath the waves. The sea closed in and swallowed up the crazy man who claimed to be some kind of assassin.

"Good riddance to weirdo rubbish," Bald Spot huffed. He yanked out a handkerchief and dragged it across the greasy sweat that was rolling down his face.

Captain Schnook returned to the cabin and restarted the engine. High above, the clouds suddenly parted, bathing the scene in the brilliant white of a full moon.

Steering in a wide arc, the fishing boat retraced its route. The chugging engine drowned out the sound of the bobbing waves as the boat began the long journey back to shore.

The instant he dropped below the waves Remo saw why the Mob had an affinity for this particular method of execution.

The combined weight of cement and metal pan was more than half that of his body. The heavy mass at his ankles sliced through the increasingly cold water, dragging him remorselessly to the bottom of the sea.

Most men in the same situation would not have been able to keep from drowning. Panic was the first instinct of man; death the inevitable outcome.

Most men, however, were not Remo.

As the tub of cement worked its foul purpose, Remo reached calmly down between his calves. He tapped one index finger against the hard cement.

Once, twice.

Once, twice, three times.

Then back to once, twice. His finger became a miniature jackhammer, repeating the same one-two, one-two-three pattern until he could feel the vibrations from the cement being conducted through the water that whizzed by his ears.

Fissures erupted in the grainy cement like spider-web cracks in a pane of glass. One downward thrust of his knuckles and the cement shattered into a thousand pieces.

As he kicked the jagged remnants of cement away, Remo's only regret was the loss of his hand-stitched Italian loafers that spiraled along with bucket and debris toward the black infinity of the ocean floor. He only had one other pair of identical shoes in his closet. He'd have to remember to order another dozen when he got back home.

Remo gave a few sharp kicks that launched him like a fired torpedo through the gloom and back up to the moonlit surface. Instinct propelled him in the direction of the turbulent water that was being churned up in the fishing boat's wake.

The boat had already completed its arc and was heading back toward the Rhode Island shore. Remo shot in behind the fishing boat.

He found a rust-encrusted bolt that was too small for anyone to grab onto. Remo latched onto the bolt with fingertips more secure than any wrench. Going limp, he allowed the boat to drag him like an empty net in its wake. The boat continued to shore, the dead man who'd been left at the ocean's bottom latched like a remora to its stern.

There was no need to worry about oxygen. Remo could go for hours underwater with the air he currently carried in his lungs.

Remo brought his free hand up to the side of the boat. In it he clutched a single sharp chunk of cement that he'd salvaged from his cement overshoes.

He was disappointed that he couldn't whistle underwater. He had to settle for humming "Whistle While You Work" as he jammed the savagely sharp tip of the cement shard into the side of the boat and began carving a foot-long hole.

The four would-be murderers of the Patriccone crime family didn't realize their boat was taking on water until it suddenly began listing heavily to one side.

"What the hell is going on?" Bald Spot demanded. Like the others, he found himself grabbing onto whatever was nearby to keep from pitching over the side.

Imminent Heart Attack was nearest, and managed to climb the crooked stairs into the hold. He lurched back up a moment later, his trousers soaked to the knees.

"We's sinking!" Imminent Heart Attack cried.

There was momentary panic as the men attempted to assess their situation.

The shore was still too far away. They'd never make it before the boat flipped over and sank. Luckily Bald Spot, who was a landlubber at heart, had made sure before they'd left the dock that there was a lifeboat. Except when he grabbed onto a railing and spun around in the direction where he'd last seen it, he discovered it was gone.

"Where the hell is the goddamn lifeboat?" Bald Spot demanded.

"What're lookin' at me for?" Unibrow asked. "I ain't took it."

"You's closest to where it was. You shoulda kept a eye on it!"

"Quiet! Quiet!" Imminent Heart Attack hoarsely whispered. He'd gone unhealthily pale. "Do you hear that?"

All three men strained their ears. A voice that belonged to none of the three men on deck, nor their compatriot Captain Schnook who was still desperately attempting to pilot the listing boat to shore, rose ominously over the sound of the engine.

"Dah-dum, dah-dum."

"Where's that comin' from?" Bald Spot hissed.

The sound came again.

"Dah-dum, dah-dum."

It was quiet, menacing. It was the opening of the theme to *Jaws*.

"Dum-dum-dum-dum-dum-dum-dum-dum, ba-da-dum!"

A figure broke through the waves on the sagging port side of the boat.

A man-eating shark would have been a far more welcome guest than the owner of the cruel, deepset eyes and the even crueler smile who rose in the air like a playful dolphin.

At the apex of his jump, something launched from the man's fingertips. The chunk of cement rocketed into the forehead of Unibrow, taking off most of the top of his head and turning his brains to chum. Unibrow collapsed, dead. His body struck the listing deck and he slid rapidly through the railing and splashed into the Atlantic.

"Dah-dum, dah-dum!"

Somehow the voice had already migrated to the opposite side of the boat.

"Shit!" Bald Spot said. He repeated the curse an instant later when the engine abruptly spluttered and died. The sea grew ominously quiet.

The lights of Sakonnet Point had not yet faded up out of the gloomy Atlantic night. They were still far from shore.

Bald Spot yanked his automatic from under his armpit. Beside him, Imminent Heart Attack was a panicked lost cause.

Imminent Heart Attack's already pasty face had grown ghastly white and was painted in a glistening sheen of sweat. His breath was ragged, launching clouds of irregular steam into the cold night air.

Captain Schnook made an appearance on the deck, hustling as

best he could and clinging to the railing as he hurried toward the others.

"What the hell is going on —" the boat's pilot began.

He was cut off by the sudden appearance of the intruder whose advice for a burial at sea Bald Spot now fervently wished he'd ignored.

"Chips Ahoy!" Remo announced, grabbing Captain Schnook by the ankle and yanking him overboard.

Bald Spot managed to get off one shot. Unfortunately he was pretty sure he only managed to land a round in Captain Schnook's chest. Either way, his vanishing companion was almost certainly dead the minute he hit the water.

"Keep your eyes peeled," Bald Spot ordered Imminent Heart Attack.

But the other man had dropped to his knees and was clutching his chest. By the time Bald Spot became aware of a soaking wet figure standing immediately behind him, Imminent Heart Attack's heart attack was no longer imminent.

"I called that one perfectly," Remo said, as the kneeling man's heart gave one final, feeble beat before stopping forever.

Imminent Heart Attack flopped face-first to the deck, as dead as a mackerel.

Bald Spot wheeled around and attempted to aim his gun at Remo's head. Except somehow the gun wasn't pointed where it was supposed to be pointed. He'd fired the weapon at several men in his life as hired muscle working for the Patriccone crime syndicate, and each time the dark end of the barrel had been aimed at the target. This time the black eternity of the barrel was pointed squarely between his own eyes.

Bald Spot wished his brain hadn't already ordered his finger to squeeze the trigger. Sadly for him, the command had been given.

The last living thing he saw on earth was the stranger's eyes. He'd never seen someone with eyes like that. It was as if the eyes were set into a living skull.

And then there was a very bright flash, followed by a very, very black, burning void in which existed only an infinity of torment and regret.

Remo waited for the boat to lurch heavily to one side, then lift impossibly high in the air before sinking rapidly beneath the waves. The lights on the deck shuddered beneath the inky depths as the boat sank, then winked out.

Treading water, Remo surveyed the scene with approval. A couple of bodies bobbed to the surface. He recognized Bald Spot and Imminent Heart Attack. Maybe they'd be swept out to sea, maybe they'd wash up on shore. Either way the message was sent. There had been payback for the murder of an informant. The Patriccone syndicate wasn't as strong as it or the rest of the criminal world imagined.

Remo could not enjoy the satisfaction of a job well done. The easiest part of his night was dealing with a bunch of mobsters. The really tough work was going home.

He wished fervently that another ten boatloads of Mafia goons armed with machine guns and flamethrowers would decide to sail out in front of him and extend this happy time away from hearth and home, but the freezing ocean waters remained calm. No such luck.

Cursing the unreliability of organized crime killers, Remo began swimming swiftly in the direction of the invisible Rhode Island shoreline.

CHAPTER 3

THE PLAGUES OF OLD ARRIVED IN THE NEW WORLD aboard wooden ships. Immigrants and sailors. Pets, rats, and farm animals. Fleas hidden away in paupers' rags and in the fine linens of men and women of means. All carried deadly diseases.

The latest plague to arrive in America was unwittingly brought into New York City by a pair of American brothers who had spent the better part of the most boring afternoon of their lives sprawled on the worn plastic seats in the lobby of the North American Air Terminal at New York's John F. Kennedy International Airport.

Elliot and Peter Lindstrom had long ago worn out conversation. Worn as well were their wristwatches, cell phones, and eyes as they continuously checked the time. The more they checked, the slower time seemed to pass. At one point Elliot swore he saw the second hand on his Junghans Meister Telemeter wristwatch tick backwards, an optical illusion he shared with his brother.

"Maybe you should go for ophthalmology," Elliot suggested, exhaling boredom as he flopped the arm with his watch to the seat between them. "You can operate on the cataracts I'm going to have by the time we shuffle out of here."

"I don't think so," Peter said. "I'm thinking podiatry now."

His brother sat up straight in his chair for the first time since he went to track down a vending machine for some candy bars an hour ago.

"Really? Feet? You know pop will kill you, don't you?"

"I bet their malpractice insurance is lower than anybody's," Peter said. "What can you screw up about feet? They're just feet. You spend a day on corns and ingrown toenails, and you're out of the office by five. And every weekend is free. Whoever heard of anybody ever having a foot emergency?"

"I don't think that's true," Elliot said.

"No, probably not," Peter admitted with a shrug, "but can you imagine the look on pop's face when I tell him I'm going into feet?"

Both boys chuckled. Not as much, however, as they might have had they not wasted the entire afternoon hanging out in a drafty airport terminal.

The two young Lindstrom brothers were students at New York's Columbus University in the Morningside Heights section of Manhattan. Elliot was a junior with an eye on a law career, his brother Peter was a freshman who had started classes that fall. At the moment, Peter was leaning toward medical school, but nothing was certain.

Almost nothing.

Their father would murder them if they didn't land jobs in either the legal or medical field. Lawyer was good. Judge was better. And no dentists.

"You spend your whole day with your hands in people's mouths. They can put 'doctor' in front of their names, but those people aren't doctors," the boys' father said when he'd dropped his sons off at the train in Boston in late August.

"How about Pete becomes a gynecologist, pop?" Elliot had suggested.

"That's not funny. And keep that smart mouth of yours shut, because I know 'proctologist' is next. Ah! Ah! I knew it! Don't listen to this comic brother of yours, Peter. Nephrologist would be good. Heart surgeon would be better. Something with organs would make your mother happy. You," he said to Elliot, who was already sniggering. "Keep that gutter mouth of yours shut."

He kissed each of his sons on the forehead, told Elliot that there would be hell to pay if he failed to look out for his younger brother, and left them both with a warning that they'd better both be home for the holidays or they'd break their mother's heart.

Both boys had managed to get through most of the fall semester without breaking anyone's heart or deciding whether or not they'd be able to mend it if they had.

The only mistake the Lindstrom boys had made was agreeing to pull Good Samaritan duty and shepherd a foreign exchange student new to the United States from the airport through his first day at Columbus U.

What should have been an easy back-and-forth trip became an hours-long ordeal when all flights from LAX were delayed due to some kind of bad weather in the Midwest. To make matters worse, North American Air had apparently allowed some lunatic access to their flight information display system. The overhead FIDS board had been randomly updating with incorrect times all afternoon. The confusion wasn't merely limited to the boards in the main concourse. Both Lindstrom boys had repeatedly checked their phones, and Elliot had checked a couple of the nearby kiosks. All erroneous flight times were in agreement. They had made a few attempts to ask North American Air employees when the flight they were waiting for was due in, but massive lines deterred them.

When a voice came over the public address system apologizing for the computer glitch and vowing that the problem had been addressed, Elliot and Peter glanced up at the main concourse FIDS screen. They were relieved to find that not only had the delayed flight arrived, it had done so twenty minutes before.

"Finally," Elliot exhaled, climbing to his feet.

The brothers were near enough to the guarded and roped-off arrival doors to see through the windows. The first travelers to deplane were already walking down the bright white corridor, and seconds later began streaming wearily into the concourse.

The first trickle of hustling passengers thickened to a glut of men and women shoving through the doors. Some hurried to hug waiting loved ones, most headed for the baggage carousel, while those only with carry on luggage stepped numbly through the nearby automatic doors into the dying autumn light. The main herd thinned and turned back into a trickle as the last passengers to deplane entered the huge concourse.

For a minute the brothers began to think they'd wasted the entire afternoon, and that the student for whom they'd been waiting had missed his flight. Finally, a lone figure stepped through the doors in the wake of a young family consisting of father, mother, toddler, and infant. The little blond-haired boy was about two years old, and walked with his head nearly on backwards, so fascinated was he with the man who'd been the last to leave the plane. The child's father held him by the hand and continued to yank him forward, quickly ushering his entire family away from the college student.

"That's him," Elliot announced. "I mean, I guess."

The two of them hurried over to intercept the last North America Air arrival.

"Are you Hop Yung?" Elliot asked.

The young student admitted this was he with a slight bow of his head.

"Nice to meet you," Elliot said. "Pete and Elliot. Hey, I don't want to rush you or anything, but we'd better get to the train. It's going to be packed this late in the day."

"Help me with my bags," the young Asian man commanded, in English more precise than most modern young Americans could manage.

Without another word, Hop Yung led the way to the baggage carousel.

As they fell in behind the young man, Elliot turned to Peter and mouthed the words, "friendly guy," to which Peter mouthed, "this was your idea."

As they went to collect Hop Yung's suitcases, both Lindstrom boys wondered what kind of fashion statement their Chinese chemistry student charge was trying to make by dressing all in black like some kind of undertaker.

And what was with the single, long fingernail? It looked sharp enough to be dangerous.

CHAPTER 4

THE WIZENED FIGURE sat cross-legged on the living room floor, the ancient skin of his face bathed in the dull glow of the TV screen.

His age-speckled flesh was like tan parchment drawn tight over bone. His scalp was bald but for cotton-candy tufts of hair at his ears. A similar thread of yellowed-white beard extended from the point of his chin.

He wore a golden morning kimono that settled on the carpet around his body like a deflated parachute.

His frail body was like an ambulatory skeleton, although at that precise moment a statue would have seemed more capable of movement. His chest did not rise and fall with rhythmic breathing, nor was there so much as a twitch of one digit on the slender hands that rested on his folded knees. Even the tufts of hair at ears and chin did not move in the natural eddies of air that circulated through the room. It was as if the frightened breeze thought better than to disturb the ancient figure.

The only thing that suggested he was not a mummified corpse that someone had set down to monitor the television like some ghoulish Nielsen family member was his eyes. Sharp hazel eyes, seemingly much younger than the rest of the aged figure, twitched every so often in order to track the action on the screen.

Chiun, Reigning Master of Sinanju Emeritus, watched the television but did not enjoy what he saw. And, as was so often the case for the sweet and kindly old man who had earned only love and respect in a very long life, it was all Remo's fault.

At the thought of Remo, whom the kindhearted old man had embraced as a son only to be forced to endure endless heartaches, the wisp of beard at Chiun's chin finally twitched ever-so-slightly.

Remo Williams. The foundling that the old Asian had discovered wallowing in filth and decadence, and eventually raised up to the pinnacle of all that man could be but rarely attained. Remo, the adopted son he had drawn to his bosom and to whom Chiun had shown only love. Remo, who seemed to go out of his way to grieve his elderly father, did not believe there was honor in killing. He had said as much that morning after breakfast in this very same living room of the Connecticut condominium the two men shared.

Chiun had responded to such insanity in the only sensible way.

"Aaaiiii!" was the Master of Sinanju's high-pitched reply.

"I knew you'd say that," Remo had said.

The old Korean was holding a universal remote control when Remo made his announcement. At Remo's words, the remote became a cluster of brittle plastic strips exploding from a tightly clenched fist.

"Repeat what you just said," Chiun insisted. "My ears are quite old and I am certain I could not have heard you correctly."

"Here we go," Remo said, rolling his eyes to the ceiling and praying to the paint for strength. "I said I don't believe there's honor in killing."

"Aaiiii!" repeated Chiun, of the House of Sinanju, the most deadly assassins ever to trod the face of the earth.

There was a sudden knock at the front door. Remo, relieved for the reprieve, hurried over to answer it.

A mailman in blue uniform stood on the front step. He clutched a bundle of weekly supermarket flyers in his hand.

Remo did not get mail. The only regular items that would have been sent to him were bills, and those were directed to a post office box that was overseen by his employer. Remo had seen the mailman around the neighborhood, but never before had the man ventured up his front sidewalk.

The concerned mailman remained on the step, even as he attempted to stick his ruddy face through the crack in the door.

"Is everything all right in there?" he asked. "I heard screaming." He was sweating and mostly bald, with a lousy comb-over held in place by grease, perspiration and spit. He glanced around the room but saw only the two men he had seen only rarely at the condo to which he never delivered mail. There was no sign of a half-skinned cat, which was a surprise considering the shrieks that had just emanated from the house.

"Everything's hunky-dory," Remo said to the mailman. "I'm just about to get a lecture on how there is great honor in killing. How killing is the highest honor one can bestow on someone, provided it is done quickly and cleanly. How the only dishonor in killing is doing it sloppily or for free. Remember, no freebies. Therein lies the greatest dishonor."

"At least you heard *one* thing," announced the old man sitting on the floor in front of the television called over.

"Ah," the mailman had said. He looked from the thin white man in the black T-shirt and chinos standing just inside the front door, rotating his thick wrists absently, to the old Asian in the brocade gold kimono surrounded by a scattering of plastic remote control debris who, despite his apparent frailness, looked like one of those cobras in a nature documentary, coiled and ready to strike. There was something frightening about these two men. The mailman was suddenly glad the pair of them never got any mail, and he deeply regretted the do-gooder impulse that had drawn him to their door.

"Why don't I get out of your hair?" the mailman had said, backing slowly away.

"You. Postman," Chiun had called, aiming a slender finger at the perspiring fat man in blue who was inching off the front step. "Do you have a dagger in your sack?"

"I don't know," the mailman said, shrugging. "Maybe. Stuff comes in boxes."

"Search. I will wait. If you have a dagger, kindly hand it to my son."

"I've *really* got to go," the mailman said told Remo.

"Take the postman's knife, Remo," Chiun wailed. "Quick! Plunge it in your father's broken heart."

The mailman didn't know what else to do. He stuffed the bundle of supermarket ads in Remo's hands before hightailing it down the walk.

"Thanks for getting us labeled the biggest nuts in the neighborhood," Remo had said, closing the door.

"*Now* you care what the neighbors think. You didn't care that time when you were shaming five thousand years of the Masters of Sinanju who preceded us when you said you did not find honor in killing."

"I remember that," Remo said. "Mostly because it was two goddamn minutes ago."

"Have I taught you nothing?" Chiun demanded.

"You taught me everything, Little Father," Remo had said. "Everything I know that is worth knowing I learned from you."

"So you say now," Chiun snapped, waving Remo's words from the air with a flutter of long, bony hands. "Yet you choose to thank me by maligning our entire profession. In case you have forgotten, we are assassins."

"I haven't forgotten, Chiun," Remo had said. "In fact, I've got to get going. Smith's got a job for me in Rhode Island. I've got a herd of Mob bastards to thin."

"You malign them, but they have probably not shamed their fathers."

"I'm sure they haven't, Chiun," Remo said, sighing. "We can pick this up when I get back home. Can I get you something while I'm out?"

"A son who doesn't shame me at every opportunity."

"I walked right into that one. See you in a bit."

That was hours ago. Morning had given way to afternoon, and eventually to late night, yet the Master of Sinanju had not stirred.

It was the dead of night when he heard the car drive up the road and park in the garage. Moments after the engine stopped, the sliding glass door in the kitchen opened then closed. An instant later, Remo stepped into the darkened living room that was illuminated only by the light of the television screen and from a streetlight whose amber rays managed to battle through the closed picture window blinds.

"What is more," Chiun said, as if seconds and not hours had passed since Remo had walked out the door, "we are not just any old killers. We are Masters of Sinanju, with skills unequaled in human history."

Remo's shoulders slumped wearily.

"Didn't you break the pause button when you busted the remote?" he asked, waving at the remnants of the remote control that still littered the carpet. "Have you really sat here all day long just to ambush me the minute I walk in the door?"

"I was not finished," Chiun sniffed.

"*I* was."

Remo padded, barefoot, for the stairs.

Chiun rose like a puff of steam from a whistling teakettle and dogged Remo up to the second floor.

"For five thousand years the Masters of Sinanju have plied our art for pharaoh, emperor and king, punishing the wicked, removing the disloyal, steering ships of state through treacherous and tempestuous seas. We ply our deadly and *honorable* trade — yes, Remo, *honorable* — so that the hungry children of our village of Sinanju, the pearl of the Orient, are fed, so that the crippled and the aged of our home are cared for in sickness and infirmity. What greater honor is there than to give someone else's life in service to our fellow villagers?"

"I don't think that's quite how that saying goes," Remo said.

"So now he corrects me," Chiun said to the upstairs linen closet door. "This is gratitude? This is respect?"

"Fine. Whatever. I'm tired. All I'm saying, Chiun, is it's like a doctor. A doctor can be honorable in how he conducts himself professionally, but taking out an appendix isn't honorable or dishonorable. It just is. It's honor neutral."

They had reached Remo's bedroom. He'd hoped Chiun would cut him a break until the next morning, but the old Korean followed him inside.

Chiun's stern face, a leathery mask of sharp lines drawn tight around mouth and eyes, suddenly relaxed. A spark appeared in the depths of his hazel eyes.

"Ah, I see," the old Korean said, a sly edge creeping into his voice. "You nearly had me, Remo, I must confess. But I see now what is going on. This is a joke. I am being *Prank'd*. Where are the television cameras hidden? Where is Ashley Kutchty?"

He peered at Remo's closet door as if expecting it to burst open at any moment. Remo pulled the door open and removed a tatami sleeping mat, which he rolled out on the floor. The mat and Remo's spare pair of loafers were all the closet housed. There was no hidden camera crew to be seen.

"It's not happening, Little Father," Remo said. "That asshole's show has been off the air for years."

Chiun's eyes bored into Remo's and saw that his pupil was speaking the truth. He allowed his shoulders to sink in disappointment.

"Believe me," Remo said, "I'd love that gangly douchebag to charge through the front door, if for no other reason than to send him sailing right back out the window."

"What about Allen Funt?" Chiun asked.

"Sorry to break it to you, Little Father, but *Candid Camera*'s been off the air for half a century."

Remo stripped off his T-shirt. It, like the rest of his clothes, stunk of salt water. He headed into the bathroom and turned on the shower.

Alone in Remo's bedroom, Chiun's frown returned, less stern than before but seemingly more firmly set. When he shook his head, the wisps of yellowing white hair that clung like tufts of cloud above his ears danced sadly around his otherwise bald scalp.

"Then I do not understand," he called into the bathroom. "Nor do I want to."

Remo stepped back into the bedroom for a moment, a towel in hand.

"It's not that I think we don't perform a service, Chiun. And we get paid to do it, and that's fine. I get that. But, look, there's the sunrise. It's great when the sun comes up, and the sun is a wonderful thing that the earth couldn't live without. It's nature, it's perfection.

But is it honorable? No, it just is. I was just pointing out — approximately twenty goddamn hours ago — that there are people out there who are saying there's something called honor killing and that just rankles me. It should you, too. If for nothing else because they're amateurs, and amateurs take the beer and Skittles out of our mouths."

"I cannot decide, Remo, if you are being deliberately dense in order to upset me, or if this is just your usual disappointing dense self," Chiun said.

"Pick one," Remo replied. "I've got to get some sleep."

He stepped back into the bathroom and shut the door.

Chiun listened to the shower curtain being drawn.

"I will consider forgiving you for insulting five millennia of Masters of Sinanju if you purchase a new control device for the television," the old Korean called through the closed door.

"Done," Remo's disembodied voice shouted from the bathroom.

Chiun had only extracted the promise from his adopted son because it was late and, during his many hours frozen in place in the living room, the lack of a remote control had forced him to endure the entire daytime, prime time, and late night lineup of an American television network. Once Remo bought a new control device, Chiun fully intended to revisit this topic, since it was clear that in this, as in all other matters, Remo was in desperate need of his teacher's guidance. No honor in killing, indeed.

Shaking his head at the insanity of a land that would put such fool ideas into the heads of its youth, the Master of Sinanju glided silently from the room.

CHAPTER 5

"God knows I'm not a prude, but *every* night? You should see the one she brought back tonight. Some Goth wannabe. I felt like saying to him, 'Hello? 1998 is on the phone. It wants its counterculture back.' I can't *even*."

Rebecca Cooper threw up her hands in histrionic surrender.

"You could try to get a new roommate," Lucy Pierre suggested.

"Hello? Tried it twice already. They won't let me because I switched two times freshman year and once sophomore. Nazi RA says *I'm* the problem. As if. *I'm* not the one who's banging Johnny Cash back in my room right now."

The two girls were in a small coffee shop just outside Columbus University's Manhattan campus.

Rebecca was happy to run into Lucy, who'd stepped in for a minute to grab a double espresso on her way back to the dorms. Lucy was a fellow member of Dr. Portnoy's The Phallus class, which dissected archaic theories on the phallus through the prism of feminist and queer studies. At least Rebecca had someone of equal intellect to grouse to while her roommate was back at Lexington Hall doing the nasty with skinny Darth Vader.

"I don't know where she finds these guys," Rebecca said. "She's just getting back at her father for leaving her mother when she was in high school. I mean, paging Dr. Freud! Any first year psychology student could see that from a mile away. Last month she kept dragging in some minimum wage barista, if you can believe that. Like she had a future with a loser like that. *Not.*"

Rebecca didn't notice that the same loser, futureless barista who had dated her roommate the previous month was two feet away from her and was in the process of preparing her to-go cappuccino.

After her server had ducked into the backroom for a moment to add a dash of spit to her order, Rebecca paid the smiling young man without so much as deigning to make eye contact with him, grabbed her coffee, and left the shop with her friend.

"You wouldn't happen to want a new roommate, would you?" she asked Lucy as they headed back to campus. "See, if *you* switch, I can move in with you, and it's all on you. I'd be doing *you* a favor, and Herr Hitler RA can't say it's me this time."

Lucy nearly burned her throat choking on her espresso.

"No, sorry, Becca," Lucy coughed. "Jane and I get along great."

"You get along with *everyone*," Rebecca complained. "Why am *I* always the one who gets stuck with the lemons who can't get along with *anybody*?"

Lucy could not offer an answer. At least not one that would have kept her one of the few girls on campus not on Rebecca Cooper's enemies list.

It was night in New York. Squares of light were shining from nearly every window on campus. From the quad, Rebecca saw that the curtains were drawn on the lone window of her third-floor Lexington Hall dorm room.

"It's been an hour," Rebecca said. "Mr. and Mrs. Addams Family must be done by now."

"You shouldn't say that, Becca," Lucy said. "The phrase 'mister and missus' is an artificial social construct of the patriarchy designed to keep women subservient. Not only does 'mister' come first, thus relegating women to second-citizen status, but marriage itself is an institution created with the sole purpose of enslaving women."

Rebecca was glad that Lucy hadn't accepted her roommate proposal. She could never have gotten along with an insufferable know-it-all like Lucy Pierre, who was prettier and smarter than Rebecca and was also acing Dr. Portnoy's The Phallus class.

The two girls parted at the great granite steps of Lexington Hall.

Rebecca mounted the steps and passed into the lobby.

Young men and women chatted in groups or wandered in and out of the building. A table was set up in a corner of the lobby at which some activist students were collecting signatures to change the name of Lexington Hall. Barely legible magic marker scribbles on sheets of cardboard taped to their table explained that Lexington was a city in Kentucky, that Kentucky was a Southern state, and that the dorm's name was, therefore, racist. No one had bothered to research the fact that Lexington Hall had been named after John Lexington, one of the founders of Columbus University. John Lexington originally hailed from Lexington, Massachusetts, which was not a Southern American state, and had been an officer in the Union Army who led his troops to victory in several battles against the Confederacy during the Civil War. Columbus University charged its students two hundred thousand dollars per year.

Rebecca took the elevator up to the third floor.

She encountered only one fellow student in the hallway, a stuck-up girl who she'd considered rooming with the previous year until she found out the girl was at Columbus on a full scholarship and that her father drove a bakery truck.

Rebecca didn't acknowledge the other girl's existence as they passed at the elevator. The elevator doors were sliding closed at Rebecca's back as, now alone in the hallway, she approached her closed dorm room door.

Her roommate generally hung on the doorknob a plastic "do not disturb" sign that she'd picked up ostensibly as a joke from a hotel in Atlantic City, but which Rebecca was sure was going to melt from overuse. The sign was not hanging on the door.

Rebecca rapped a knuckle on the door.

"Hello?" she said.

No response from within.

The rudeness was infuriating. First kicking Rebecca out of her own room again, then not even having the civility to answer her.

"Okay, Gail, I'm coming in. You guys had better be decent."

Rebecca pushed open the door and stepped boldly into the room, making certain to look anywhere but her roommate's bed.

"I don't want to be a bitch here, but this has got to stop," Rebecca announced.

She was looking in the direction of her desk. A young man stood there. Although he possessed similar features, it was not the boy her roommate Gail Ritter had brought home.

"Oh," she said. "I didn't realize —"

She suddenly noticed three other men in the room. They were dressed similarly to the Goth student Gail had brought back to the room.

"Oh, no," Rebecca angrily insisted. "Gail, I was clear on this rule. *No* parties. I don't know what kind of gross orgy you guys have got planned, but this is the last straw. I'm not putting up with this roommate bullshit anymore. I don't care how expensive he says it is, daddy can get me something off campus."

She turned, prepared to storm out the door.

One of the young men blocked her path.

"Excuse me. Rude much?"

She tried to step around the young man. He grabbed her arm as she reached for the doorknob and spun her back around.

"What the hell is all this? Gail, who are these guys?"

It occurred to her that her roommate had not said a word since Rebecca had entered the room. She had continued to assiduously train her eyes on everything but Gail's bed. She'd made the mistake of stumbling in on her roommate once before, and was scarred for life. She'd vowed never to make that mistake again.

Rebecca shot a nasty look in the direction of Gail's bed.

Gail was there. At least what was left of her.

The face of Rebecca's roommate was ghostly white. Her eyes were open wide, as was her mouth in a final scream that had apparently gone unheard by her fellow students.

Gail was naked. Her abdomen had been sliced wide open. Yawning wide was the empty, bloody cavity that had for two decades been home to Gail's internal organs.

There was blood. So much blood. Soaked into the bedcovers and seeping deep into the half-exposed mattress. Spilling over on the funny little *Power Puff* rug that Gail had brought from her bedroom back home, which she'd had since childhood and which she had confided to Rebecca brought her comfort all alone at school in New York City.

Rebecca screamed. Or she tried to.

A hand had clamped vise-like over her mouth, muffling her cry.

The young men closed in around her, some pinning her arms, others grabbing her legs. Rebecca struggled wildly but futilely as the men lifted her in the air and carried her over to her own unmade bed.

The pain was horrific, but fortunately short-lived. There was intense pressure in her abdomen like nothing she ever imagined a human could withstand. Then there was blood, but this time it did not belong to her roommate.

In some lucid part of her mind she wondered how the pale young men in the black robes — who were perhaps not Goths after all — had sliced her so effectively without her seeing any evidence of a knife. Then one of them raised his hand and in the dim light cast by the lamp on Gail's desk she saw a viciously sharp fingernail cut at an angle.

Oh, that makes sense, Rebecca thought.

She thought the final mystery of her short life should have been revealed to her less anticlimactically, but there was no one to complain to and no more time left to do so since the last ounce of blood had just pumped through her fluttering heart, and there was nothing left for Rebecca Cooper to do on this earth but die.

CHAPTER 6

IN RYE, NEW YORK, JUST UNDER twenty miles up the coast from Columbus University, a somber brick building that had been constructed in the same era as the old dorms at that exclusive Manhattan institution of higher learning sat nestled on several wooded acres on the shore of Long Island Sound.

A high brick wall separated the grounds from the road out front. A pair of granite lions capped columns at an open gate at which a sleepy security guard manned a small shack. A chain could be drawn across the entrance to the gravel driveway, but was rarely deployed. Few people were interested in anything that transpired beyond the front wall.

Folcroft Sanitarium was a convalescent and retirement home. Guests came and went as they pleased during visiting hours.

Most similar institutions were ordinarily not terribly rigid about enforcing their posted hours. If a family member stayed a little longer than official closing time while visiting an ill or elderly relative, what was the harm? One difference between Folcroft and other such institutions was a rigid enforcement of sanitarium visiting hours. Guests were explicitly told not to arrive before nine a.m. and, with the sole exception of a loved one's imminent death, were expected to be off the grounds no later than 8:05 p.m.

"I'm sorry," the nursing staff would apologize when dealing with complaints from someone they were shepherding through the halls to the exit at eight p.m. "We don't set the rules, they come from above."

Once the doors were locked for the night, staff that was forced to deal with family members angry over Folcroft's unyielding enforcement of the rules would quietly complain about the inflexibility of sanitarium management.

"You know it comes right from the top," they'd say. "The old sourpuss doesn't care because he's not the one kicking people out the door the second the clock strikes eight. Does he think if they stay a minute longer they'll all turn into pumpkins or something?"

It was currently well after eight o'clock, and the last of that day's visitors had long since been ushered out the sanitarium's main exit.

There was a reason for the strictly enforced visiting hours that was unknown to the staff at Folcroft. On the surface the strict visiting hour mandate was just another of the compulsory rules instituted by management that was expected to be obeyed without question. Privately, however, the rule was for the well-being of visitors as well as to protect the great secret that was hidden behind Folcroft Sanitarium's ivy-covered walls.

It might prove to be a fatal mistake for a lost guest to wander through Folcroft's halls alone at night, for only to the public was Folcroft a private hospital. The actual purpose of that somber brick building on the shore of Long Island Sound was a secret so damning that those not meant to learn the truth had in the past paid the ultimate price.

Some who had learned the secret had been enemies, others had been innocents. Every single death weighed heavily on the shoulders of the man who had ordered each execution.

At that moment, in a darkened office at the rear of the building illuminated only by the dull glow of an old banker's lamp, toiled the man who rigidly enforced Folcroft's visiting hours in part to avoid the guilt of having to sign another death warrant.

Dr. Harold W. Smith tapped swiftly away at the alphanumeric computer keyboard that was buried under the gleaming surface of his high-tech black desk.

Smith's public face was that of director of Folcroft. It was in his private capacity that Harold Smith was still at his desk at so late an hour.

An endless scroll of data rolled across the computer monitor housed within the desk. The information was reflected in the spotless lenses of the wireless glasses that were perched with architectural precision on Smith's patrician nose.

Smith had trained his eyes to perform a rapid scan of the constant data stream. Just as muscles could be trained to react automatically, so had Smith taught his own well-ordered mind. Certain words or phrases unconsciously leapt out at him, and the data to which they were connected was either dismissed upon closer scrutiny or set aside for further inspection.

Smith's analytical skills had served him well in a previous life working as an anonymous cog at the CIA. Although back then, unknown to Smith at first, he was not so anonymous as he had imagined himself to be.

It was a surprise to Harold Smith that he had ever attracted the attention of his superiors. There were blind spots in the emotionless former CIA analyst's personality, particularly when it came to what was considered normal social interaction, but one thing Smith knew about himself was that he was not the type of person people tended to notice.

"I don't understand what is expected of me," Smith had said to his immediate superior when he was singled out for psychological testing.

"I don't get it either, Smith. Just take their tests and jump through their hoops and try not to put everybody to sleep."

Smith had done all he was asked, even though he had no idea why he was the only person at Central Intelligence going through what it soon became clear was the most rigorous security and psychological testing he had ever encountered.

Eventually it was revealed that Smith's meticulous work, uncompromising honesty, and unfailing patriotism had brought him unexpected attention.

A secret meeting with a president — now long dead — had presented Smith with an opportunity to serve his country in a capacity that the younger Harold Smith had never imagined. Crime was running out of control. Corruption was rampant at the highest levels of government. Social and political upheaval was threatening to tear the country apart. Smith — the incorruptible man — had been selected as the one person out of millions of Americans to take on the impossible burden of saving the republic from the barbarians who were already within the gates.

A new agency was to be established, answerable directly to the president. The commander in chief could suggest assignments, but could not order them. It was to be called CURE, and it would be utterly autonomous. And Smith was to be its director.

It had taken some persuasion, but Harold Smith had at last accepted the burden of responsibility for saving the nation that he loved.

"There was just one thing, Smith," the president had said as the newly appointed CURE director was on his way out of the Oval Office. "The ink blot test. You said it was just ink. The tests said you weren't very imaginative, but you know what that ink-blot test is all about. Why couldn't you have a least said you saw a naked lady or a bunny?"

"It was spilled ink, Mr. President," Harold Smith had replied, still baffled that anyone could be expected to see something in the Rorschach test that was evidently not there.

To Dr. Harold W. Smith, spilled ink was nothing more nor nothing less than spilled ink.

This lack of imagination had served him well in his decades as director of America's most powerful clandestine agency. Other men in the same post might have had the imagination to use CURE's vast resources for personal gain. Not so, Harold W. Smith. CURE's mission was CURE's mission, just as ink blots were ink blots.

To ensure that his agency's mission succeeded meant many long, lonely nights sitting at his post in that darkened office in the back of the old brick sanitarium on the black waters of Long Island Sound.

This particular night Smith's attention was directed at information coming out of Rhode Island.

CURE's enforcement arm had dropped the ball with the Patriccone syndicate. There were other, stronger ways to state that fact, but Smith abhorred profanity.

Remo had been given the simple assignment of terrifying one of Patriccone's top men into testifying against his Mafia boss. Instead, Remo had mixed up the target's name with that of a low-level bagman and wound up persuading the wrong man into turning state's evidence. The bagman knew next to nothing. As a result of the screw-up, Don Patriccone was alerted to a plot against him. What's more, the bagman had been killed.

The whole affair had been a massive bungle, and when CURE's enforcement arm had been informed of the mess his response had been less than concerned.

"Zip-a-dee-doo-dah, who cares?" Remo had said. "So one meatball rolls off the plate. There's still a hundred more bubbling in the pot on the stove."

"Unacceptable," Smith insisted.

"Yeah? Well, accept it, Smitty, because shit happens."

Accepting it was unacceptable, therefore Smith had not.

The CURE mainframes were able to calculate with a high degree of certainty the probable location of several individuals involved in the Rhode Island Mob's drug trade. Ideally, the men would have been just a small fraction who would have eventually been sent to prison based on the information of the man Remo was supposed to have turned. That option was no longer on the table. The public execution of the worthless bagman Remo had mistakenly converted required a swift and unequal response.

Smith had sent Remo back to Rhode Island to the warehouse where the CURE computers had decided several members of the Patriccone crime syndicate would be gathered alone that night. After he had given the command to CURE's enforcement arm, all Harold Smith could do was wait.

A report finally came in just after two o'clock in the morning. The Providence warehouse to which Smith had sent Remo was on fire. The brief story said that the building was expected to be a total loss, but mentioned that rescue personnel were optimistic that no one was in the warehouse when the fire broke out.

That was it. Remo had dispatched the men elsewhere and then returned to the scene to destroy the drug warehouse. Smith didn't need CURE's basement mainframes to help him reach this conclusion. He had worked with the younger Master of Sinanju long enough to recognize Remo's fingerprints.

The deed was done. A message had been sent to a criminal organization that assumed it was above the law.

Smith pulled off his glasses and rubbed his eyes wearily. His wife would not be waiting up for him when he got home. She had spent too many late nights alone to expect her Harold to keep anything remotely like normal hours. But hopefully she had left dinner in the oven. Smith suddenly realized that he had not eaten anything all day except a small yogurt for breakfast. Maude Smith was a terrible cook, but even some of Mrs. Smith's charcoal-flavored macaroni and cheese would hit the spot right now.

Smith was reaching out to shut down his computer when the buzz of a muted alert caught his attention. A fresh window had opened up on the screen.

The CURE director replaced his glasses and glanced down at the buried monitor.

A computer program Smith had written many years before had kicked in. The program, which had only rarely activated during his tenure as CURE director, was an urgent red flag from the basement mainframes. It only alerted Smith when something directly related to CURE appeared in the news.

The risk of discovery was omnipresent in Smith's job. When the window opened he felt his mouth go dry, fearing the worst from his algorithm, and that a front page exposé on CURE's activities was splashed across the *New York Times* Web site.

Smith scanned the columns of text.

The mainframes had flagged an API story out of New York that had just appeared on the Internet. The bodies of two young girls had been found on the Manhattan campus of Columbus University. A double homicide. A sad reality in modern New York, but hardly anything on its own to warrant CURE's attention.

Smith briefly wondered if his program might be faulty. Midway through the article, a brief description was given of the condition of the bodies.

As Smith read the report he felt his tongue dry to dust. His blood began to pound like thunder in his ears. He suddenly became aware of the pacemaker that shocked his heart into regular rhythm, and hoped that it would not malfunction, since it felt as if his heart had shrunk to half its size beneath his thin ribcage.

Clutching the edge of his desk for support, Smith swallowed hard.

It was impossible. It simply could not be. He read the text again.

The bodies of the girls had been discovered an hour before, hanging from a tree off the main quad of the university. The corpses had been skinned, their stomachs slit open and the organs bundled in packages of skin buried at the base of the tree.

The story concluded that, as of publication, there were no leads.

No leads.

The thunder continued to pound in Smith's head. It was impossible. It simply could not be; not after all this time. Yet there it was in black and white.

It suddenly felt as if his green-striped Dartmouth tie was strangling him. Smith used his fingers to loosen the half-Windsor knot.

His computers were not malfunctioning. The four basement mainframes were working perfectly. The emotionless computers did not care that the world had just opened up and swallowed Smith whole. Information delivered, they returned to their work of remorselessly searching both public and private data for every potentially nefarious fact, figure, and scheme that might merit CURE's attention.

As the mainframes resumed their work, so too did Harold Smith.

Steeling his spine, Dr. Harold W. Smith reached for the blue contact phone at the corner of his desk.

CHAPTER 7

REMO AND CHIUN DROVE into Manhattan just after dawn.

The ride from Connecticut to New York had been tense. The Master of Sinanju appeared to have completely forgotten his irritation with Remo's comments on honor killings. A cloud had settled on the elderly Korean's features.

As they headed up Broadway Remo glanced at the old man, who was staring unflinchingly out the windshield at the early morning city traffic.

Once the silence became too much to bear, Remo cleared his throat.

"It's probably fine, Chiun," he promised. "The last time I took a head count there was something like six billion people on the planet. It stands to reason that some maniac was going to come up independently with the same method of killing people."

"No," Chiun replied with certainty.

"Okay, then a copycat," Remo suggested. "Those old murders made it on the news. Maybe not all the details, but probably enough of them. Or maybe it's some psycho who works in law enforcement. The FBI, state police, and even local cops would've had records from those two times before. Some Jack the Ripper wannabe got his hands on the old files and decided to go nuts with them."

The Master of Sinanju shook his head.

"It is he," the old man intoned.

"The Leader? No way. That blind bastard is dead. It was a barrel of laughs sticking him in that nursing home the first time we met him, but that was only because we never thought he'd heal up and get loose. We didn't take a chance last time around. We made sure we finished him off. The Leader is dead, Chiun. Case closed."

The tufts of hair over Chiun's ears seemed alone in shaking disagreement. His eyes remained trained firmly ahead, as if on some dark destination only he could see.

"There is as much unknown of the *gyonshi* Creed as there is known, my son," the Master of Sinanju said, using the hated name for the cult of Chinese vampires which they had twice met; a name that neither of them had spoken that morning until now. "The evil ones have existed since before the ancient mists from which our own discipline emerged. Yes, the Leader died. But does the Leader live?"

"You're either dead or you're alive, Little Father. There's no middle ground when it comes to dead."

"You know from our own experiences that there is much more to the world than that, Remo," Chiun chided. "You yourself have put the lie to your own assertion on more than a single occasion. For most, dead is dead. Not for all."

His tone was gentle, yet resolute.

Remo shook his head.

"He's dead, Little Father," Remo said, no longer as certain as he was a moment ago. "He *has* to be."

When they arrived at the campus of Columbus University, Remo performed the New York miracle of immediately finding an available parking space in the street. He did not, however have change for the meter, so he ripped it off its post and skimmed it down Broadway.

"See? A parking space in New York City on the first attempt," Remo said. "That's a good omen, Chiun."

The Master of Sinanju merely thrust his hands deep into the voluminous sleeves of his green kimono, turned from his pupil, and proceeded to pad wordlessly down the sidewalk. Remo hustled to catch up.

The two men walked side by side onto the university campus.

While Chiun seemed certain, Remo could not be faulted for having doubts. Who could blame him? After all, it was impossible to believe.

The article Smith had read to Remo over the phone in the dead of night must have gotten it wrong. There was no way the Chinese vampires could still be around.

The Leader had been as old as the hills when CURE first encountered him. Back then, Remo had damaged a portion of the old man's brain, since it was said that only in death did the members of his Creed truly live. The attack had made the Leader an invalid. However, the blow Remo had used was faulty.

Chiun was always carping at Remo to keep his elbow straight. It had never really mattered before. But Remo's flawed technique had given the Leader the chance to recuperate. It had taken nearly a decade for the *gyonshi* cult leader's brain to repair itself, but when it had he had returned to seek revenge against the House of Sinanju.

That second time, Remo had finished the Leader off for good. Legends or no legends, mysterious hidden skills or no, Remo had personally killed the man. He had watched the final breath pass from the old bastard's dying body.

Remo had seen the orange mist — which in life infected the cadaverous old man and all other Chinese vampires — slip into the air and evaporate. Gone for good. Remo had even duplicated the ritualistic slaughter of the Creed that was intended only for the victims of the ancient cult. A final insult against the twisted old mind that had brought horrible death to so many.

No. The Leader was dead. And with him had died the ancient Creed.

The bodies of the girls at Columbus — no matter how gruesomely similar to *gyonshi* murder victims — could not possibly have anything to do with the ancient cult.

Chiun padded silently beside Remo along a sidewalk that cut through the snow-dusted lawn in the direction of the university dorms.

"A penny for your thoughts," Remo said.

"You should have kept your elbow straight the first time," Chiun replied.

"I want my penny back," Remo grunted.

They found the campus to be virtually deserted so early in the morning. The first classes were ordinarily not scheduled to start for over an hour, but with a killer on the loose the university had suspended morning classes. Hungover students in every dorm were expressing gratitude to the two juniors who'd been slaughtered the previous night.

Remo and Chiun followed the neatly shoveled path from the main quad to the science center. Up ahead they spotted some flapping yellow police tape that ran from a storm drain at the corner of the science building to a light post.

A wide, shaded alley of bushes and trees ran alongside the building. Although the bodies had been removed during the night, uniformed police still guarded the area.

One of the two officers stopped Remo and Chiun as they approached the scene.

"Turn right around and get outta here," the cop commanded.

Remo fished in the pocket of his tan chinos and flashed a plastic card.

"Remo Bednick, Homeland Security," he said.

He didn't wait for permission. He lifted the police tape so that the five-foot tall Master of Sinanju could pass beneath without stooping.

"Hold on, pal," the cop said. "So *you're* Homeland Security. Who's he?" he pointed to the wizened Asian, already heading deeper into the crime scene.

Remo looked the cop square in the eye and uttered only one, magic word.

"Racist."

The cop looked as if he'd just stumbled on a scene even more horrifying than a pair of twenty year-old disemboweled coeds dangling from a tree. He held up his hands, palms forward, in immediate surrender.

"Sorry," the cop begged. "I didn't mean anything by it. It's just — You know what? Forget I asked. *Please* forget. Okay?"

His tone and eyes pleaded desperately.

"I'll forget it," Remo said. "*This* time. But when you get back to the station you need to sign yourself up for sensitivity training. Six months, not a day less. Don't try to worm your way out of it. I'll check." He pointed at the cop's partner. "You, too."

The other man's bobbing head joined that of the first cop.

"Yes, sir," the first cop said. "*Thank you*, sir."

Remo gave a crisp nod before ducking under the tape and entering the alley next to the science building.

There was a time when Remo might actually have had to explain the Master of Sinanju's presence at a crime scene, since Chiun refused to carry around the phony identification with which their employer supplied them. But Remo had found the current hypersensitivity on the subject of race to be a terrific time saver. Men in authority now folded like rickety card tables at the slightest suggestion of racial insensitivity. The world might be rocketing to hell on greased skids, but at least there was one corner of the insanity that Remo had managed to turn to his advantage along the way.

Remo was whistling as he headed after the Master of Sinanju.

A crime scene investigative unit was scouring every square inch of the area. They worked under the watchful supervision of several plainclothes detectives.

The bulk of the activity was around the base of an old maple tree. Even from a distance, Remo could see that the thin snow had been trampled to mud at the trunk. Here and there, patches of snow that should have still been white were awash in crimson.

Chiun was over by the tree, poking around at the ground with the toe of his sandal and refusing to acknowledge a red-faced detective's demand for him to leave.

"It's okay," Remo said, hustling over to Chiun's side. "He's with me."

Remo showed the same card he'd flashed to the uniformed cops at the police tape.

"That's a Blockbuster card," the detective said.

"Evidently your health plan doesn't include glasses for anyone below detective," Remo said.

He fished out his Homeland Security I.D. and waved it under the cop's nose, satisfying the plainclothes officer.

"Detective Sturgis," the cop said.

The detective was portly and in his late fifties, with sagging jowls and a stocking hat tugged halfway down his ears. He reluctantly hung his hand out in the air before him. The hand was red and chapped, and the fingernails were chewed down to the raw skin.

"Do not touch it, Remo," Chiun advised. The Master of Sinanju didn't look up from his examination of the ground. "With skin like that he should be ringing a bell while begging for alms outside this filthy city's gates."

The cop hastily withdrew his hand, shoving both hands in his overcoat pockets.

"Your friend's a real charmer," the cop grunted. He looked Remo up and down. "Aren't you cold?"

Although the morning was freezing, Remo wore only a thin white T-shirt along with his chinos and loafers.

"Washington's idea for our new uniform," Remo said. "First they took away our fedoras, now this. If they take our rubber hoses, I'm lodging a complaint with Elliott Ness."

Remo joined the Master of Sinanju in examining the area where the girls had been found.

"They were not killed here," Chiun said.

There was an insufficient amount of blood for the murders to have taken place in the wooded alley between two buildings.

"No," Sturgis said. "The murders took place in their dorm room over in Lexington Hall. Place looks like a slaughterhouse."

The bodies had been removed for autopsy. Despite their absence, Remo did not need Sinanju-trained eyes to see the twin scrape marks in the bark on a thick overhanging branch from which the girls had been suspended by ropes.

Trampling feet had not removed the smell of blood. Remo's sensitive nose detected the metallic scent in the packed dirt that had been churned to thin mud, as well as in the untrammeled snow.

Remo crouched alongside Chiun to examine the ground. The snow immediately beneath the branch where the bodies had hung had been cleared away. Two small cavities had been excavated in the cold ground.

"I've got to admit, Little Father. I'm feeling a little déjà vu."

Chiun straightened back up. He indicated the holes in the earth with his toe.

"The organs were here," the old man said. "I know of only one sect that desecrates its victims in this precise way."

There was no doubt about it. The entire scene was eerily reminiscent of the Chinese vampire cult.

"What do you mean, sect?" asked Detective Sturgis, who had been hovering irritatingly close by. "You guys have a clue what's going on here, I'd like to be filled in."

Remo had been gazing in the now-empty holes; staring into the past. He pulled his eyes away from the ground.

"Who were they?" he asked the NYPD detective.

"The victims?" Sturgis said. "Just a couple of juniors here at Columbus. Guess they saved their parents the price of one year's tuition."

He gave a little snort of laughter. Remo refrained from removing his head and skipping it out into the quad like a decapitated parking meter.

"Who found the bodies?"

"Two other students. A couple of brothers. That's not fraternity-speak, I mean two actual brothers." The cop consulted his notes. "Elliot and Peter Lindstrom. The older one bunks at Crane Hall. Big dorm on the other side of the medical school. Both of them said they were heading back there, last I spoke to them."

He gave Remo Elliott Lindstrom's dorm room number.

"Did they know the girls?" Remo asked.

"Older one said he knew one of them in passing. He was a junior, too. Younger one's a freshman, just started here this fall. He said he didn't know either girl. The two of them were pretty out of it. Shocked. No big surprise. I nearly tossed my cookies."

"Anybody else see anyone around here?"

"Just those two brothers," Sturgis said. "They're not suspects, at least for now. They said they spotted the blood trail and followed it in. Just curious, but they managed to mess up whatever prints the killers made in the snow pretty good."

"Are we finished here, Chiun?" Remo asked.

The Master of Sinanju nodded.

"I would see the bodies," the old man announced.

"First things first. We should talk to the kids who found them."

They turned from the tree where the girls had been suspended.

"So what's Homeland Security's interest here?" Sturgis called after them. "You see anything like this before? Because sixteen years in homicide, this is a first for me."

"We've seen it *all* before," Remo replied grimly.

Sturgis let the cryptic reply hang in the frosty air for a moment before flipping his notebook closed and pocketing it. The detective kept a suspicious eye trained on Remo and Chiun as the two men passed beneath the yellow police tape and headed off in the direction of the older Lindstrom boy's dorm.

Crane Hall had been home at one time or another to authors, entertainers, captains of industry and dozens of state and federal lawmakers. Even a past President of the United States had spent part of his youth in the Columbus University dormitory.

In spite of the early hour, more than a few young faces dotted the many windows that overlooked the path that led up from the spot where the bodies had been discovered.

None of the Columbus U students in the windows seemed interested in Remo and Chiun. Although both men sensed a stray gaze drop over their approaching forms, most eyes were aimed off to where the coroner's office had only recently hauled away the bodies of roommates Rebecca Cooper and Gail Ritter.

The light of the rising sun that was beginning to glint off the upper story windows was a cheery contrast to the grisly scene Remo and Chiun had just left.

Remo wondered how long the students in the windows above them had forced themselves to stay awake, perhaps worried that they might be the next victims of some unknown killer. Although maybe they would have been up anyway. Most kids these days seemed to survive entirely on coffee and energy drinks.

"I'm amazed college kids learn anything with the hours they keep," he commented to the Master of Sinanju.

The main building of Columbus University's medical school was at their backs as they headed up the broad staircase of the ivy-covered dorm.

"I am amazed that you still think American youths are capable of learning anything of value at all," replied Chiun. "Their skulls are impenetrable granite whether they are wide awake or comatose."

Remo had to admit the old Korean was right. He had met many college students in his life and had found very few were even capable of learning. He had found as he'd gotten older that their lack of knowledge and concomitant certainty over that which they didn't know only got worse the more time they dithered away in school.

This thought flitted through his mind as he glanced up at the dorm's façade. He caught a glimpse of movement at a window on the fifth floor. A pale face was visible for an instant before a curtain dropped down to obscure the room beyond.

Remo noted that — unlike all the other floors of Crane Hall — shades, blinds or curtains were drawn on every window on the fifth floor. Except for the brief glimpse of a single face, no students on that floor appeared to be interested in the activity below.

"Someone doesn't like the light," Remo commented.

The Master of Sinanju had seen as well the solitary face five stories above.

"Evil thrives in darkness," the old Korean ominously replied.

Remo and Chiun crossed the short landing and entered the building.

With classes suspended, there was no activity in the lobby. The two men encountered no students on their way to the elevator, nor on the ride up to the fifth floor.

When the doors to the car slid open five stories up, the two Masters of Sinanju sensed the utter stillness of death. It was a feeling greater than mere uninhabited stillness. The sensation that emanated from the walls was that of a place recently humming with life, but one in which that life had been abruptly extinguished.

Although they saw no blood on the narrow carpet that ran up the center of the old wood floor, the stink of it poured from underneath every closed door.

The two men shared a dark glance.

"Have a care, my son," Chiun whispered.

"You, too, Little Father."

They exited the elevator.

Remo paused outside the first door. He sensed no movement from within. Still, he remained alert as he turned the knob and nudged the door open.

A vision from a horror movie greeted him.

The young occupants of the room had been hung on the walls like cattle in a butcher shop. Vertical incisions opened the soft tissue of their abdomens. The killers had not bothered with the ritualistic skinning and binding-up of the organs in flesh which had been practiced on the girls whose bodies had been discovered outside. These organs had been dug out and slopped onto the floor at the dangling toes of the two bodies.

Remo didn't bother to check any of the other rooms. The stillness from within and the blood scent pouring into the hall told him what he would find.

Detective Sturgis had said that the elder Lindstrom boy was in room 5-J. As he and Chiun closed in on that room, Remo was unsurprised to find it was the one from which the pale face had looked down at them as they entered the building.

He paused outside the door.

"Do we knock?" he whispered, grimly half-joking.

Chiun answered the question by raising his foot and launching the sole of his sandal into the center of the door. Metal hinges tore apart with a shriek, the bolt on the opposite side ripped the frame from the wall, and the entire door exploded in a thousand splintering wooden darts into the dorm room.

In a swirl of green kimono hems, the Master of Sinanju swept into the room in the wake of the exploding door shards. Remo darted in behind him.

Inside was a typical dorm room. Books were piled on a pair of desks. Clothing littered the floor, pretentious art hung from the walls. A pair of unmade beds sat on either side of the window on the far side of the room, opposite the hallway.

The two occupants of the room looked up at their guests with expressions of calm amusement.

Elliott and Peter Lindstrom sat on the edge of the bed to the left of the window.

"Yes, you *should* have knocked," Elliot informed Remo.

Peter nodded agreement. "It's the polite thing to do."

The young men had evidently heard Remo whisper the question out in the hallway. Their hearing was clearly much more acute than that of normal men. There was no telling what other senses were likewise enhanced.

"Watch yourself, Little Father," Remo warned.

The Master of Sinanju was already moving in an arc around the right side of the room. Remo performed a mirror-image dance to the left.

"Where is your foul master?" the old Korean demanded as he closed in on Peter Lindstrom, sitting placidly beside his brother.

"Never met him," Elliott replied. "We're looking forward to it though. After we take care of you two."

Remo was passing the partially open door of a closet. He sensed nothing living inside, but was unsurprised due to the smell to see a pair of glassy eyes staring out at him through the gap in the louvered doors.

Elliott saw Remo glance inside the closet, noting the look of quiet revulsion on Remo's face when he looked back at the two boys sitting on the bed.

"Meet Dave, my roommate. Dave snored. Dave won't snore anymore."

Peter giggled.

The laugh was like a cue. The two boys got to their feet.

There was a confident poise to the Lindstrom brothers that the greater mass of humanity did not possess.

Remo found that there was no bracing for a conventional attack, as from an ordinary human foe. It was as if some feral switch suddenly flicked on in the two boys.

Although Remo knew an attack would come, he was surprised by its speed.

Both Lindstrom boys shot forward at once, one left, one right.

Elliot's hand ripped from his pocket in a blur. His heretofore unseen *gyonshi* nail tore part of the thick denim layers of his jeans en route to Remo's chest.

The sight of the sharpened *gyonshi* fingernail, the first he'd seen in years, was not unexpected by this point. Even so, with the appearance of that ugly memory thrust forward into the present day, coupled with the surprising swiftness of the attack, Remo nearly allowed the elder Lindstrom boy's blow to register.

The instant before the cutting edge of the viciously sharp nail pierced the flesh of his chest, Remo twisted to one side. With his target suddenly gone, Elliot's forward momentum launched him past Remo.

Remo shot a sharp knuckle into the boy's temple as he soared past. Enough to graze, not kill. Elliott Lindstrom was unconscious before he hit the floor. He plowed through a pile of discarded laundry and crashed through the louvered doors of the closet.

Peter had lunged for Chiun simultaneous with his brother's attack on Remo.

The young Lindstrom boy's eyes flashed with murderous glee as he leapt at the Master of Sinanju, his *gyonshi* nail slashing the air like a mugger brandishing a stiletto.

"Don't kill him, Little Father!" Remo said.

Chiun shot the younger Sinanju master a foul look.

Peter Lindstrom's hand slashed left. Chiun pivoted from its path.

Remo could see the edge of the younger boy's nail sparkle in the wan light of a desk lamp. Then the hand slashed down across the lamp's shade, opening a wide gash and exploding the bulb in a spray of sparks and glass.

The boy tore his hand from the lamp, which spun off the edge of the desk and crashed to the floor. His hand slashed right, aiming for Chiun's wattled neck.

The fingernail did not come close to contact with the old man's flesh.

Chiun's hand lashed out, fingers curled, palm flat. The old man's hand met the forehead of Peter Lindstrom with a dull crack. Enough to incapacitate, not to kill.

The boy's eyes rolled back in his head, the bones in his legs suddenly turned to jelly, and he dropped to the carpet.

When the second Lindstrom boy had been subdued, Chiun looked up from the crumpled body at his feet. His hazel eyes locked on Remo's.

"*Now* do you believe?" the Master of Sinanju said.

In a swirl of kimono hems, the old Korean swept from the dorm room.

Remo had not wanted to believe it, yet the truth was at his feet. Somehow the *gyonshi* had returned, and with them their ancient Creed that baptized in blood.

Remo focused his attention on the two young men. Their breathing was shallow, yet both lived.

Remo knew from experience that while some joined the cult of Chinese vampires voluntarily, many of their foot soldiers were conscripted against their will. These latter were not responsible for their actions while under the influence of the Creed's mind-controlling poison. Remo had at least learned how to deal with that toxin in the past.

Remo hauled Peter Lindstrom up over his shoulder, then pulled Elliott up under his arm. Ever mindful of the rhythmic breathing of the pair of dangerous bundles he now held, Remo carted the two unconscious boys from the room.

CHAPTER 8

THE GRAY CLOUDS WERE SWOLLEN with stubborn snow that clung to the sky and refused to fall to earth as Captain Gao Tiaphang of the Chinese People's Liberation Army halted his convoy at the edge of the great dark Manchurian forest.

The jeep he rode in was an old Russian knock-off of the superior American model. Its aged shocks squeaked as the captain climbed down to the frozen ground.

There were three troop transport buses behind him, each carrying a dozen men. Captain Tiaphang signaled the men in the trucks to stay where they were as he walked around to the front of his jeep.

A dead zone of brown weeds filled the space between the edge of the forest and the rough road of frozen mud on which the convoy had stopped.

There was evidence of a recently abandoned outdoor market that had been set up along the road side of the band of dried brown weeds. Several booths remained, stripped bare of whatever items the peasants had been peddling.

The village Guizhou sat on the southern edge of the vast forest. It was a small peasant village that spent its summers harvesting far too little rice and survived the harsh winters by rationing what little food was grown during the warmer months.

The entire village consisted of fewer than thirty homes, which were arranged around a central dirt street. A large pile of ox-droppings had been left on the roadway, and as he entered the town Captain Tiaphang viewed the frozen excrement with the disdain of a man born in the city. He pounded on the door of the nearest hut.

After some shuffling inside, an old man with razor-slit eyes and a long drooping mustache at last opened the door. He held a curving pipe in his shaking hand. Curls of smoke rose up around his wrinkled face.

"May I help you?" the old man asked.

"I am in need of a guide, old one," Captain Tiaphang demanded.

The ancient peasant tapped the stem of his pipe with shaking fingers.

"There is only one place in this region where one would need a guide," the old man said. "It is not a place anyone from here has ever gone."

He nodded in the direction of the dark forest.

"I seek a convoy that vanished in those woods three days ago," the captain said.

The old man nodded, both sadly and wisely.

"This is not unexpected," he said shaking his head. He sucked at the chewed end of his pipe. "I was last to see your fellow soldiers. A terrible thing."

"You did not see them come back out?" the captain said, pointing to the gnarled, black trees beyond dead field that ran alongside the rural road.

"No. None who enter those woods ever leave them. The world should live in fear of the day they do. I warned the other soldiers not to go there," the old man said. "They came to the village and asked about two missing women. They were told they entered the forest whose name we do not speak, and that they were therefore dead. Perhaps worse even than dead. The soldiers did not listen. They entered the forest at the place where the two white women went. Of course they never returned."

The weathered old man, as ancient and gnarled as one of the distant forest trees, blew a somber smoke ring at the swollen winter sky.

Captain Tiaphang knew about Ellie McGlone and Peg Sampson, the two women who worked for Ranch Micro Industries. The Sampson woman had informed coworkers that the pair of them were going sightseeing. That was five days ago, and they had not returned to work. Closed circuit television cameras near their hotel had found them boarding a bus that traveled out of the city. The driver of that bus had informed authorities that he had driven the women to this location.

The bus driver was now in prison. This was not a place to which he was ever supposed to bring Americans, who were only tolerated in China and certainly were not permitted to wander around freely. The driver had insisted that the McGlone woman had persuaded him to deviate so far from his route. Under extreme questioning, he suggested that there was something about the woman that had made him surrender his free will.

Captain Tiaphang did not care about some superstitious bus driver, who would soon be on his way to a forced labor camp. He cared about possible American spies.

"You will find someone to guide me through the forest," the captain demanded of the old peasant with the pipe.

"Impossible," the old man replied. "None who are now alive have ever been in there. We would be as lost as you. The other soldiers are dead. As you will be if you seek to learn their fate."

The old man's face puckered. He held the bowl of his pipe and pointed with the curving stem to the nearer trees of the great black woods.

"Would that your comrades had listened," the aged one said. "Demons have always haunted these woods. It is the home of the City of the Dead. The other captain who came here led his men to slaughter."

Captain Tiaphang's lips curled in contempt.

Although he was stationed more than fifty miles away, he had heard whispered hints of this city of death and of the creatures of the night that the locals insisted lived in this ancient forest. But Captain Tiaphang was an educated man. He did not believe in fairy stories. More importantly, neither did his superiors.

The first group of soldiers had been sent on a simple mission to locate the missing women. When they failed to return, Captain Tiaphang was dispatched. And Captain Tiaphang had no intention of turning back until he successfully completed his mission.

At a signal from the captain, four men from the lead truck trundled up the frozen dirt path and bullied their way into the tiny, squalid hut. At gunpoint, they forced the old man to prepare himself for a long journey into the forbidding woods.

"I cannot be of assistance," the old one wept.

"You will lead us, or we will shoot you here," the captain said.

Shaking and sobbing, the old man was led to the jeep and forced into the seat behind Captain Tiaphang's driver

The caravan rumbled back to life, and the row of vehicles turned off the road and headed across the strip of dead grass to the great forest. One by one, the military vehicles were swallowed by the black trees.

As the woods consumed the last of the transport trucks, the people of the village of Guizhou, who had been hiding and watching the from the chilly silence of their shabby huts, stepped cautiously out into the gray winter light.

Many offered silent prayers to their gods that the demons of the woods would be satisfied with their latest meal, for Guizhou and all that existed beyond its borders was unprepared for the full evil in that forest to spill out into the world.

The convoy was only able to drive half a kilometer before the last of the vehicles to make it between the thickening growth of wild trees got hung up on a rock and refused to move any further. Captain Tiaphang climbed down from his stuck jeep.

The captain gave a foul look back at the trucks that had likewise become snared on rocks or fallen logs. One was even jammed between two trees.

The captain ordered his men to abandon their vehicles.

The band continued on foot.

They soon found the trucks of the previous expedition. The

earlier group had found a slightly easier path, and had gotten similarly caught only a few minutes walking distance from Captain Tiaphang's abandoned vehicles.

There were only two trucks, each stuck in a heavy rut formed in spring by the rush of a melting stream. There was no evidence of foul play. It appeared as if the previous expedition had had also left their vehicles voluntarily.

Captain Tiaphang's soldiers forged ahead, between primordial trees that were bare and black. Only a little dull daylight, filtered through thick clouds, reached the forest floor.

The old man from the village — whose name Captain Tiaphang had learned was Oi — proved as useless as he had claimed. The old one tramped back amidst the soldiers, his rheumy eyes peering fearfully at every barren branch and fallen leaf.

Eventually a path revealed itself, which was almost a shocking thing to Tiaphang. The forest had appeared as if it had never seen a single footfall of man or beast.

The path led over a hill and down to a clearing near a small brook.

Tiaphang and his men found themselves in an abandoned village. The place was even more pitiful than old Oi's little rural community on the edge of the woods.

The captain had the old one dragged to the front of the column.

"Is this collection of hovels the great city of death that so many have feared?" he laughed.

Oi shook his head.

"No," the old villager said. "I heard stories in my youth that the inhabitants of the City of the Dead had abandoned it until the return of its master. This is where for one hundred years they awaited his return. If they have left now, it can mean only one thing. I beg you, captain, leave these woods now."

Captain Tiaphang's face clouded, flashing anger.

"Fan out!" he commanded. "Find where they have gone."

His men followed the command, quickly discovering another path. This trail led from the opposite end of the little shanty village, deeper into the woods.

He ordered his men forward. When Oi hesitated, the captain slapped the frightened old man across the face. The skin of Oi's fragile cheek split, and a trickle of blood oozed from the narrow wound.

"No injury you inflict on me can be worse than that which is to come," Oi said. "Your men are yours to command. I will go no further."

Tiaphang clicked the hasp on his holster and stared down into the old man's upturned face. Oi did not flinch. Finally, the captain snapped his holster shut and spun away from the old villager.

"He will only slow us down," the captain announced.

The soldiers left old Oi in the abandoned village and marched single file up the hidden path. They had not traveled another ten minutes before one of the youngest men let out a gasp so loud that it halted the entire company.

Captain Tiaphang and the others followed the young soldier's shocked gaze.

A shadow had descended on the path ahead. At least, at first it appeared to be a shadow. On closer inspection it appeared more like a dark, dense fog.

It soon became clear that the fog was comprised of several clouds, distinct from one another at times, at others rolling in to join with the larger mass.

The captain had to order the soldiers of the Chinese Liberation Army under his command not to disband and run screaming from the woods. As it was, he had to permit them to draw their weapons before they would proceed.

"You cannot shoot a cloud," Captain Tiaphang muttered angrily as he led his men up the path and through the fog.

The heavy black mist seemed to have a mind of its own. Rather than roll down the hill to where the company had left old Oi, it floated alongside the soldiers.

Occasionally a patch of the fog would disengage from the rest and float across the path, forcing the soldiers to walk through it. The sensation was unsettling. It was almost as if there was something...*alive* in the fog. When it passed over the soldiers, one had the feeling that one was hearing fragments of another's thoughts.

Captain Tiaphang blamed the old man Oi, who had been worthless as a guide and had only contributed to the apprehension of the men under his command.

The ancient City of the Dead soon appeared in glimpses through a thick copse of black trees. It was revealed fully when the company reached the end of the path.

Stumbling across the place of mythical death was like being the first man in centuries to set foot in Machu Picchu or some other abandoned place forgotten by time.

Many buildings at the edge of the city had surrendered to the elements, crumbling to piles of jagged stone in the eons since the terrible place was inhabited.

Further in, what would have been older structures in an expanding settlement seemed to have managed to weather the years far better. Even so, trees and other forest vegetation had found purchase in every available crevice, cracking stone and rising high above the City of Death. The forest canopy was so great that Captain Tiaphang understood why no airplane had ever spotted the ancient ruins from above.

A surprise came near what had once been the center of the city. The place of evil was not so abandoned as the legends had suggested.

Although no people were visible, open fires burned in pits in a communal square around which were arranged several intact stone buildings. Bubbling, brackish soup of some sort boiled in cauldrons set on the fires.

Whoever had been cooking in the dead city appeared to have run off at the approach of the People's Liberation Army soldiers.

The steps of a hideous black temple rose to the east of the square. Perhaps the squatters had heard the approach of the soldiers and had run up into the temple.

At the top of the staircase, between the black hollows of two huge doors that led into the bowels of the evil shrine, a stone throne was set into an alcove, all carved from solid rock. Before the forest had reclaimed the site, he who sat on that ancient throne would have had the entire City of the Dead spread out before him.

"Captain!"

Tiaphang had been staring up the ancient staircase, wondering about who had once ruled from that stone throne and feeling an unaccustomed shudder of ice brush his spine as he imagined this terrible place in a younger world.

The shout shook him from his reverie. He hurried over to join several of his men, who were crowded around the open door of one of the stone dwellings.

"What is it?" the captain demanded.

The men were too frightened to speak. They indicated the door. Tiaphang scowled at the soldiers before sticking his head under the stone arch.

The color drained from his face.

His men had found the previous expedition.

Two dozen officers and men had comprised that first group. At least a dozen of them were hanging from iron hooks that were fitted into fresh wooden beams at the ceiling of the single large room. The bodies had been defiled. The stomachs had been cut open and the organs had been removed. Buckets made of wood harvested from the forest were stained dark near the dangling feet of some of the victims.

It was not only soldiers who had been treated like slaughtered cattle. A more recent addition hung at the front of the gruesome collection.

The dead eyes of old Oi, their useless guide from the village Guizhou, stared blankly at Captain Tiaphang. The old man's tunic had been torn open, and his abdomen had been slit from sternum to pelvis. His organs lay steaming near the cold entrance to the stone hut. Fresh blood dribbled from his naked feet into a nearly overflowing bucket.

Tiaphang wheeled around. He now knew exactly what it was that bubbled in the cauldrons over the abandoned fires.

"What is this wicked place?" Captain Tiaphang hissed.

A titter of echoing laughter was his reply.

The black fog that had dogged the captain and his men through the woods was slowly rolling up the road that he and his men had taken into the heart of the City of the Dead. More of the strange mist poured from the doors of the stone buildings that surrounded the square beneath the great temple.

The fog became so dense that Captain Tiaphang could no longer see back in the direction he and his men had come.

A voice seemed to come from nowhere and everywhere at once. It echoed through the square and spoke in the quite recesses of Captain Tiaphang's own mind.

"Do you invite us in?"

"Who is there!" Captain Tiaphang demanded. "Show your faces!"

"All will become clear. You need only invite us in."

Another voice. Cloying, taunting.

The captain spun around. There was no one other than his own men standing in the strange black fog at the temple stairs.

Captain Tiaphang was an officer in the People's Liberation Army of China. He would not be frightened by some forest peasants playing pranks.

He commanded his men to raise their weapons. Though afraid of that which they did not see, the younger men did as commanded.

The fog continued to swirl between and around them. At one point, Tiaphang swore he saw the shadow of a satisfied face congeal from the mist.

"You are invited in," Captain Tiaphang announced.

The instant the words had passed his lips, the air around him came alive.

The black fog seemed to sprout arms and faces. His troops were instantly infiltrated by ghastly, ghostly men and women. They were hemmed in on every side and within their ranks by gaunt, flat faces.

Swish-swish!

Screams rose to the forest canopy.

Swish-swish!

A sharpened fingernail poised in the air above a horrified soldier. Another blood-curdling scream as the fingernail blade slashed down.

Blood. It was everywhere. Flooding the ground. A sea of viscera; sloshing organs. Bodies dropping one by one. His entire company decimated in seconds.

The last scream died in the throat of a soldier who spit a fountain of crimson as he collapsed to the ground. Clouds of warm white steam fled the shredded corpses of Captain Tiaphang's men, already cooling in death on the ground of the legendary City of the Dead in the primordial Manchurian forest.

Captain Tiaphang staggered backward. He felt something brush against his cheek. A hand. A sharpened fingernail.

A face appeared before him. Sightless eyes stared into his own.

Despite the man's apparent blindness, Captain Tiaphang felt that those unseeing orbs could penetrate deeper than those of a sighted man. It was as if his soul were naked and shivering beneath the gaze of the blind figure dressed in black.

The blind man removed his hand from the captain's cheek. A dollop of blood clung to the jagged tip of his viciously sharp index fingernail.

Captain Tiaphang was certain the nail would drop to his belly, and that his own organs and blood would join that of his men.

The blind man leaned in close. His breath smelled like a rotting corpse.

"Leave," he commanded.

Captain Tiaphang of the People's Liberation Army was accustomed to following orders, and this was one he definitely did not need to be told a second time.

He turned and ran for all he was worth. Slipping, falling into a puddle of steaming, muddy blood. Scampering back to his feet. Running. Out of the accursed city, back to the path, through the woods and to the world of the living.

All the while, the captain's frantically beating heart raced the poison that had been delivered by the scratch on his cheek through his bloodstream to every cell in his body.

Those who dwelled once more in the City of the dead watched the People's Army captain flee from their midst, covered in mud mixed with the blood of his own men.

When the soldier was gone, the figures in black congregated around the Leader.

"What must we do now?" they asked.

The Leader turned and mounted the steps of the temple, taking his seat in the shadows that bathed the ancient stone throne. When at last he spoke, his voice carried to the upturned faces, standing amid a sea of blood and corpses.

"The message is sent. The time of vengeance is fast approaching. Now, we feast. After, we prepare for the arrival of the Master of Sinanju."

CHAPTER 9

THE DORM STAIRWELL down which Remo and Chiun stole was deserted; a result of the two disemboweled girls who had been discovered hanging from a Columbus University campus tree in the wee hours the previous night.

The entire fifth floor of the dorm that had been turned into an abattoir sometime before dawn had yet to be discovered. So many more deaths would likely result in the school being shut down indefinitely, and the building would soon be crawling with local and federal police. For now, the pair of Masters of Sinanju encountered no prying eyes on their silent way from the fifth to the ground floor.

Remo carried the two Lindstrom boys without a sign of strain on his face. The two bundles were awkward, however, forcing him at ground level to make a request of the old Korean who had yet to speak a single word since they had exited the fifth floor room where they had encountered their attackers.

"Grab the door, will you, Chiun?"

"Forgive my ignorance, Remo. Was I drafted into servitude while I was sleeping and no one informed me?"

"I've schlepped these things down five flights of stairs. It's just one goddamn door. If it makes you happy, you can sing 'Swing Low Sweet Chariot' while you do it."

Chiun reluctantly held the door open for Remo as the younger

Master of Sinanju carted the bodies of the unconscious Lindstrom boys from the stairwell of Crane Hall.

"Keep their hands away from me," the old Korean warned as Remo passed by. "Acting as doorman for you will not be my last act on the mortal plane."

"Hey, *mine* isn't waking up," Remo said. "I can't account for what you may have botched with yours."

He barely managed to yank the college kid that was dangling under his arm out of the way of the slamming stairwell door.

The entire brick building shook from the force of the door's impact. Ivy leaves and dislodged mortar dropped to the steps of the short side staircase down which Remo hurried. Chiun trailed reluctantly behind.

"Did you ever hear the phrase 'kill with kindness?'" Remo muttered.

"*I* am not kind?" Chiun replied. "I? Not kind? Forget all that I have done for you throughout the years, Remo. That should be easy for you, as you have much experience forgetting the countless acts of kindness I have bestowed upon your ingrate self. It is you who did not wish to put these two out of their misery, which would be the kindest thing one could do for them. You are keeping them alive, not I. Kindness, indeed."

"It's not their fault their minds have been messed with. Besides, we've got to question them. Not to mention we know what to do about this vampire virus this time around."

They hustled across a stone path to a side door of the nearby Columbus Medical School.

Rather than ask Chiun to open another door for him — which was as likely an event to occur as an unexpected return of Halley's Comet over the Super Bowl on the 4th of July — Remo used the heel of his shoe to smash open the locked side door of the medical school building.

A security pad with a punch-code keyboard was mounted on the wall in the foyer just inside the door. It blinked and beeped, waiting for the proper code to be entered.

"Crap on a crust," Remo said.

He knew he probably had a minute to key in the right code

before an alarm that would wake the dead would start blaring across the campus.

"Can you get that, Little Father?"

The old Korean's eyelids drooped to half-mast.

"Do you wish me to open a door for it?"

"Jesus, Mary, and Joseph, it's not like I'm lugging around a couple of bodies or anything. Just stand there. I wouldn't want you to strain yourself."

Remo put down the two unconscious boys like a perturbed housewife dropping a pair of shopping bags on the kitchen table. He examined the blinking pad.

He had no idea what the code would be. It was a medical school. For all he knew the code was Marcus Welby's birthday.

Since the device was meant to accept information that was punched into it, Remo decided that the best course of action was to punch it.

He launched his fist dead center into the small box. It exploded in a spray of thin plastic chips, wires, and tiny metal screws. A small computer chip on colored wires dropped out and slapped against the wall. The blinking lights winked out.

"I could have done *that*," Chiun sniffed, arms stuffed deep inside the voluminous sleeves of his kimono.

Remo was too busy waiting for an alarm to start shrieking to shoot the old man a foul look. It turned out the building's security system was about as worthwhile as a modern college education. Remo's improvised reprogramming worked.

In the silence that ensued, Remo scooped up the unconscious college boys once more and the two Sinanju masters hurried through the darkened halls of the building.

A timer on the ancient boiler in the basement had not yet turned up the heat. The building was as cold as a crypt.

Remo was used to the fact that he and Chiun no longer sent out visible huffing puffs of steam into freezing air. He found it disconcerting that neither did the two men he was carrying, who otherwise superficially resembled ordinary college students. Whatever other horrors the cult of Chinese vampires might have ready to unleash on Remo and his teacher, at least they'd soon have the two Lindstrom boys back to normal.

In their previous encounter with the *gyonshi*, Remo had discovered that a powerful enough electric shock would purge the victims of the virus that infected them.

Since this building was part of the Columbus Medical School, he assumed somewhere in it would be a portable defibrillator. The devices were becoming so cheap to produce they were springing up hanging on walls everywhere, from campgrounds to malls to corner convenience stores. They were everywhere, Remo soon discovered, but the main medical school building of Columbus University.

The two Masters of Sinanju were halfway down their second gloomy corridor and not a single defibrillator wall unit was in sight.

"I'm going to plug one of them into a wall socket in a minute," Remo grumbled.

Their footfalls had been silent, but his voice echoed down the vacant hall. A balding head abruptly stuck out from a room three doors down.

"What are you two doing here? Classes have been cancelled this morning."

The professor wore a white lab coat with "Dr. Kovaks" stitched in blue over his left breast pocket. He was a parody of a university professor, with a shiny, plucked scalp that descended into a fringe of uncombed white hair. A pair of bifocals were attached to the tip of his nose, above which two watery blue eyes studied Remo and Chiun with suspicion as they approached up the hall.

The two intruders had been cloaked in shadows, but when Remo stepped into a shaft of light, Dr. Kovaks inhaled shock at seeing the two bundles he was carrying.

"What's the meaning of this?" Dr. Kovaks demanded.

"Off the top of my head, I'd go with 'a hernia,'" Remo replied. "Listen, doc, put your eyes back in their sockets. Everything's fine. We just need one of those things with the two paddles on them. You know, like they shock people's chests with on TV. Stat," he added with what he determined was an appropriate medical flourish.

"A defibrillator?" Dr. Kovaks asked, baffled.

"Yeah, one of those," Remo replied. Off Chiun's look of disgust, he said, "Oh, like *you* knew."

Dr. Kovaks hesitated, asking what was wrong with the two boys that required a defibrillator. Remo replied by squeezing the portly professor's earlobe. Dr. Kovaks decided that he concurred with Remo's diagnosis — whatever it was — and, rubbing the side of his head, waddled to a classroom at the end of the hallway.

A human skeleton hung from a metal stand in the corner. Its dead eye sockets stared eternity at the motley group that hurried into the classroom.

Dr. Kovaks waddled over to a closet next to the skeleton.

As the doctor fussed around inside the closet, Remo first eased Elliot Lindstrom onto a lab table at the front of the room, then stretched out the second Lindstrom boy on the next table. Both Elliot and Peter continued their shallow, rhythmic breathing.

"Here we go," Dr. Kovaks announced.

He hustled over from the closet and presented a white plastic box to Remo.

Remo was never particularly good with gadgets, and so was glad to have a real-life college professor on the scene to pitch in. He was even happier Kovaks was there when he popped the lid on the plastic box and got a look at the contents.

Dr. Kovaks noted the baffled look on Remo's face.

"Do you know what you're doing?" the professor asked.

"I could tell you stories," Chiun confided.

"I've seen them do it a million times on TV," Remo said, perturbed, to both men. He was poking around in the case. "Where are the goddamn paddles?"

TV doctors were always rubbing paddles together before giving a patient's heart a shock, but there were none visible inside the case. Just a couple of sticky pads that looked like the business end of a fly swatter.

"Here, I'll do it," Dr. Kovaks said.

He pulled open Elliot Lindstrom's shirt and attached the sticky blue fly swatters to either side of the young man's chest; one high, one low.

"This could be dangerous if there's nothing wrong with this young man," the professor warned.

"There is," Remo assured him.

As if taking a cue from the professor's warning, Peter Lindstrom began to groan. Chiun was keeping watch over the younger brother as Remo and Dr. Kovaks worked around the older boy. After the low groan, Peter snorted softly. The Master of Sinanju shot a dark look at Remo.

"Whatever this quacksalver intends to do with that device, do it quickly," the old Korean warned. "They will not sleep forever."

Remo nodded to the professor. "Do it," he insisted.

Dr. Kovaks turned on the defibrillator, hesitated for a moment as he looked first from the boy stretched out on the lab table to the two men standing watch beside both tables, and then sent a jolt of electricity through the pads on the boy's chest.

Elliot Lindstrom's back arched and he bounced once, roughly. His head snapped back against the polished black surface of the table, and his fingers curled into weak fists.

At the next table, the brother groaned once more.

"Knock that one out again if he comes to, Little Father," Remo said.

His eyes were trained on the older brother.

Elliott Lindstrom was awakening, but there was no telling yet who would be behind the waking eyes. The boy's head rolled slowly from side to side.

For a quiet moment, nothing happened.

The jolt had apparently been insufficient to release the poison.

Remo was about to order Dr. Kovaks to shock the boy a second time, upping the dose this time, when a faint orange mist suddenly began to slip from Elliot's nostrils.

It looked like a thin curl of cartoon smoke from an orange cigar. At first it was a barely visible vapor, but then the boy's pale lips parted and, with an accompanying low belch, a cloud of thick fog poured from the young man's mouth.

The *gyonshi* poison. Remo had seen it before. It was a hard-learned lesson from their previous encounter with the ancient vampire Creed.

Remo reached for the defibrillator patches on Elliot Lindstrom's chest.

"Okay, this one'll be fine," he said. "Let's get the other —"

All at once, Elliot Lindstrom let out a blood curdling scream.

The young man's eyes snapped open. He took in the room, but seemed not to see it. His eyes were focused on some incomprehensible terror visible only to him.

Desperate hands snatched the edges of the table, knuckles grew white as snow.

The boy violently twisted left and right, repeatedly banging his head on the surface of the table.

Remo grabbed the wildly convulsing boy by the shoulders, pinning him to the table.

"Remo! His hand!" Chiun snapped.

At the next table, the second Lindstrom boy's groans increased.

"I know!" Remo snapped.

He was acutely aware of the potential damage the young man's fingernail could inflict, and was careful to keep the hand with the *gyonshi* nail away from his own body.

The shock should have purged the poison. It had done so in the past. The orange cloud had passed his lips. The kid shouldn't be reacting as he was.

As Remo held on, Elliot Lindstrom kicked and twisted for an excruciating half-minute before his back arched a final, agonizing time. The convulsions stopped as if a string had been cut, and the boy collapsed like a deflated balloon to the table.

This time when the final breath passed his lips, there was no accompanying orange cloud. The young man grew still in death.

Numbly, Remo released his grip. He had no idea what could have gone wrong. He focused his hearing on the boy's chest. As expected, there was no heartbeat.

"It should have worked," Remo insisted.

The exact same technique that worked before had failed. Purging the toxin this time had not been a cure, but had hastened death. Somehow the Chinese vampire Creed had altered the virus, and the hard-learned lessons from the past were no good.

He had no time to dwell on this failure.

A wild, animal growl issued from behind him.

Remo wheeled to find Peter Lindstrom fully awake, furious eyes directed on the frail figure closest to him.

The boy lashed out at the old Korean with the sharpened edge of his fingernail.

The *gyonshi* was fast. The Master of Sinanju was faster.

In a blur of motion the fine details of which were visible only to Remo's eyes, Chiun produced his own deadly sharp fingernails from the folds of his kimono sleeves. The Master of Sinanju raked his sharpened nails with bloody precision across the young man's throat. Four bubbling crimson trails sprang up in the soft tissue in the wake of the older Sinanju master's Knives of Eternity.

The boy's attack on his elderly victim was instantly forgotten. The surviving Lindstrom boy snatched at his own throat with both hands in a vain attempt to hold in the precious red fluid. From between the gaps in his fingers, a thin cloud of orange smoke seeped along with the gurgling blood.

There was a moment where the boy seemed suddenly to be himself again. His eyes cleared and he looked in terror from face to face, pleading for help. And then he pitched forward and toppled off the table, landing in a crumpled heap at Chiun's feet.

Remo had no time to process the most recent brutal death to plague the campus of Columbus University.

As he watched the second Lindstrom boy's body fall, he felt a faint scratch draw across the exposed flesh at the back of his neck.

He wheeled around to discover Dr. Kovaks withdrawing his hand, a look of triumph on his pale, blubbery face.

Remo slapped a hand over the thin wound. He raised a clawed hand to deal with his grinning attacker, but the green kimono blur that flew past him got there first.

Chiun sent a flying heel into the chest of Dr. Kovaks.

The professor might have been able to tell his students exactly which of a dozen bones were broken in the initial assault, but for the fact that the explosion of bone shrapnel from the precision blow pierced every major organ in his body. All that was undamaged in the attack was his brain, which ceased working when his rocketing body crashed through the wall of the classroom and burst out into the darkened hallway, coming to a skidding stop against a water fountain on the far wall.

The old Korean spun from the professor-shaped hole in the classroom wall.

"Speak! What do you feel?" the Master of Sinanju demanded.

"Pissed off," Remo snarled. "That old wobble-bottom shouldn't have gotten within a country mile of me."

"The poison," Chiun directed. "With what have these devil apothecaries infected you, my son?"

As a Master of Sinanju at the height of his abilities, Remo was sensitive to every cell in his body. He concentrated inward, from the point at which the dead professor's fingernail had scratched his neck to the blood coursing through his veins.

Remo shrugged.

"Nothing," he said. "Maybe he was a fat dud." He paused, a hint of worry suddenly brushing his face. "Hold on a sec."

It had taken a moment to take hold. But it was there. He detected the alien presence before he felt its effects. It did not, however, come exclusively from the scrape on the back of his neck.

The tainted blood coursed through his veins, but it mixed with something else. Something in the air in the classroom.

The dying breaths of the Lindstrom boys had released the orange *gyonshi* poison into the room. Even though the clouds had broken up, the aerosol droplets were still suspended in the air that Remo was breathing in.

"Shit," he said. "*Go*, Little Father."

He tried to push the old man from his side. Chiun was rooted to the floor.

"It wasn't only in the scratch, Chiun," he insisted. "Whatever escaped from their lungs was the second part of the poison."

Remo staggered backwards. He could feel the warm intermingling toxins invading his system. His body was already going on defense. He could feel his blood growing sluggish like syrup as it attempted to filter the virus, forcing it away from the body's vital centers. It had gotten in, but it wasn't getting far. Not yet.

Something moved in his peripheral vision. Remo turned woozily, just in time to spot the looming figure of Dr. Kovaks.

It was impossible. Chiun had killed the man. Yet he stood before Remo now, blood drooling from his grinning mouth. The professor's eyes had changed. They were totally white, staring at the world with milky malevolence.

The professor now possessed a fully formed *gyonshi* fingernail, which he brandished above his head like a blade. The Master of Sinanju stood with his back to Kovaks, his concern for Remo making him oblivious to the sudden danger.

"Look out, Chiun!" Remo yelled.

Too late. The zombie professor slashed down. His sharp nail pierced the old Korean's spine, severing it at the midpoint. Chiun's mouth dropped open in silent pain. Not a sound escaped his lips as his hazel eyes locked onto those of his adopted son. The Master of Sinanju had never looked so frail to Remo as he did in his dying moment.

Chiun's grimacing face twisted back into an expression of stoic surrender, the master of his own emotions even unto the end. And then the delicate figure collapsed dead to the floor amid the deflating shape of his shimmering green kimono.

CHAPTER 10

THE MASTER OF SINANJU lay dead at Remo's feet.

The frail colossus who had withstood the battering forces of an entire century; who had triumphed over armies; who had decimated legions of the most skilled killers known to man had been felled by the hand of some anonymous *gyonshi* vermin.

Such an insignificant death for a figure so towering was an insult to the man who had taught Remo Williams everything. The Master of Sinanju was no more. The only father Remo had ever known was gone forever.

The anguish and rage would come soon enough. At the moment it was taking all the focus he possessed to deal with Chiun's killer.

Remo's head spun. The poison Kovaks had delivered to the back of his neck, coupled with the particles expelled into the air by the dying Lindstrom boys had apparently given a one-two punch to Remo's nervous system.

The zombie form of Dr. Kovaks didn't care that Remo was stumbling against a lab table, attempting to straighten up in preparation for battle. The portly professor with the milky white eyes stepped over the body of the Master of Sinanju as if Remo's teacher were a piece of garbage tossed in the gutter.

Although seemingly blind, Kovaks made a beeline for Remo. The professor raised his arm high. His *gyonshi* fingernail glinted in the streams of sunlight that poured into the classroom through six tall windows in the far wall.

Kovaks slashed at Remo's throat.

For an instant it seemed as if Remo's hands would refuse to listen to years of training. Thanks to whatever *gyonshi* filth was poisoning his system, he was offering himself up like a lamb to slaughter. It was only through sheer force of will that his hand shot out and he was able to parry the blow.

The professor's arm was insubstantial. Remo nearly dislocated his shoulder when his own hand passed through the wrist of his attacker.

Dr. Kovaks lashed out again, this time in a cutting blow horizontally across Remo's chest.

Remo blocked the second blow. This time there was substance to the arm.

He heard a voice. Someone shouting deep inside his own brain.

No time to listen. He was in a fight for his life.

Dr. Kovaks' hand shot out repeatedly at Remo. Two, five, ten times. With fumbling forearms Remo managed to block each blow. But with each subsequent blow it grew more difficult to stop the relentless barrage. Remo's brain felt as if it had been pumped full of helium. The room spun crazily around him.

He was on defense, unable to land a killing blow. Not that he had much hope of killing the professor. Chiun had already killed the man once. Could one kill a zombie?

The voice in his head was growing more insistent. He was too engrossed in battle to listen to some hallucination, but the voice would not be ignored.

For one second, Remo backed away from the grinning ambulatory corpse with its mouth dripping blood and concentrated on his own hazy brain.

He finally heard the urgent words, spoken in the familiar singsong voice that he thought he would never hear again.

"Stop fighting! It is me!"

The voice of his dead teacher spoke not only in his head, but echoed in his ears.

It came not from the great beyond, but from the Columbus University classroom.

Remo looked at the floor where Chiun's body had fallen. The kimono-clad corpse faded from existence like a desert mirage. He snapped his head up to his attacker.

The bloodied, blind face and portly body of Dr. Kovaks melted away, replaced by the ancient visage and wizened form of the Master of Sinanju.

Chiun held his hands out in a defensive posture; alert, ready to deflect any other blows his pupil might launch in his direction.

Remo attempted to make sense of the scene before him. He was lucid enough to know now that he had been hallucinating, but what was real and what was illusion? The poison continued to course through his system. He felt his brain grow light.

"How do I know it's you?" he croaked.

"Don't be a retard," Chiun said.

"That's you," Remo said, and promptly passed out.

The Master of Sinanju caught the collapsing body before it hit the floor. With great delicacy and a strength belied by his ancient form, he lifted the limp form of his pupil in his arms.

When Remo had begun blindly lashing out at him, Chiun's sensitive ears had detected the flutter in the younger man's heart that signaled intense emotional pain.

Remo's clouded mind had given the younger man a terrible waking dream visible only to him, but from the grief that tripped his heart and the subsequent attack, Chiun had surmised the hallucination which the *gyonshi* poison had presented to his pupil.

The Master of Sinanju offered a tight smile that reflected both concern and deep affection for his slumbering adopted son. With great care, he carried the much younger man from the classroom.

The twisted body of Dr. Kovaks was nestled in the deep dent it had made in the side of the water fountain. A trickle of water ran from a tear in the thin metal, mixing with and diluting the puddle of blood that had spread across the floor.

Chiun found something waiting for him in the dark hallway.

An amorphous black cloud swirled before the fire doors at the end of the hall.

The Master of Sinanju's mind had not been influenced by the poison that had afflicted his pupil. Remo had said something about there being two components to this toxin: one introduced directly into the bloodstream by a scratch, the other inhaled from molecules dispersed by the dying college student brothers. Chiun had been exposed to the latter but not the former, and was therefore immune to whatever terrible effects were plaguing Remo. He could therefore see clearly through the swirling black cloud at the end of the hall and at the dark figure of a young man who stood placidly within it.

The man stepped forward. The cloud came with him, moving closer to the Master of Sinanju and his precious cargo.

"You are Sinanju."

The voice seemed to come from nowhere, aided by the composition of the swirling cloud, yet Chiun could clearly see its source. The young man was smiling.

Chiun stared into the belly of the fog and the man standing within it. Their eyes locked.

"You see me," the young man dressed in black said.

"I see a *gyonshi* dog who murders without thought and believes he can hide with the aid of trickery," Chiun spit.

"That you can see me or not matters not," the young Chinese vampire said. "Look upon the face of your son whom you love. It is your future, old one."

The man in the mist hung back, studying the old Korean before him.

"You tell me my future, I tell you your past," Chiun said. "Yours is a Creed of cowards. You look for weakness and rarely attack one-on-one. What pitiful strength you possess is only ever due to greater numbers. If you think me as weak as you, worshiper of evil, attack me now and I will give you the Final Death your cult craves."

"You assume I am alone, old man," the young *gyonshi* teased.

"One or a hundred, it does not matter. I tell you this, jackal. Though you send one thousand against me, I will dispense them all to protect this one man."

The young man within the cloud considered the Master of Sinanju's words. When he eventually spoke, his voice held the same strange disembodied quality.

"And I tell you, old one. Those things you slaughtered are but vassals. The true keepers of the Creed have returned. Fear you us, Sinanju. For death has kissed these shores and we will have our harvest."

With that the mist began to recede down the hallway, and the young man with it.

Even Chiun's sharp eyes lost the shape of the figure as the *gyonshi* killer closed in on the fire doors. It was not the man but the black cloud that seemed to open the distant doors. The mist flooded out, the fire doors closed and, but for the gentle gurgle of the ruptured water fountain, all in the hall grew quiet.

Chiun trained his ears on each classroom that he would have to pass, tuning up to the straining point in order to detect the slightest noise within them. He heard nothing.

Holding his precious cargo close to his heart, the Master of Sinanju glided carefully down the hallway. To seek out a telephone.

CHAPTER 11

DR. HAROLD W. SMITH scanned the latest report from Columbus University with tired eyes and a growing sense of dread in the pit of his acid-churned stomach.

A bottle of pink liquid antacid sat on the corner of his desk. Smith had taken the bottle out of his bottom drawer minutes before but had yet to open it. The antacid was on standby in case it was needed. So, too, was Harold W. Smith, who was currently helpless to do anything but monitor the situation as it developed in New York City.

The two dead girls that had been the reason Smith had sent Remo and Chiun to the Manhattan university's campus were no longer the only victims. In a horrific turn of events almost impossible to comprehend, an entire dormitory floor had been a scene of unprecedented carnage. Dozens of young lives ritualistically snuffed out in the dead hours of a cold New York night.

The bodies had only just been discovered. Not a living soul had escaped the slaughterhouse. It was an appalling crime. One that the national news media had only just gotten wind of. Reporters would soon be descending en masse on the university. Columbus would soon be a madhouse, with all eyes trained on it, and so far Remo — CURE's top secret enforcement arm — had failed to check in.

The manner in which the first two bodies had been prepared

after death had suggested the work of the Chinese cult with which CURE had dealt twice in the past. Despite the grisly display that had been made of the two girls, Smith had not been convinced that they were dealing with the same cult. Remo had handled the Leader with finality the last time he'd stopped the aged head of the Chinese sect. This latest news, however, had nudged Smith into accepting the very real possibility that the *gyonshi* cult had returned. Not headed by the Leader, of course. That old fiend was long dead. But perhaps a protégé who had decided to take up the cause of his deceased cult leader.

The invisible electronic tendrils of Folcroft's basement mainframes extended into the computer systems of every domestic and foreign government agency. When photographs of the latest crime scene were downloaded into the FBI's system in Washington, the images were automatically and secretly rerouted to the computer screen buried beneath the gleaming surface of Smith's onyx desk.

The photographs were more gruesome than the initial descriptions.

Image after image taken from the hallway repeated the same terrible scene of bodies hanging from dorm room ceilings. The bellies of the corpses had been sliced open and their organs had been harvested. The skin of some had been peeled away and wrapped around the ghastly bundles that sat beneath the dead students.

The photos gave Smith a chilling sense of déjà vu.

In only one dorm room was the scene different.

A body had been discovered in this room as well, but it had not been dangling from the ceiling like the others. This one had been hanging in a closet.

It was difficult to tell if there had been a struggle in the room. The boys who had lived there had apparently been typically disorganized college students. But when Smith saw the smashed louvered doors of the closet, he made an intuitive leap.

"Remo," he said aloud.

The instant the name passed his lips, the intercom on his desk buzzed.

"Dr. Smith," his secretary's voice said. "I know you asked not to be disturbed, but there's someone on the phone."

"Take a message, Mrs. Mikulka," Smith sternly replied.

"I *can't*, Dr. Smith," Eileen Mikulka said, her voice worried. "He's yelling in some foreign language. I can't get a word of what he's saying. I thought it was a wrong number the first time he called, so I hung up on him. He called right back. It sounds like he could be in some kind of trouble, but I don't know what it could be. I don't know what I should do. Do you think I should call the police?"

Smith's natural state was that of a man at constant attention, even while seated. At his secretary's suggestion, he somehow managed to sit up even straighter in his chair.

"No, Mrs. Mikulka," he said. "I will take the call."

"Yes, sir," his secretary said, clearly relieved.

The call was transferred to the Folcroft business phone at the corner of his desk. When Smith picked it up, his eardrum was instantly assaulted by a torrent of frantic gibberish. He had to hold the phone away from his ear as the speaker on the other end of the line jabbered desperately away. The first time the man paused to take a breath, Smith charged into the breach.

"I am sorry," the CURE directed said. "You have a wrong number."

The man began talking once more.

"Wrong number," Smith repeated. "Please don't call here again."

He hung up the phone.

In the next room, Eileen Mikulka had apparently been watching for the light on the phone to wink out. The instant it did, she buzzed the intercom once more.

"I'm sorry about that, Dr. Smith. It just sounded so urgent."

"I have dealt with it, Mrs. Mikulka. Now, please. I don't wish to be disturbed."

"Yes, sir."

He permitted his secretary to return to the humdrum of sanitarium business as he resumed his perusal of the data coming out of Columbus University.

He had no sooner redirected his gaze to his computer monitor than the blue contact phone jangled to life. He snatched it up on the first ring.

"Report," Smith said.

He had expected to hear Remo's voice. He was instead surprised to find the Master of Sinanju on the other end of the line.

"We are in need of transportation," Chiun tersely announced, in place of the usual effusive salutations with which he greeted his employer.

Smith placed a flat palm on the edge of his desk.

"Why? What's wrong? Chiun, where's Remo?"

The elderly Korean's response did not fill CURE's director with confidence.

"Remo lives," Chiun said. "More than that I cannot now say. I require transportation to Fortress Folcroft where I can examine him away from prying eyes. We are in the filthy city that everyone hates, near one of those yellow metal objects on which dogs relieve themselves. A vender of sandwiches is across the road. *Hurry.*"

Precise directions to his location delivered, the Master of Sinanju broke the connection.

The old Korean was not on the line long enough to be traced by conventional means. However, thanks to CURE's mainframes, Smith was quickly able to trace the call to a Manhattan phone kiosk near a fire hydrant and across from a Subway sandwich shop.

He did not like the idea of CURE's field operatives spending time at Folcroft. Remo and Chiun were a physical link to the work that Smith carried on in secret from his office. However, there had been times in the past when it was necessary to bring CURE's agents home. Judging by the urgency in Chiun's voice, this was one of those times.

The acid in his belly surged. Smith uncapped his antacid and took a deep swig. King Canute had a greater chance of stopping the ocean from rising than a slug of Pepto-Bismol had of quelling the rising acid tide in Harold Smith's stomach.

Smith screwed the cap back on the bottle and turned his attention to his keyboard. He had scarcely started typing than his intercom buzzed again.

"Dr. Smith," the hesitant voice of his secretary said.

Smith noticed one of the sanitarium line lights was blinking once more.

"Not now, Mrs. Mikulka," he snapped.

Smith worked his computer keyboard like a concert pianist. The mainframes at the CURE director's disposal might not have the power to move mountains, but they had the power to reduce the tallest peaks on the planet to rubble. That awesome power at the tapping fingertips of Harold Smith was brought to bear on the single task of arranging transportation for Remo and Chiun out of Manhattan.

Smith finished with a flourish. He quickly shut down his computer and climbed to his feet. It was a contest between his chair and aging bones to see which would creak loudest. He checked his trusty Timex as he hustled across the threadbare carpet.

When he passed through the outer office, his matronly secretary was looking at her ringing phone and shrugging helplessly.

Smith didn't have time to deal with wrong numbers.

He hurried through the administration wing of the sanitarium. In the medical wing he collected a pair of orderlies, commanding the men to grab a gurney.

The two men followed the Folcroft director out a side door of the brick building to the landscaped lawn.

The grass was brown and matted. A low, white sun was burning off the remnants of thin snow that had barely blanketed the lawn the previous day.

Smith checked his watch every minute, face pinched in lemony concern, until the sound of an approaching helicopter could be detected over the ambient everyday morning noise of Rye.

The noise of chopping rotor blades quickly increased, soon eclipsing all other sounds. The medical helicopter appeared over the wildly bending treetops, swooping up from the south.

The orderlies who had accompanied Smith onto the lawn struggled to cover their ears while attempting to keep the white sheet on the gurney from blowing away in the hurricane winds that were being produced by the landing helicopter. Both men were so preoccupied that they did not notice that their employer did not yield to the wind.

Harold Smith was rooted to the ground. Sharp gray eyes behind spotless, rimless glasses were locked on the helicopter as it settled to the brown grass.

The side door of the helicopter opened just over eighteen minutes after Smith had ordered the nearest NYPD black-and-white to collect two men across from the Subway sandwich shop and transport them to a waiting hospital helicopter. It might have been a world's record in the efficient deployment of government resources. Smith did not stand around waiting for accolades.

"Bring the gurney," Smith commanded.

The two orderlies did as they were told, hustling across the grass behind their employer to the waiting helicopter.

A tiny figure sprang from the door. When a pair of helping hands reached out, he swatted them away.

The Master of Sinanju refused the assistance of the helicopter's EMT crew. He was alone in assisting Remo to the ground as Smith reached the chopper.

When Smith saw that Remo appeared alert, if a little shaky on his feet, the CURE director exhaled Pepto-Bismol-scented relief.

"I'm fine, Little Father," Remo was grousing.

"He is not fine," Chiun assured Smith.

"Who are you going to believe," Remo asked the CURE director, "him or me? Don't give me that look. I don't need the mother hen stuff from you, too."

Although it was not unprecedented for patients to arrive at the facility by helicopter, it was still out of the ordinary. Smith was concerned by the prying eyes he knew must be watching from the windows at his back. It was important to keep up the appearance that this was merely another guest of Folcroft Sanitarium.

"Please get on the gurney," he said.

"You get on the gurney," Remo said. "We can take turns popping wheelies in the goddamn parking lot."

"Do as Emperor Smith suggests," Chiun insisted.

Remo suddenly seemed to get the situation. It was broad daylight in Folcroft's front yard, and he was standing with his back to a helicopter staffed by emergency medical staff while facing a pair of sanitarium orderlies. The windows before him were not currently filled with gawkers, but there were a few curious faces. Remo doubted it was coincidence that Smith had chosen the side lawn which meant the squinting onlookers were facing the direction of the blinding, midmorning sun.

"Fine," he said, shoulders slumping.

He climbed onto the gurney, but drew the line at accepting assistance from the Folcroft orderlies. He slapped their hands away.

Smith noted that the gesture was identical to that which the Master of Sinanju had used to ward off help from the helicopter EMTs.

The helicopter had been ordered not to linger. As soon as the small group began heading back to the building, the chopper was lifting off.

The treetops were dancing crazily in the wind once more as Smith ushered orderlies, gurney, and the Master of Sinanju into the side door of the sanitarium.

They bypassed the main medical wing. A special basement ward was set up ostensibly for difficult cases that could not mix with regular patients. In truth it had never been used for Folcroft business, but was there in case of emergencies connected to the secret work conducted under the sanitarium's roof.

Only two rooms were occupied, as they had been for years. The first door was open. A man of indeterminate age slumbered in the lone bed. The door to the second room was closed as Remo was wheeled past it, but Dr. Smith noted through the small window the emaciated figure with a splash of long blond hair across his pillow lying comatose beneath a crisp white sheet. Another reminder of old CURE business.

Remo was brought into one of the remaining empty rooms, and Smith immediately dismissed the two orderlies and shut the door.

The Master of Sinanju was already ministering to his patient when Smith stepped over to the gurney. The ancient Korean tapped every joint and squeezed every muscle. When Smith stopped beside him, the old man nodded to the CURE director.

"Whom do you see?" Chiun asked Remo.

"Joan of Arc," Remo replied. "Who do you think I see? I see Smitty, in all his pinched-sphincter glory. No offense, Smitty."

"What happened, Chiun?" Smith asked.

Remo snapped his fingers in Smith's face.

"Hello. I'm sitting right here."

"Please, Remo," Smith said. "I don't care which of you answers. Was it the Chinese vampire cult?"

"It sure looks that way," Remo said.

"It was," Chiun solemnly intoned.

Smith shook his head. "All those students murdered. I assume it is some follower of the Leader. Did you at least stop him or them?"

"At least?" Remo mocked. "I was busy at least getting poisoned and nearly at least dying to at least stop anybody. We didn't meet whoever is behind this. We only met a couple of kids who they conscripted into service with that junk they pump into their veins. Also some dweeby college professor who Chiun put through a wall. At least I think he did." He turned to the Master of Sinanju. "You did, didn't you, Little Father? Things got a little hazy for me back there at the end."

The Master of Sinanju nodded crisply.

"That was it," Remo said. "Whoever the big cheese is this time around, we didn't get a chance to root him out before I started seeing zombies swinging from the chandeliers, which was just around the same time I tried duking it out with Chiun."

"Explain," Smith commanded.

Remo had pushed himself to his elbows on the gurney. The fight drained out of him, and he dropped to his back once more. His face was covered in sweat. Perspiration soaked his T-shirt. He felt like he was battling an old childhood flu.

Remo took a deep breath, then quickly filled the CURE director in on that morning's events at Columbus University, including the attempt to save the Lindstrom brothers using a defibrillator, which had only resulted in the deaths of the two boys and the dispersal of fifty-percent of the latest *gyonshi* poison into the air.

"The good news is that it looks like you need to mix the gin with the tonic for this particular cocktail to work," Remo said. "The scratch only introduced part of it. It was when it mixed with the water particles in the air that it got me. Chiun didn't get scratched, so the vapor didn't have any effect on him."

"And you're saying this caused you to hallucinate?" Smith asked.

"Among other symptoms," Remo said. "I feel like I got run over by a bulldozer for one. But, yeah, hallucinations are right up at the top symptoms. I swore Chiun was the body of the corpse he'd killed. The *gyonshi* do that with their drugs, don't they, Chiun? They're famous for potions that mess with your mind?"

"Their Creed is possessed with a vast knowledge of wicked draughts," the old Korean replied, his tone dark with ancient knowledge.

"Then close the window," Remo said. "What the hell do drafts have to do with anything?"

"Not drafts, draughts," Smith said.

Remo closed his eyes. "Did I mention my head hurts, too?"

"Elixirs," Smith explained.

"Isn't English anybody's first language around here?" Remo said.

"They are not limited to potions that dominate the will and cloud the senses," Chiun informed them. "The ancient Creed knows more about death than any who have ever walked on or under the earth. Their dark knowledge surpasses even the Masters of Sinanju, for we are dealers in death, not worshippers of it. It was rumored that the Leader of their cult possessed mastery over death itself."

For this, Remo opened his eyes.

"Are you suggesting what I think you're suggesting?"

Chiun stuffed his hands into his kimono sleeves.

"I have suggested nothing. I merely am open to the possibility that when we thought we had encountered our ancient foe for the last time years ago that we may have been mistaken. Mostly you. I was far less mistaken. Sixty-forty," he added, lest Smith place the unequal burden of blame on his shoulders.

"I don't think it can possibly be the Leader himself," Remo said, not attempting to mask his deep skepticism.

"Seventy-thirty," Chiun confided in Smith.

"I am having an impossible time accepting that this could be the work of the Leader himself," Smith said. "When the story broke of those two girls who were found in that tree, I pulled up his old autopsy report. He is dead. There is no doubt."

"His body died," Chiun conceded. "I cannot say what happened to that which gave it movement."

Smith had seen much as director of CURE. Despite having many of his beliefs challenged over the years, he was still uncomfortable with such metaphysical conversations. Perhaps, he conceded, he was less comfortable because of all that he had seen. No matter. Harold W. Smith preferred dealing with the corporeal, and the reality was that at that very moment there was a killer or killers using techniques of the ancient vampire cult terrorizing a college campus in New York City, and the men who were best suited to deal with the crisis were currently sidelined in a small basement room in Rye.

"How soon can you get back to New York?" Smith asked.

"Geez Louise, Smitty, give me a minute to catch my breath," Remo said. "It's not like I just took a stroll through the valley of the shadow of death or anything."

The biblical phrase rattled loose a thought that he had not even realized had been lurking in the back of his mind.

"That's weird," Remo said. "Speaking of shadows, I think I just remembered something. Chiun, when I was out of it back at that school, were you talking to a cloud?"

The Master of Sinanju studied the younger man's face carefully.

"What do you remember seeing?" Chiun asked.

Remo closed his eyes once more, trying to recall the hallucinatory images.

"I was floating. That professor wasn't a zombie after all. He was dead. There was a water fountain, I think. I was in a hall. There was a cloud. A black cloud. It spoke." He opened his eyes, and scrunched one side of his face in confusion. "Did all of that really happen?"

"What did you see within the cloud?"

"Nothing. Just a swirling black cloud."

Chiun nodded.

"It is as I feared. We of Sinanju are not susceptible to the false images these conjurers use to trick the weak minds of lesser men. Unfortunately for you, Remo, your mind was not much to begin with. The addition of this poison to your system has dulled a brain already prone to slow-wittedness. There was a man within the smoke. You are certain you did not see him?"

"No," Remo said. "And thanks a bunch for all that other stuff."

Chiun shook his head.

"I am sorry, Emperor Smith, but until Remo purges this toxin from his system he cannot return to that city of rats and falling buildings."

"Will he be able to do so, Master Chiun?"

"Hey, bedside manner," Remo said. "I'm sitting right here."

Chiun ignored the younger man. Instead, he pried Remo's eyes open wide and carefully examined them. He then touched the tips of his fingers to Remo's jugular. Finally, he pressed a palm flat on his pupil's chest.

"I believe so," the Master of Sinanju concluded. "Even now his body works to purge the poison. A man not fortunate to have been trained by me would likely be under the thrall of the cult now, or lost in the nightmare of his own thoughts."

"May I remind you that that last thing is pretty much what happened to you last time around?" Remo asked.

"Hush, Remo," Chiun said. "You are delirious."

"How soon can he return to active duty?" Smith asked.

"That is impossible to say. Hours. Perhaps days."

"That can't be," Smith insisted. "There is a madman slaughtering college students on the loose in New York City."

"I agree, even though you're not exactly making your case, Smitty," Remo said, "Everybody hates college kids. But even they didn't deserve what we saw."

He started to sit up. Chiun pressed his hand on Remo's chest, this time not to feel the younger man's heart. Remo found himself unable to move.

"Quit it, Chiun," Remo said.

"Do you see, Emperor Smith? Remo is as helpless as the day we discovered him as a foundling in a basket on the steps of Fortress Folcroft."

"Not how I remember it," Remo said.

He struggled against the pressure on his chest, but was unable to move. It was as if the old Korean's palm were a ten thousand pound weight. He finally gave up and collapsed to his back, his brow gleaming with perspiration.

"I will send you alone, Master Chiun," Smith said.

"A wise decision, Smith the Shrewd," Chiun said. "The Master of Sinanju will be a typhoon that will lay waste this Chinese filth who dare profane these shores with the evil rituals of their wicked death Creed. I will slaughter them to a man, and when I have finished with this vermin it will be their carcasses that will hang from the tallest trees in the rat city. When I am done, all will know the name of mighty Harold Smith, and none from this accursed sect will ever show his ugly Chinese face in this land again."

"Er, yes," Smith said.

He was imagining what an unsupervised Chiun loose in Manhattan could mean. It was possible that this was not just the Master of Sinanju's typical flowery language, and that the picture he had painted was exactly what Smith could expect if the old Korean returned to Columbus University alone.

"On second thought, you say you've seen the face of one of them?" Smith asked.

"I have," Chiun said. "But in truth, Emperor Smith, once you've seen one Chinaman, you've seen them all."

"Perhaps there is a way to narrow our focus. Please accompany me to my office."

"I will be there momentarily, Emperor Smith," Chiun said. "Please permit your humble servant a moment alone with Remo. I do not wish to embarrass him by chastising him in your presence for his great failure in this matter."

Smith nodded once, in what Remo interpreted to be the CURE director's attempt at encouragement for a speedy recovery, then left the basement room.

"The guy's a regular walking Hallmark get-well card," Remo grumbled.

"Silence," Chiun said.

He helped his pupil from the gurney. Remo found that his legs felt rubbery, but they managed to keep him upright for the three steps it took him to reach the bed. He did not need much assistance from the Master of Sinanju to climb under the sheets.

"Whatever that stuff is, it packs a real wallop," he said. "Still, I'm glad it was me that got zapped and not you."

"I see your sense of humor is returning, feeble as it is," Chiun droned.

"I'm not kidding, Little Father. I don't know who's behind this. I don't know if it's some new asshole or if it's the Leader's ghost come back to kick us in the nuts one more time for old time's sake. Whoever it is, these *gyonshi* bastards have meant business in the past, and they don't look like they've slacked off. You watch yourself."

The concern the younger man felt for his teacher was deep and genuine. The old Korean felt his chest swell with love for his son-in-spirit.

Chiun pressed his hand to Remo's forehead.

"Rest now, my son. You will be recovered soon enough, and then side-by-side the Masters of Sinanju will vanquish these demons once and for all."

In a swirl of green kimono hems, the elderly Korean swept from the room, leaving a buzzing florescent light and a dripping tap in the sink as Remo's only company.

"You could've left an old *People* magazine," he grumbled.

He allowed his sweating head to sink back into the soft pillow with the pristine white pillowcase. It took only a few short seconds for sleep to overtake him.

CHAPTER 12

EILEEN MIKULKA WAS SIMPLY BESIDE HERSELF.

Generally Mrs. Mikulka's job as secretary to the director of Folcroft Sanitarium was predictably uneventful. Some would even say her work was boring, which was also a word that was very often applied to her employer.

Dr. Harold W. Smith was an easy enough man to work for, even though he was not without his peccadilloes. But wasn't that the same with all men who had reached a position of authority? So what if her employer locked himself in his office most days? Mrs. Mikulka had figured out long ago what Dr. Smith was up to behind that door.

Dr. Smith was addicted to online chess. She had come to that conclusion many years before, even when the Internet wasn't a household word like it was these days. A mind as sharp as Dr. Smith's had to be devoting itself to intellectual pursuits, and the one time she had tiptoed around the subject her taciturn employer had not denied it. That was all the proof Eileen Mikulka needed.

That the little game Dr. Smith played as a pastime had turned into an addiction explained the late hours her boss often kept.

The possibility that Harold Smith might have been fooling around online with some of that, frankly, filthy nonsense Eileen Mikulka had heard about was simply out of the question. Dr. Smith was a strange one, but he was certainly not a dirty old man.

Online chess. Probably with some Russians. They were the ones who were so smart with all those sort of things, weren't they? Rockets, sending dogs into space, chess, and the like.

The fact that Dr. Smith spent so much time devoted to his online avocation meant that the responsibility of running most of the day-to-day operations of Folcroft fell to the plump shoulders of his trustworthy secretary.

Mrs. Mikulka was not one to shirk her duties, even though over time those duties had wound up including most of those of her employer. She was pleased to help. Dr. Smith always looked so worn down all the time that she saw it as a moral obligation to relieve the poor man's burden. She never discussed her work outside of sanitarium walls, but in her private thoughts she had decided that if online chess sapped the life out of you that much, Eileen Mikulka was happy to stick with a deck of cards and an occasional game of solitaire before bed, thank you very much.

And even though she was responsible for keeping things running smoothly around Folcroft, her duties were, to be completely honest, not terribly difficult. Dr. Smith had set Folcroft Sanitarium up to be a smoothly running machine, and so the most Mrs. Mikulka usually had to do was to make sure the wheels didn't come off.

That was most of the time. Today was proving to be the exception to the rule.

She was so distracted this day that she had set aside all of her normal duties just to stare at the phone on her desk in Dr. Smith's outer office.

It had fallen silent once again. Still, she was certain it would ring. The usually quite phone had been jangling off the hook all morning.

She wished Folcroft's assistant director, that nice Mr. Howard, was at work. He might have been able to help with this phone craziness. Unfortunately there had been a death in the family, and so Mark Howard was taking a few personal days off. His absence couldn't have come at a worse time for Eileen Mikulka.

At first, she counted down in her head the seconds since the previous call. She eventually had become so exasperated that she found herself counting aloud.

"...ten Mississippi, eleven Mississippi, twelve Mississippi..."

Ring!

"Jiminy Christmas," Mrs. Mikulka complained.

Eileen Mikulka was not one to grumble, but her morning might be going much better if Dr. Smith had invested in a phone plan with caller I.D.

She stabbed the blinking light and picked up the phone.

The same foreign voice that had called Folcroft more than three dozen times that morning began shouting at her without preamble. The man didn't take a breath. Just launched right into it. In fact, she had no way of knowing if he was stopping during those gaps when he wasn't on the phone. For all she knew he had been reading the dictionary nonstop all morning. His finger must have been worn out from dialing.

"I don't understand you!" Mrs. Mikulka shouted very slowly into the phone, like a tourist who assumed that increasing the volume would somehow magically pierce the language barrier. *"You have a wrong number! Please do not call here again!"*

Exhaling exasperation loud enough into the receiver that she hoped the man would understand her in whatever language he was yelling, she hung the phone back up.

She'd no sooner hung up than her employer marched into the room.

"Oh, Dr. Smith," Mrs. Mikulka said, half-standing. "The phone's been —"

"Deal with it, Mrs. Mikulka," Dr. Smith snapped. "Someone will be joining me in my office in a minute. Please let him in."

Director Smith hurried straight past her and into his office, clicking the door shut behind him. He did not slam it, although he marched with such urgency it looked as though he might do so. Mrs. Mikulka knew better. Dr. Harold Smith was not a door slammer.

She had no sooner dropped her ample backside back to her chair than a second man breezed into her office.

She recognized the elderly Asian gentleman. The man had been a patient at the sanitarium for a time, and came back for occasional visits. He could be very friendly at times — almost insincere in his effusiveness — and at others could be a bit of a prickly pear. Mrs. Mikulka didn't know the old man's name. He was often accompanied by a much younger, ruder man whom Eileen Mikulka assumed was some kind of nurse.

She had surmised some time ago that the old Asian was one of Dr. Smith's chess opponents. Their latest game must have somehow been going poorly for both players, for the old gentleman in the kimono swept through Mrs. Mikulka's office with the same determination as had her employer a moment ago.

Mrs. Mikulka hopped to her feet and hustled to intercept the old man at the door to the Folcroft director's inner office.

No sooner had she left her desk than the phone began ringing again.

"Oh, dear," she said about the phone. She ignored the ringing for a moment and addressed the old gentleman. "Dr. Smith said that you should go right in."

She offered a kindly smile as she reached for the doorknob.

"Begone, wench!" the old Asian gentleman announced, at that moment being even more rude than the nurse in the T-shirt who usually accompanied him.

The elderly man barged straight past the matronly secretary and into Dr. Smith's office, slamming the door behind him with such force that Mrs. Mikulka had to grab a spider plant that was spinning in a pot on a file cabinet before it could drop to the floor.

The chess game must have been going even worse than she'd imagined.

Ring!

She eyed the ringing phone with frustration.

"No rest for the weary," Eileen Mikulka sighed.

She reset her spider plant firmly in the center atop the file cabinet and headed back to answer her phone for the umpteenth time that morning.

Smith was settled into his creaking chair behind his high-tech desk when the Master of Sinanju glided into his office.

"I had a thought," the CURE director said. "Was it a young or an old man you saw in the smoke back at the university?"

He had been typing away at the touch-sensitive keyboard at the edge of his desk when Chiun entered the room. His fingers were poised now, awaiting input from the Master of Sinanju just as his computer was awaiting input from Smith himself.

"Young," Chiun replied.

"Excellent," Smith said. "That eliminates teachers from the search."

He attacked his keyboard with renewed vigor.

Ordinarily the Master of Sinanju would have sunk to a lotus position on the worn carpet in the center of the room. This day he was in no mood to rest. He stood at attention like a carved cigar store Indian in front of the CURE director's desk.

Whitecaps danced on the black waters of Long Island Sound through the one-way picture window at Smith's back. A trio of seagulls rose on eddies of air, then plummeted back to the churning waves. It was the birds that Chiun watched, not Smith.

"If you are sure it was a young man, then we are looking for students," Smith said as he worked. "Perhaps we need only review the faces of exchange students from China. I'll pull up the most recent arrivals, then work back from there. There we have it."

He finished typing with a flourish.

"Please have a look, Master Chiun," Smith said, beckoning the older man to join him at the computer monitor.

When Chiun rounded the desk he found himself looking down at six Chinese faces arranged in two rows of three.

"Are any of these the man you saw?" Smith asked.

Chiun studied the images on the screen.

"It is difficult to tell with Chinese, Emperor Smith. I will not say that they all look alike. Remo has told me all about political correction, and I strive to be correct in all things. On the other hand, I could scatter a handful of sand on your desk and have an easier time telling one grain from the next. Why their mothers bother naming them at all, I have no idea. They could call that one Boy Number One and the one next to him Boy Number One Billion and One. Who would know the difference?"

Even under such trying conditions the old Korean was pleased to demonstrate to his emperor that he had embraced a new concept.

Chiun was nothing if not capable of learning new things, even ones as stupid as political correction.

"How about these?" Smith asked.

He clicked to a second page of mug shots, then a third and a fourth. Twenty pages in, Chiun still had not identified the man he'd seen at the university.

"It is not this lowly servant's place to advise the emperor how he directs his oracles to conduct their mechanical searches," Chiun said when they reached page thirty-seven. "But perhaps I was not clear in my inadequate attempt to inform you earlier. The individual I saw was foreign born, not native to America."

"I know that, Master Chiun," Smith said. "These aren't Chinese-Americans, these are all Chinese exchange students currently attending Columbus University."

"How many foreign Chinese do you allow to take the places of your own children at this school?"

Smith had seen that information when he was setting up his search of Chinese nationals enrolled at the Manhattan school.

"There are just over ten thousand Chinese exchange students in a total student population of a little over thirty thousand," Smith absently replied as he pulled up the next page of mug shots.

"Begging the emperor's pardon, but the Chinese hate your nation. They have made their intentions for you clear. They will see you a ruined husk, begging for scraps from other nations."

"I am aware of China's ambitions."

"Yet your nation permits their young to attend your schools, learn your ways, and steal whatever information they can collect on you to use against you? For that is what the Chinese are most known for: thievery. That and fireworks. But mostly thievery."

"Those decisions have nothing to do with me," Smith said. "Please, Master Chiun, the latest pictures." He indicated his computer screen.

Chiun had lived and worked in America for many years, and had found that the self-destructive stupidity of Americans was a flower that bloomed every day, then immediately set to work trying to figure out the best way to sever its own stem.

When the old Korean glanced down at the screen, he raised his hand.

"Hold!" he commanded. "That is the one."

The old Korean extended a slender finger at a photo in the bottom row.

"Hop Yung," Smith said. He quickly pulled up the boy's information. "Arrived at LaGuardia two days ago. From Manchuria."

"Legend placed the *gyonshi* City of the Dead in Manchuria," Chiun said. "It was said to be in a forest. It was abandoned when the Leader left those shores a hundred years ago."

"We had assumed that the Leader was the last of his sect," Smith said. "Perhaps we were in error. All this time there could have been others like him in Manchuria."

"I do nor err," Chiun sniffed. "If an error was made, it was only because I was not in possession of all of the facts. However, just because this boy hails from Manchuria does not mean he is from the City of the Dead. The *gyonshi* have often expanded beyond their borders to conscript agents for their wicked cause."

Smith studied the image of Hop Yung. When the photo had been taken he had been a kid of eighteen in a red polo shirt. But even in the attempt to blend in there was something off about Hop Yung. The boy's skin was overly pale and his cheeks and eyes were sunken and shaded in black.

"He almost looks normal," the CURE director said, frowning.

"He was even more sickly white and was dressed entirely in black when I encountered him. He was like one of those morose American teenager Visigoths."

"I believe they are called Goths, Master Chiun," Smith said absently.

He was distracted by the sudden buzzing of the intercom.

"What is it, Mrs. Mikulka?"

"I'm terribly sorry to interrupt, Dr. Smith," his secretary's frantic voice announced over the tinny speaker. "I know you didn't want to be disturbed, but it's this man on the phone. He's called another eight times since you came back to your office. Now he's started repeating what sounds like the same nonsense word over and over. I really don't know what to do. I'm at my wits' end out here."

The CURE director's already vinegary expression soured even more.

"I will deal with it," Smith snapped.

He'd had enough of this man and his wrong number, whoever it was. There were urgent matters that needed tending to, and a pest on the phone was not one of them.

Smith snatched up the Folcroft line.

"Listen here —" he began.

Mrs. Mikulka was right. The caller had changed tack. He was no longer spouting a stream of unintelligible gibberish, he had moved on to a single word. It was said quickly and in a foreign tongue, but Smith recognized it clearly enough.

"...Sinanju! Sinanju! Sinanju! Sinanju!"

Smith had heard the Korean language spoken enough by Chiun and Remo that he should have picked up on it the first time. The stranger on the line was so frightened and desperate that he had made his panicked shouting impossible to comprehend.

The CURE director barely had time to glance up at the Master of Sinanju standing at his elbow when the phone was being spirited from his clenched hand.

Chiun barked a few words in Korean into the mouthpiece.

The man calmed down a little. Smith still could not understand a word he was saying, but the mangled shouting at least became recognizable as language.

Chiun listened only for a few seconds before his face blanched. So shocked was he that it seemed as if he wanted to squeeze the receiver until it exploded in his hand, but he needed the device to bark out a few phrases at the caller.

The conversation was brief. When he was finished, the Master of Sinanju handed the phone off to the CURE director and ran for the door.

"What is wrong?" Smith asked.

"I must see Remo!" Chiun snapped over his shoulder.

And then Smith heard the words he had least expected and least wanted to hear.

"I must return to Sinanju at once!" the Master of Sinanju cried.

He did not give his employer a chance to question him further.

The old Korean raced from the office, slamming the door behind him.

The walls shook. A black-and-white photo of Folcroft taken many years before hopped on the wall and nearly fell off its hook.

Smith did not realize that he'd left the intercom on until he heard what sounded like a clay pot crash to the floor in the outer office.

"Oh, dear," he heard the voice of Mrs. Mikulka say.

Smith had the presence of mind only to snap off the intercom. After he fumbled the button to off, he looked helplessly from the silent intercom, to the phone now back in its cradle, to the Columbus University I.D. photo of exchange student Hop Yung staring up from his canted monitor like some demon from the bottomless pit.

Something had just happened. Something earth shattering. And Dr. Harold W. Smith had no idea what that something was.

CHAPTER 13

WHEN REMO AWOKE, he recognized the room he was in even though he had never spent very much time there.

He was in a bed that was not his own. Another five beds were arranged around the walls of the small ward. Sunlight streamed in through the big windows that were protected by wire mesh to prevent the other boys from breaking them during recess.

He was seven years old, he was in second grade, and he was in the infirmary at St. Theresa's Orphanage in Newark, New Jersey.

His schoolwork had been piled on the little table next to the bed. He had not lifted a pencil or cracked a book in the two days he'd been in the small hospital ward.

A very worried face hovered above him, framed in black and white. The nun was removing the damp washcloth from his forehead.

Sister Mary Brigid placed her hand on Remo's forehead. It felt freezing cold, as if she'd been out making snowballs to toss at police cars, which some of the bigger boys had tried goading Remo into doing. Remo had refused, and so they had run away and left him to find his way back to the orphanage. He'd returned late and sick. So sick that he had been taken directly to the infirmary which he'd only ever visited when the nurse from the Catholic high school came that one time last year to administer physicals.

Sister Brigid had assisted the nurse back then, since the infirmary was her domain. The elderly nun never ventured elsewhere at St. Theresa's. Remo had thought she was scary that day of the physicals. She didn't look so scary to him now. The old nun seemed kindly and concerned. When she spoke, her voice was even more worried than her expression.

"He's burning up," she said.

She shifted her hand, as if trying to cool his overheated forehead with the wrinkled skin of her palm.

Remo saw another face at the foot of his bed. He would know that face anywhere. It was Sister Mary Margaret, the nun who ran the orphanage. She had been the only mother Remo had ever known all those years ago.

All those years ago? No, that wasn't right.

It was not many years ago, it was right now. Remo was seven years old, and he was going to get in trouble with Sister Felicula because he hadn't done any of his English homework in two days.

Sister Brigid took a fresh compress from a pan next to Remo's homework and pressed it to his forehead. At the foot of the bed, Sister Margaret smiled.

"It's all right, Remo," Sister Margaret said. "You don't have to stay with us."

"I can't leave, sister," Remo croaked, his voice barely audible. He had never felt so sick in his life. "I don't have anywhere else to go."

"You have family now, Remo," Sister Margaret said. "Go to them."

Remo didn't understand. Didn't Sister Margaret know that he had no family? She had to be aware there was no one out there for him. He lived in an orphanage. In her orphanage. No one wanted him. There was no family he could ever call his own.

Beside him, Sister Brigid wrung out the warm compress and dropped it in the pan. She pressed her palm to the fresh washcloth on his forehead.

At the foot of the bed, Sister Mary Margaret, still smiling.

No. No longer smiling now. Frowning. Her cherubic face suddenly very drawn and gray. People did not have faces that gray. Certainly not Sister Mary Margaret. And why had she traded in her black-and-white habit for a three-piece gray suit?

"Wake up, Remo," a voice close to his side gently commanded.

It wasn't Sister Brigid at his side any longer. It was an old man with strange eyes like none of the boys at St. Theresa's possessed. He knew the man. He felt his heart swell. He wasn't an orphan after all. The man was his father.

At the foot of the bed was the man in the suit, wearing a look of concern that mirrored that of the wizened figure at his bedside.

Remo's family.

"I'm up, Little Father," Remo said.

But his voice was as weak as that of the little boy who had gotten the flu after refusing to throw snowballs at police cars all those years ago.

Chiun leaned over and spoke gently to Remo. Remo replied as best he could in a voice barely strong enough for Smith to hear. Remo tried to argue with his teacher, but there was sad determination on the old man's face.

Their conversation lasted for several minutes, and when it was finished the Master of Sinanju slipped from the basement hospital room.

"Smitty, don't let him go," Remo managed to say loud enough for the departing CURE director to hear. It took all his strength to get the words out.

"I am sorry, Remo," Smith replied from the door. "His mind is made up. I must make the arrangements."

The head of CURE ducked from the room, leaving Remo struggling to determine what was real and what was illusion. He prayed that the whispered conversation he'd just had with his teacher was another hallucination resulting from the poison in his system. If it was not, the Master of Sinanju was almost certainly heading into a trap.

Remo attempted to push himself out of bed. A fresh wave of exhaustion overcame him and he was once more carried back to his distant past and the four walls of the orphanage that housed his earliest memories.

Abandoned in the basement of Folcroft Sanitarium, Remo collapsed back to the bed and was enveloped by an invisible blanket that smothered all conscious thought.

His final wish before total darkness overcame him was that the news not be bleak upon awakening, for if he were to wake to a world in which the Master of Sinanju was no more he would prefer that he continue to sleep forever.

CHAPTER 14

WHEN THE POUNDING on his front door began in the wee hours of the morning, Captain Ralph Chauncy first incorporated the noise into a dream in which someone was repeatedly slamming a car door. An aunt who had been dead for many years was there, as well as a brother-in-law whom Captain Chauncy couldn't stand.

Reality only sunk in when his wife ground an elbow into his back.

"Get that, Ralph," Sylvia Chauncy grunted.

Captain Chauncy's late aunt, his jerk brother-in-law, and the car door his brother-in-law had been slamming vanished. Real life asserted itself.

Chauncy looked at the clock on the nightstand.

"It's four o'clock in the morning," he groused, his voice thick with sleep.

Sylvia didn't reply verbally, but she did roll over and offer the back of her nightgown to her husband.

The pounding at the front door of the bungalow continued unabated. It was joined by a rustling in the Hala tree outside his bedroom window. Through the blinds and with the aid of the motion-detecting lights that suddenly switched on, he saw a shadow in a military police uniform pushing away drooping branches a few feet from where he sat on the edge of his bed.

"Captain Chauncy, sir," the young man called from outside.

The hoarse voice was a half-hearted attempt to shout while not actually shouting. It was a whispered yell, and it was totally unacceptable.

Captain Chauncy didn't live on base. His bungalow was on a residential Honolulu street. Ralph Chauncy had civilian neighbors, and he was sure Bob next door, the manager of the Waikiki White Sands Hotel, as well as Bob's middle school teacher wife wouldn't appreciate an M.P. whisper-shouting in the bushes at four a.m.

Chauncy attempted to locate his slippers in the dark, but failed to stab his feet into them. He wasn't about to turn on the light to find them.

"Get the damn door, Ralph," Sylvia complained from underneath the pillow she'd stuffed down over her exposed ear.

The Peeping Tom M.P. was now directly on the other side of the window. He was cupping his hands over his eyes and attempting to peer into the room.

"Captain Chauncy?" the voice muffled only by a pane of glass asked the shadow he thought he saw moving at the edge of the bed.

Chauncy waved an angry, dismissive hand, which the man at the window failed to see.

"Goddamn it," the captain muttered.

Barefoot and in his underwear, Chauncy picked his way across his bedroom and through his dark house to the front door, at which the banging had not subsided.

Chauncy yanked the door open. A second M.P. nearly fell into the front hall.

"Captain Chauncy, sir?" the young man asked.

"What is it?" Chauncy demanded, rubbing sleep residue from the corner of one eye. "Do you have any idea what time it is?"

"Johnson! I have eyes on him!" the M.P. called at the corner of the house on the other side of the driveway.

"Dammit, keep it down," Captain Chauncy hissed. "What is all this about?"

"I don't know, captain," the M.P. said. "Our orders were to collect you on the double."

The M.P. who had been peeking into the Chauncy's bedroom from the backyard came stumbling around the corner of the house and into the driveway. Just before he stepped onto the asphalt he stomped down on the big maroon leaves of one of Sylvia's Ti Leaf plants. He left the plant in ruins and crossed the driveway and front lawn to join his partner on the front walk.

"A minute ago you two only had a court martial to worry about," Chauncy grunted. "Now you've got worse. You're going to have to deal with my wife. Wait here."

As he turned back inside, the M.P. who had been knocking stopped him.

"We were told to take you right away, sir. No time for anything."

Chauncy fixed the soldier with a glare.

"Son, I don't know what this is all about, but if you try dragging me out of here in my underwear you really will be facing a court martial. Two minutes."

His instinct was to slam the door in their faces, but he was already going to catch hell from Sylvia and probably Bob next door for the racket this pair had made.

Mustering all the patience that remained in his sleep-deprived system, Captain Chauncy closed the bungalow's front door as quietly as exhaustion and frustration permitted.

Four minutes later, Captain Ralph Chauncy was speeding through the dark, deserted streets of Honolulu in the back seat of a military police jeep.

Dawn was still a few hours off. Palm trees were sinister, swaying shadows arching their spines beyond the weak light cast by energy-saving streetlights.

"You can't give me a hint?" Chauncy asked, irritated.

"Sorry, sir," the driver replied.

Captain Chauncy glanced out the window, eyes at half-mast, and sighed.

"Well, I know it's not my birthday, so it's not a surprise party."

In point of fact, Captain Chauncy had a fairly good idea what this was about, at least in a very broad sense.

Chauncy was the commander of the U.S.S. *Darter*, a submarine homeported at Naval Station Pearl Harbor. The *Los Angeles*-class sub was not part of the official fleet of submarines for whom Pearl Harbor was home. It was an off-the-books vessel which, aside from the occasional shakedown cruise, rarely left port.

The U.S.S. *Darter* had only one main duty. Once every year the submarine under Captain Chauncy's command departed on a secret mission to the Far East.

Captain Chauncy had no idea what was being delivered to that rocky shore on the West Korean Bay. He only knew that somebody above his pay grade thought that it was of vital importance enough to risk a shooting war with North Korea to deliver some crates by rubber raft to some inconsequential fishing village.

Chauncy knew that the village was a nothing little backwater because when he first pulled this assignment he had hauled out some maps and tried to locate anything of significance in the area. There was nothing. Only a crummy little nothing-of-a-village that nobody other than the Norks gave a rat's ass about.

He soon learned that this assignment was deemed so important that his was the third sub to make the annual roundtrip into enemy waters.

The submarine immediately prior to his own had been the U.S.S. *Harlequin*. Not much was known about the loss of that ship. Rumor had it that she had been sunk off the North Korean coast, but there was nothing in the official record. It was disconcerting that such a tight lid had been kept on the fate of the *Harlequin*. She had been more or less written off, as if she and her crew had never existed.

Before the *Harlequin* had been another *Darter*, which had been decommissioned after its final run East. Chauncy figured that after they'd lost the *Harlequin* under hush-hush circumstances, some superstitious higher-ups had decided to christen her replacement after her more fortunate predecessor. This new U.S.S. *Darter* under Captain Ralph Chauncy's command had successfully made the annual run in and out of North Korean waters for several years.

From the back seat of the jeep, Captain Chauncy watched the swaying of the ominous palm tree shadows as they sped past. He was being whisked to his ship. That was the only possibility he could think of. But he'd already made the annual crate delivery to communist North Korea two weeks ago, on the regular November 12 date. The fact that Chauncy was being shanghaied into going back again so soon could only mean one thing.

On rare occasions, the Darter under his command had been given one other repeat assignment. In addition to the annual mysterious crates, Chauncy had been charged with transporting human cargo.

It was the old man. It had to be.

He was a hundred if he was a day, weighed ninety pounds soaking wet, and had the disposition of a rattlesnake after it had been shaken in a burlap sack.

The little old Korean pain-in-the-ass was the only person on earth who could get the Navy to drop everything else and drag Captain Chauncy out of a sound sleep in order to use a United States military submarine like a Pacific Princess cruise ship.

Captain Chauncy was sure he was right. He was therefore surprised when the jeep flew past the entrance to the naval station where the *Darter* was berthed and sped onto adjoining Hickam Air Force Base.

"I think you missed my stop," the captain dryly noted.

"No, sir," the M.P. in the passenger seat replied.

The jeep raced deep into the base and stopped inside a hanger where Chauncy found waiting for him a flight suit, a helmet, and an F-15E Strike Eagle. The plane had already been prepped for takeoff. An Air Force colonel stood at the boarding ladder, waiting only for the arrival of his passenger.

"What the hell is going on here?" Captain Chauncy demanded.

He had practically been rolled out of the back of the jeep by the M.P.s, who had already turned around and were speeding out of the hangar.

"Captain," the colonel said, "I've been ordered not to discuss anything with you beyond this sentence."

The Air Force colonel proved to be a real martinet when it came to following orders. The flyboy kept his mouth screwed shut as the two men boarded the craft, as the plane taxied over to the runway that the Air Force shared with Honolulu International Airport, and during takeoff into the lightening Honolulu sky.

Oahu was a fading dot of glittering lights in their wake, as were the remaining scattered islands in the Hawaiian archipelago.

Once they had reached maximum elevation and acceleration, the pilot dropped the external tanks that had helped them achieve full fuel efficiency for takeoff. The F-15 roared into the night in excess of mach 2.

"How about you give me a clue now?" Captain Chauncy demanded once the fighter jet was tearing through the heavens high over the Pacific.

His Air Force pilot kept his mouth screwed shut.

"It's going to be a long flight," Captain Chauncy grunted.

While the distance was far, the duration of the flight was not. The plane had to refuel in the air several times to reach its destination. They had flown into the night, but dawn was just beginning to break behind them when the F-15 screamed out of the heavens.

From the cockpit, Captain Chauncy watched the ocean race up to meet them. Something resembling a misshapen gray shoe box sat alone in the water, with nothing visible near it for miles in every direction.

It was ridiculously small when he first spotted it, but distance belied its great size. The shape of the aircraft carrier grew so quickly that it was mere seconds before it was a massive floating impossibility whose great size should have dragged it to the ocean floor.

And then they had dropped below the shadow of the bridge and were screaming across the flight deck. The F-15's tail hook snagged an arresting cable, absorbing the energy of the landing plane, and the Air Force jet jolted to a stop.

As soon as they had climbed down from their respective cockpits, the Air Force colonel hustled wordlessly across the flight deck.

Captain Chauncy hadn't a clue what was going on. The *Darter*'s captain only knew that his best guess put them within spitting distance of Japan.

"You look about as lost as I was, skipper," a familiar voice chimed in behind him.

Chauncy turned to find the amused face of the U.S.S. *Darter*'s executive officer.

"What the blazes is going on, Platt?" Captain Chauncy demanded of his first officer.

"Wait'll you see, sir," Commander Geoffrey Platt replied. "You won't believe it."

Captain Chauncy wasn't so sure. At this point he was inclined to believe just about anything.

The *Darter*'s first officer led his captain to the furthermost point of the aircraft carrier's deck. Only when they were at the railing did Chauncy finally see it.

It had been hidden by the last remnants of night and by the aircraft carrier's towering immensity. Dwarfed beneath the looming shadow of the carrier, a *Los Angeles*-class submarine identical to the U.S.S. *Darter* slid stealthily through the crashing waves.

"It's ours," Commander Platt said, grinning. "At least for the next day or so. It's a rental, so we don't want to get any dings in the fender."

Commander Geoffrey Platt had been pulled from leave and shanghaied much the same as had been Captain Chauncy. So too had several key members of the *Darter*'s crew. Chauncy's men were to take temporary command of this new sub — the U.S.S. *Jezebel* — for a special mission for which no other crew was qualified.

"The *Darter* was too far away, skipper," Commander Platt explained after they'd boarded the Jezebel and began to make their way down the conning tower ladder. "We had to get there fast, and she would have taken days to cross the Pacific."

"Why, Platt?" Captain Chauncy demanded when he reached the deck at the bottom of the ladder. "What's so goddamn important that it's got the entire Navy doing backflips through flaming hoops?"

His answer came from behind him in the form of a squeaky, sing-song voice that managed to be angry, condescending, and infuriating all at once.

"It is about time," the familiar voice accused. "Had I thrown a bottle with a note in it bemoaning the incompetence of this navy into the ocean four thousand miles away, it would have floated here faster than you."

Captain Chauncy closed his eyes, took a deep breath, and turned around.

The little old Korean passenger for whom Chauncy had been forced in the past to act like the captain on the *Love Boat* stood impatiently just on the other side of the open bridge door at the end of the short hall.

"Enough lollygagging," the passenger said. "A boat from the Spanish Armada would have reached my village by now. Although being Spaniards it would crash into the rocks. Do that at your peril. I have my eye on you."

Warning issued, the old man in the red kimono with the rearing black-and-gold dragons spun on one sandaled foot and disappeared from the door. If past experience was any indication, he was off to take up residence in the captain's cabin.

Captain Chauncy shut his eyes and counted to ten. Next time he would close his bedroom blinds back in Honolulu and go back to sleep.

His executive officer noted the weary look on his skipper's face.

"At least it's a short trip this time around," the exec offered.

Captain Chauncy didn't take comfort in the fact that the trip into dangerous North Korean waters would take less time than usual.

"Just a faster trip to our own funeral," Chauncy said.

The newly appointed captain of the U.S.S. *Jezebel* barked the order to seal the hatch, then headed down the short corridor. Before he'd even reached the bridge he was shouting out commands for the sub to get underway.

Captain Chauncy was buoyed by the knowledge that if he was going to get torpedoed by the Norks, at least the little old pain-in-the-ass passenger would be coming along on the express elevator down to Davy Jones' Locker.

CHAPTER 15

REMO WAS BACK IN THE INFIRMARY at St. Theresa's Orphanage.

The night was over. Dust danced in the sunlight of the new day that streamed through the tall windows.

Sister Brigid was no longer doling out cold compresses from a pan at his bedside.

Remo's fever had broken during the night. The elderly nun who acted in place of a proper nurse whenever the orphan boys wound up with inevitable scrapes and bruises was fussing around in an office adjacent to the infirmary. From his bed Remo could see the back of the old nun's black habit as she rearranged items inside a wooden cabinet with glass doors in which she stored her aspirin, mercurochrome, and off-brand band-aids.

He turned his head in the other direction. Someone was sitting in the chair next to his bed. She had been there all night. He had seen the placid figure seated there even during the worst of his delirium. A beacon guiding him back from the darkness.

Sister Mary Margaret Morrow stood and smoothed out her black skirt. She placed a palm flat on his forehead. He remembered that touch. So caring. So long ago.

"You've stayed with us long enough, Remo," Sister Margaret said. "You need to go now."

His heart ached at the thought.

"I don't want to, sister."

"I know. But it's time."

It pained him, yet he knew it to be true.

"I missed you." His voice cracked. The words were difficult to get out.

Sister Margaret smiled. He remembered the smile, too. On his most hopeless days as a boy, when he was certain that he would never find a home or a family of his own, that smile had made him feel that the world was not as terrible a place as he imagined it to be. How could it be when a smile so kind existed in it?

Sister Brigid had returned to his bedside. He heard her fussing next to him. He didn't turn to the older nun. He was studying Sister Margaret's face. He had forgotten all the little details. The crinkles at the corners of her eyes, the little white scar on the chin. How had a face so important to him ever faded from his memory? He was using this opportunity to sear every feature into his brain so that he never forgot again.

Sister Margaret intuited what he was doing. She offered a knowing nod.

"I'm always with you, Remo," the long-dead nun insisted.

She suddenly looked across the little boy in the bed in the direction of Sister Brigid. Her gentle face grew harsh with concern.

"You must go. *Now*," Sister Margaret insisted, with abrupt urgency.

As she spoke, a hand snatched his shoulder. For some reason Sister Brigid had latched onto him. Her fingers were sharp like an eagle's talons.

"Remo, *go*," Sister Margaret warned.

Remo turned to see what had concerned Sister Margaret so deeply.

The figure on the other side of the bed was elderly and dressed in black, but it was not Sister Brigid who had grabbed onto him.

A pair of sinister milky eyes stared with blind malevolence at the little boy in the bed. A wicked grin split the face, revealing vacant black gums.

The Leader of the *gyonshi* vampire cult cackled with glee, his bony fingers digging deep into Remo's shoulder, gouging flesh and piercing bone.

"Go now!" Sister Mary Margaret screamed.

And the shock of the yelling woman who in life had not seemed capable of raising her voice above a stern rebuke snapped him back to reality.

The walls and ceiling of St. Theresa's infirmary collapsed down around the bed at lightning speed, Sister Margaret vanished, and the chilling laughter of the blind nightmare in black echoed through the endless void where it finally choked to silence.

Remo opened his eyes.

He was in the basement hospital room at Folcroft Sanitarium. He was home, such as it was.

The world seemed clearer now. The items around the room were in sharper focus.

His fever was gone, although he could feel the last remnants of the poison that had infected him still lurking in his system.

He was not alone.

Harold W. Smith sat on a folding chair near the door, his briefcase tucked on the floor beside him, a laptop perched on his bony knees. Smith poked away at the keyboard with furious precision. The text on the screen was reflected in the lenses of his glasses.

"Can't you peck quieter at that thing?" Remo asked. "It sounds like a hundred woodpeckers got loose in the Scrabble tile factory."

Smith glanced up from his work.

"Oh. You're awake," the CURE director said.

"I hope so. If this is a dream and I've cast your sourpuss to costar in it, I'm going to have to hire a Hollywood script doctor to punch it up."

"How do you feel?" Smith asked.

"Lousy, but alive." Remo's eyes narrowed. "Were you expecting company?"

At the question, Remo nodded to a vacant chair next to the one on which Smith sat. On the otherwise vacant chair sat the CURE director's service automatic. Smith rarely removed the gun from the bottom drawer of his office desk. It was not something that the bland director of an ordinary sanitarium would be carrying in his day-to-day work.

"I thought under the circumstances it was best to be prepared," Smith said.

With Remo now awake, Smith picked up the automatic and stuffed it into the shoulder holster that was hidden under the gray jacket of his three-piece suit. The CURE director folded his laptop, stood up, and placed the computer on the seat he had just vacated. He stepped over to Remo's bedside.

Remo was feeling his left shoulder, searching for tears in the skin and oozing blood. The skin was unbroken. His shoulder was fine.

Smith arched a curious eyebrow.

"What are you doing?" he asked the younger man.

"Nothing," Remo replied. "I had a visit from Freddy Krueger while I was asleep. I wanted to make sure all the parts were still here."

"I don't understand," Smith said.

"Neither do I," said Remo. "But I'm stuck with it just the same."

The thin sheet that covered him was damp with sweat. He pulled it off and sat up on the edge of the bed. The room failed to perform a kaleidoscopic whirl around his head, which he considered a vast improvement over the last time he'd opened his eyes.

"How long was I out?" he asked.

Smith checked his Timex. "Just under twenty-four hours."

"Were you here the whole time?"

"Most of it," Smith said. "I can work just as easily from here as I can from my office."

"You're going to fool me into thinking you might actually care, Smitty. Are you sure you weren't sitting there ready to give me the *One Flew Over the Cuckoo's Nest* deal with a pillow on my face just in case I started blabbing state secrets to some nurse?"

"There have been no nurses in to see you," Smith said. "I have been monitoring you."

"Great," Remo said. "Now I'm picturing you hovering over me in a white mini skirt. There goes my libido for the next fifty years."

"Your temperature rose much higher than a normal body can

tolerate. I would have been alarmed had Chiun not assured me that it would happen, that it was a natural response, and that you would most likely be fine."

"*Chiun,*" Remo said, suddenly alarmed.

Reality and hallucination had been playing games with his mind, testing him to see if he could figure out which was which. He had a sudden flash of memory that he was sure was real. It was of Chiun coming to him in the midst of his delirium and telling Remo he was leaving.

Remo hopped out of bed. The floor didn't sweep out from underneath him. His legs remained firmly planted beneath him.

"How much of a head start did he get?" Remo asked.

"Remo, he is there by now."

"I'm going after him."

He took only one step before Smith grabbed his arm.

"No," the CURE director insisted firmly.

"Don't 'no' me," Remo snapped, yanking his arm from Smith's grasp. "He's going to get himself killed."

"Need I remind you that it is you, not he, who spent nearly an entire day in and out of consciousness in a hospital bed?" Smith said.

The icy homicidal expression that crossed Remo's dark features was by itself a worrying reminder that Smith was in the presence of one of the two greatest killers on the face of the planet. Despite this, the CURE director stood his ground.

"You and Master Chiun spoke before he left," Smith insisted. "Remember your conversation? You knew what he was doing, and you accepted it."

The thundercloud that had crossed Remo's face evaporated. His brow furrowed at the return in sharp focus of the entire conversation that had broken through his delirium.

Remo dropped his rear end back to the hospital bed.

"Crap," he said. "I did, didn't I."

CHAPTER 16

IT WAS ONLY A DAY AGO. It seemed like months.

When the fever had fully set in Remo had lapsed into a sort of dream world, where reality and hallucination were hopelessly entangled. One minute he was in a vacant lot with some bigger boys from the orphanage where he grew up, refusing to throw a snowball at a Newark PD squad car. An instant after that, he was in the infirmary at St. Theresa's. Yet another moment and he was gazing up from his sickbed at the deeply concerned face of the Master of Sinanju looking down at him.

"Wake up, Remo," Chiun said.

"I'm up, Little Father," Remo replied, his voice thick.

Chiun rested his wrinkled palm on his pupil's forehead.

"Your fever has grown worse."

"Yeah, I feel hot. And not the way Pamela Anderson does after her plastic surgeon pumps her knobs up another eight cup sizes."

Remo suddenly noticed Smith was in the room as well. The CURE director was standing at the foot of the bed. Chiun and Smith shared a concerned glance.

"Hey, no sweat, guys," Remo assured them. "Okay maybe a little sweat. Anyway, I'll knock this out of me in no time."

"I must go, my son," Chiun announced.

"You're not going back to that college without me," Remo insisted.

He attempted to push himself to a sitting position but his body refused to listen to his will. The fight drained from his limbs, and his head fell back to the pillow.

"Just wait for me, Chiun," Remo said. "We'll go back when I'm better. You said it'll be practically no time."

"In truth, we cannot be certain how long it will take," Chiun said. "Not all *gyonshi* poisons are known to us, and not all Masters react to them the same way. You are young and strong, Remo. I have given you all the tools you require to heal. However, I cannot sit and idly wait for that time to come. I must return to Sinanju at once."

"Sinanju?" Remo asked, surprised. "I thought you were talking about Columbus U. What are you running off to that shit-smeared mud heap for? Did one of those ingrates we support break into your house and steal the copper pipes from the walls?"

"It is the Leader," Chiun replied, both his face and voice dark. "The Chinese bloodsucker has defiled the home of my ancestors. The worshiper-of-death waits for me there."

Remo tried to wrap his brain around the old Korean's words.

"How do you know?" he asked.

"My caretaker telephoned," Chiun said. "The *gyonshi* have polluted our home with their presence. Our people are hiding in fear of the ghosts that walk among them."

"The only thing the people of Sinanju hide in fear from is getting a job," Remo said. "Give me a day and we can go there together."

"No," Chiun said. "If I had another day to risk I would wait to see if you were well enough. My caretaker is trustworthy, but he was frightened. It is possible he is mistaken. We cannot know if the Leader himself is in Sinanju or here in America. My village is of paramount importance, and so I go. However, it could be that this is merely a ruse to get us both away from this land while he realizes his scheme here."

"No, this has to be the plan, Chiun. Divide and conquer. They know I'm sick. They know I probably can't travel right now. The minute I'm under the weather, you get a call to come home. That doesn't seem a little fishy to you? You're over there, I'm over here. We're weaker apart."

"Though countless miles separate us, we are never apart, my son," Chiun said.

He offered Remo a caring smile, before turning to go.

"The Leader is dead, Little Father. If his spirit somehow survived me killing him, what are you going to do with it? Hit it over the head with a Ouija board?"

"I will do that which I must do," Chiun said.

The Master of Sinanju left Remo's side and stepped over to Smith.

"I'm not entirely onboard with this, Master Chiun," Smith said. "We just sent the annual gold shipment to Sinanju two weeks ago. It will be tricky to go back this soon. The logistics of the arrangements are nearly impossible, especially given the urgency you seem to think applies to this matter in your village."

"If you will not assist me, I will find my own transportation."

Smith considered the ramifications of Chiun's suggestion. He thought of Chiun alone at LaGuardia International Airport in the post-9/11 world demanding a ticket to communist North Korea, and imagined what the old Asian might do in his current state when he was told there were no direct flights to the Hermit Kingdom. The risk of exposure to the agency was too great.

"I will make the arrangements," Smith said. "But you must give me your word to return as soon as the danger over there has passed, if there even *is* a danger."

The Master of Sinanju nodded sharp agreement.

"And you must agree to watch my son," Chiun replied.

Smith was tempted to tell the old Korean that this was not a negotiation, that Chiun had signed a contract with Smith for his services, and that the CURE director did not have to arrange for Chiun's travel at all. But in point of fact every interaction with the Master of Sinanju seemed to involve some kind of concession on Smith's part.

The director of CURE nodded crisp assent.

Remo watched Smith hold the door open to usher the Master of Sinanju from the hospital room. His teacher had never looked so frail.

"Smitty, don't let him go," Remo called over to the director of CURE before Smith could leave the room as well.

"I am sorry, Remo. His mind is made up. I must make the arrangements."

Smith had stepped from the room, leaving Remo feeling more alone than he had since he was a scared little orphan at St. Theresa's in Newark.

It had been a whole day since that conversation with his teacher. Remo now recalled every word. Leaning on the edge of his hospital bed, he accepted Chiun's decision to leave his bedside even though he didn't fully support it.

"Have you heard anything from him?" Remo asked.

"No, not since he was flown to the Pacific by Air Force jet."

Smith consulted his watch once more.

"If all went well, he has likely only just arrived."

"When does anything ever go well for us?" Remo droned. "What about that college? Where do we stand with that?"

"The situation in New York has deteriorated over the past twenty-four hours."

Remo clapped his hands, rubbing them vigorously together.

"Well let's take care of that, shall we? I mean, the world is coming to end. We might as well keep busy while the lights go out."

Remo did not like the sound of the CURE director's reply.

"That might be more true than you think, Remo," Smith said.

The older man's voice was grave.

CHAPTER 17

CAPTAIN RALPH CHAUNCY peered through the periscope of the U.S.S. *Jezebel* and inhaled deeply. He allowed the air to slowly slip from between his lips.

Despite the insanity of the whirlwind that had deposited him onto the bridge of an alien command, he felt a twinge of satisfaction that his new submarine and temporary crew had gotten them to their destination, and in record time.

"Well, we sure as hell don't need any instruments to tell us we're right where we're supposed to be," Chauncy said. "Not with those sticking up out of the shore."

He was referring to a peculiar rock formation above the bay into which the *Jezebel* had successfully navigated. The two towering columns of rock could be seen from miles out at sea. They were evidently not a natural formation. The curving rock pillars had been placed there at some point in the distant past, like Stonehenge.

They were called the Horns of Welcome, although Captain Chauncy had no way of knowing that name. To the U.S. Navy captain, they were merely a signpost to give him final confirmation that he had reached his destination. He could not know that he was looking at the same rock formation spotted by Egyptian Pharaoh Djoser's men in their ancient barques, the Dutch sailors of Maurice, Prince of Orange in their seventeenth century schooners, and by the slaves of four hundred years of Han Dynasty emperors toiling under the lash aboard their Chinese junks two millennia ago.

Captain Chauncy leaned back from the periscope, rubbing his eyes with his fingertips. His first officer stood expectantly at his side.

"Geoff, please inform our passenger that we've arrived," Chauncy said.

"With pleasure, skipper," Commander Geoffrey Platt replied.

The executive officer hurried from the bridge.

Chauncy took one last look at the ancient stone formation before ordering the periscope down, just as he'd done from the bridge of the U.S.S. *Darter* two weeks ago.

"Let's hope it's the last time this year," he muttered to himself.

Commander Platt returned a minute later, escorting their passenger who looked old enough to be Methuselah's grandfather.

"Are you certain we are where we are supposed to be?" Chiun demanded of Captain Chauncy without preamble.

Captain Chauncy had no idea why the old man would ask that question. This wasn't some Looney Tunes outfit. Did he think a captain in the United States Navy could make a wrong turn at Albuquerque and wind up at Pismo Beach?

"I have made this trip before, *sir*," Captain Chauncy replied.

He was tired, he was irritated. Maybe he answered a little more peevishly than he should have. He had no idea if he was at fault for what happened next.

The sarcastic words were no sooner out of Chauncy's mouth than the old Asian's hands flashed forward, cobra-like. The *Jezebel*'s crazy VIP passenger latched onto both of the captain's wrists.

The little bastard looked as delicate as a sand dollar, but he had a grip like a couple of vises and the brute strength of a Russian weightlifter.

The crazy passenger twisted Captain Chauncy's hands around. For some reason unknown to the suddenly worried nearby crew of the *Jezebel*, the old Korean very carefully inspected Captain Chauncy's fingernails.

"Sir?" Commander Platt said, nervously seeking from his C.O. instructions on how to proceed.

The strange confrontation was over before Captain Chauncy

could give an order. After a few seconds, during which the passenger scanned every one of Chauncy's fingernails, the old man released his death grip.

"I require a craft to take me to shore," Chiun announced.

Captain Chauncy was only too happy to comply.

Three minutes later Chauncy was on the conning tower watching as a rubber motor boat was lowered to the black waves.

Chauncy was still rubbing his bruised wrists as the old man scurried down into the prow of the boat, which was manned by two *Jezebel* crew members. Somehow the wizened figure remained standing rigidly at the front as the rubber raft bounced off across the waves toward the distant shore beneath the towering rock horns.

"Crazy old buzzard is North Korea's problem now," the captain said to his first officer, who had joined him to see their guest off the *Jezebel*. "God help the Norks."

Captain Ralph Chauncy and his executive officer didn't wait for the dot of the rubber boat to reach shore. Captain Chauncy had a bed back in Honolulu, and a wife who probably thought her husband had been dragged away in the dead of night to take part in World War Three. Given the personality of the old man they'd just set loose on enemy territory, that doomsday possibility wasn't so farfetched.

The two officers abandoned the deck of the submarine that was not their own and headed back down the U.S.S. *Jezebel*'s conning tower ladder.

The black rubber raft delivered Chiun to the rocky shore of his homeland.

Ordinarily the return of the Master of Sinanju to his native village was a major event. The men would cheer, the women would fawn, and the children would throw rose petals at the Master's feet. At least that was what the ceremony was supposed to be.

In truth, over the years the villagers had grown more lax in their dedication to uphold tradition.

"They're too busy shoveling the noodles and rice wine you and I pay for down their gullets to haul their fat asses down to the shore."

This did Remo say the last time the two Masters of Sinanju had come to the village only to find the anticipated greeting party nowhere to be found. It turned out back then that the villagers had started the celebration two days early.

"Figures," Remo had said. "Every lazy slack-ass in town is too hung over to turn out for the two guys who keep the lights on. We should set fire to the whole damn village and claim a total loss to the insurance company. You and I can split the buck-fifty this dump is worth."

Chiun had reminded Remo of the greatest vow taken by each Master of Sinanju. Although the Master could ply his deadly art anywhere else in the world, it was forbidden that he lift a hand against any villager of Sinanju.

"Yeah, we don't get to lift a hand against them, but they get to lift their legs and piss all over us," Remo had grunted.

Chiun knew that his pupil only acted as if he was dismissive of the tradition. The old Korean knew in his heart that Remo might not like it but he would adhere to it, as had all Masters of Sinanju going back thousands of years.

Even if the traditional greeting of the Master was more often than not an event for which the villagers of Sinanju failed to get out of bed, Chiun did not blame them that they were not on the rocky shore this day.

He reached down and scooped up a small handful of pebbles. Chiun rolled the small stones — the size of marbles — in his palm.

The black rubber raft was bouncing across the waves and was halfway back to its rendezvous with the American craft that traveled at great speed underwater as the Master of Sinanju picked his careful way up the path from the shore.

Chiun's elderly caretaker had been frantic on the telephone. He had spoken of mysterious black clouds of mist that had been seen drifting through the village. Voices whispered terrifying words from within the clouds. These ghosts — for what else could they be but the spirits of the dead? — threatened bloody murder on all who encountered them, until out of fear the villagers would no longer venture out of doors.

The caretaker had taken refuge in the Masters' House, where the only telephone in the village was located.

The impudent voices had come to him at the door of the Masters' House. They did not come inside, for when they asked to be invited in Chiun's caretaker had refused to permit entry. Chiun knew it was a *gyonshi* tradition to never enter a dwelling without first asking permission to do so. And so they lurked outside, shadows in both day and night, paralyzing with fear all who gazed on them.

From the windows the caretaker saw these fiendish shadows circling the Masters' House. Sometimes when they drew close enough to the windows, the frightening clouds would wear the pale faces of men in their swirling depths. They taunted the frightened old man and told him that someone called the Leader would soon arrive, and then would have his final vengeance against the village of Sinanju and its Master.

Even when no others from the village were at the shore to greet the Master upon his return, Chiun had always been able to count on one man to show up. But old Pullyang, Chiun's trusty caretaker, was too frightened to step outside of the house in which he was hiding. The same as every other man, woman, and child in the village.

Chiun felt a cold anger well up inside him. That any enemy would dare invade the home of the Masters of Sinanju was the ultimate insult.

As he walked the path from shore to village, Chiun kept his senses tuned to their utmost. He became like the spider, attuned to the vibrations of the web of the world all around him.

He had reached the dilapidated wooden racks on which the fishermen of the village mended their nets when he became aware of something gliding in his direction.

It rolled slowly out from behind a tumbledown shed, like dense fog.

The black *gyonshi* mist slipped directly into Chiun's path.

"You would have been wiser to stay away, ancient one," called a taunting voice from within the swirling mist. "Walk you now into the jaws of death."

Chiun did not break his stride.

The Master of Sinanju still held in his hand the pebbles he had collected at the shore. As he walked, he rolled one to the side of his index finger and flicked it with his thumb. The pebble fired like a bullet from his hand and into the cloud.

Thwack!

The meaty sound of rock penetrating flesh issued from within the cloud, followed immediately by that of a body collapsing to the ground.

An observer would have seen only the cloud flatten out on the road.

Unlike a casual observer, Chiun saw the dead man in the mist. The Chinese invader lay flat on his back, glassy eyes staring at the eternity of the sky. There was a small red cavity in the center of his pasty forehead. The back of his head had been blown open. Brain, bone, and hair fanned out wide around the corpse. These scattered parts of the dead man were not producing the strange black cloud. They extended outside the main body from which the fog still emanated.

How the *gyonshi* generated the mysterious cloud was unknown to generations of Masters of Sinanju. It seemed to come from their pores, and so was likely due to some filthy potion they drank. Even in death the cloud stayed with this one. It would no doubt cease obscuring him as the death the ancient sect worshipped fully claimed the corpse.

Chiun strode past the body.

The tumbledown home of the basket weaver sat outside the village proper. Chiun dismissed the pounding heartbeats of the weaver, the man's wife, his three children, and his elderly mother that came from inside the dwelling. His acute hearing was trained not on those inside the house, but on the pair of heartbeats that came from outside it.

The *gyonshi* heartbeats were abnormally calm, even under what should have been the greatest stress imaginable: coming face to face with the wrath of the Master of Sinanju. Since death was life to the cult, the two men in the pair of clouds that drifted out before Chiun from around the basket weaver's shack found themselves looking into the face of the executioner who would deliver to them that which they most desired.

"Where is the Leader, *gyonshi* defilers of the village of my ancestors?" Chiun demanded. "Speak quick and I will deliver mercifully that which you desire."

They were dressed in black robes. They did not fear the approaching wraith.

"He stands before you," the man on the right said, holding his arms out to encompass all of Chiun's ancestral village. "For where we are, there is he."

"Where you are is the grave," Chiun replied.

He rolled another pebble from his palm and, with a flick of his thumb, sent it sailing. The impact of the stone this time was so great that when it struck the man's forehead the entire top of the head lifted off like a cheap toupee. The exploding melon of his head scattered grisly chunks of skull and brains across the muddy road.

Before the man had a chance to fall, Chiun was on his companion.

The Master of Sinanju reached into the heart of the black cloud and took the Chinese vampire by the scrawny throat.

"You will tell me where the Leader is," he demanded.

The *gyonshi* only smiled. An instant later his mouth began foaming, and a moment after that his eyes bugged out of his head as if they were about to explode.

By the time a spray of blood burst from between his lips, Chiun had already hurled the body a hundred feet distant.

The dead vampire landed in some scruffy weeds. The dying impulses in his nervous system caused the body to twitch spastically, while blood popped from mouth, nose, ears, and lastly from his exploding eyeballs. The man had been a living hand grenade. No doubt some fresh poison from the twisted fiends of the ancient cult.

Chiun whirled from the body and strode into the village proper.

He found the lone main street of Sinanju deserted. The homes along the mud road were buttoned up tightly.

The early morning sky was a pale blue, colored with only a few uncertain daubs of wispy white clouds. Although it was a fine day by the generally bleak standards of the ancient fishing village, it was as if the inhabitants had taken refuge from the worst storm to hit the Korean peninsula in a hundred years.

As he strode up the center of the road Chiun sensed signs of life hidden behind locked doors and windows. Here and there a face peered through a pane of smudged glass, only to hastily withdraw when the gaze of the Master turned its way.

At the heart of the village, Chiun stopped.

"People of Sinanju, do not fear!" he called. "The Master has returned!"

Dozens of voices whispered amongst themselves. None called out to Chiun.

The citizens of the village knew that the Master plied his deadly art in foreign lands and sent the spoils back home so that the villagers did not have to work to feed their own bellies, clothe their own backs, or protect their own heads against the elements. Remo called the village of Sinanju the world's first welfare-state basket case.

Since all the hard work was done for them, not to mention far away from Sinanju, the villagers often went years without seeing the Master who supported them. Not only this, but they had very little specific knowledge of the gifts possessed by their benefactor. As long as there was stew in the pot and logs in the hearth, the people of Sinanju did not pay very much attention to how things got where they were.

The villagers, therefore, felt comfortable in the safety of the homes purchased for them by the sweat of the Master's brow to ridicule the wizened figure whom they had failed to greet, and who was standing alone in the center of the village.

The men and women of Sinanju did not know the keenness of the Master's hearing, and had no clue that the Master saw all, knew all, and heard all.

"The old fool is too late," a woman hissed. "We are all doomed."

"He should have stayed away with that white pupil he is so fond of. Neither of them ever cared about any of us. They failed us, and we will perish thanks to them."

"Let him stand out there. Don't warn him of the danger! If we sacrifice him, perhaps our lives will be spared."

One voice, braver than the rest, shouted from behind a warped door.

"You abandoned us, old man!"

It was offensive that he should converse with the people of his own village through locked doors that his labors abroad had purchased.

"The Master of Sinanju has never abandoned his village," Chiun called.

Another voice cried out.

"Then you are no Master of Sinanju!"

This insult was worse than a slap to the face.

The flesh at the corners of Chiun's eyes pinched to enraged knots. If this were anywhere else on the planet he would have kicked in the offender's door, dragged him out in the street by his hair, and flogged him until he begged for the mercy of death. But Sinanju was not like any other city, town, or village on earth.

Chiun remembered the oath he had sworn never to raise a hand against the people of the village. It was the most solemn compact between the Master and the citizens of Sinanju, and he would not break that oath no matter how ungrateful were his people.

Rather than upbraid them for their insolence, Chiun marched from the village center in the direction of his house.

As he walked away, the villagers cried out once more.

"Don't leave us!"

"He will abandon us to the forces of darkness!"

"O, that we were born now! At a time when the Master of Sinanju is no more than a weak flickering candle compared to the great bonfire of his ancestors."

The home of the Masters of Sinanju was called the House of the Many Woods, and it sat on a bluff overlooking the West Korean Bay. It was to this house of many clashing architectural styles from many different eras that Chiun headed.

A telephone wire normally ran up to a pole next to the house, then was strung onto a series of poles leading out of the village. Chiun noted as he approached that the wire had been severed. Communication with the outside world had been impossible after his caretaker had finally reached him at Folcroft.

Chiun had expected to sense the single heartbeat of his caretaker coming from the house, but two distinct pounding hearts reached his ears. One was frightened and distant, the other much calmer heartbeat was just on the other side of the closed front door.

Chiun recognized the unwavering thud of a *gyonshi* heart. Foolish old Pullyang, the caretaker of the House of Many Woods, must have made the mistake of inviting one of the invading rats in.

The pathetic attempt at an ambush would fail. The Master of Sinanju would kill the Chinese trespasser as he had his compatriots.

The old Korean mounted the steps to the home of his fathers and wrenched the door open, his free hand raised to deliver a killing blow.

The hissing figure that leapt out from the shadows was not a creature in black. Chiun hopped from its path, and the bounding figure launched past him and tumbled halfway down the steps to the mud path. In a flash, it was back on its feet.

Chiun recognized the woman as she ascended towards him. She was an ugly, childless thing that sometimes took in laundry, but never cleaned it well.

This was not a member of the Chinese vampire cult. This was a villager of Sinanju. One of the few people on earth the Master had sworn to protect, someone who tradition would never permit Chiun to kill.

"What is this, washerwoman?" Chiun demanded.

"It is death," the woman hissed.

She lunged at Chiun's throat. He easily sidestepped the latest attack, and she slammed into the open door. The impact split her forehead wide. She scurried back around, unmindful of the river of blood running from her forehead.

Her grinning triumph turned to bafflement.

Chiun instantly recognized the change. The woman herself likely did not understand what was happening. Perhaps it had been triggered when the wound on her forehead opened her blood to the air.

The instant her mouth began to foam, Chiun leapt for the open door of his house. He could do nothing to harm the woman, so he did not fling her down the stairs as he passed by her. He only slammed the door behind him.

There came a grunt of confusion from the far side of the door, then the sound of a body falling. There were a few moments during which the body jumped as if jolted by electricity, then Chiun's acute hearing heard the sickly wet pops of the woman's eyes.

After the final grisly noise, all outside the house grew silent.

Inside the house, the Master of Sinanju heard a pathetic scratching. He followed the sound to a door that led downstairs to a series of catacombs in which some of the greatest treasures of the House of Sinanju were hidden.

The door was locked. Chiun popped it open.

An emaciated figure lay across the landing at the top of the stairs.

Chiun did not sense the dull thud of a *gyonshi* heart.

He reached down and took the frail old figure gently by the bony shoulders, lifting him from the floor and setting him to his feet.

The elderly man winced at the daylight and cast a fearful eye at his savior. Only when he saw Chiun's face did the frightened man heave a sigh of great relief.

"Master of Sinanju!" Pullyang cried. "You have returned to save us!"

Chiun shook his head.

"Not all have been saved, old one," Chiun intoned to the man, who although twenty years his junior lacked the confidence and strength of the Master of Sinanju.

None in the village had ever been as faithful to Chiun as Pullyang, and so the old man was the one villager on whom Chiun smiled most kindly. Pullyang was trusted to tend to Master's affairs while Chiun was away, which was the greatest of all honors.

Pullyang cast his eyes to the floor in shame.

"I have failed you, great Master of Sinanju, who graciously throttles the universe," the caretaker said. "The demons only claimed their leader was with them. I did not know this was a lie when I phoned you. I only found out once they cut the telephone line and set the crazed washerwoman loose in your house as a trap. I have been hiding in the catacombs beneath the house for two days. I offer you my life as penance for my failure." He tugged down the collar of his tunic and turned his face away. "If you think of me at all when I am gone, I would be honored if you did not think entirely ill of me."

Chiun took his caretaker's chin in his hand and turned the old man's face to his.

"There has been enough death in Sinanju this day," the Master intoned. "Remain here where it is safe, faithful Pullyang. Leave the woman where she has fallen. I will first cleanse our village of this filth. After that, I will tend to our dead."

It was with a heavy heart that the Master of Sinanju turned from his servant. He headed back for the closed front door, the other side of which was decorated with the blood of an innocent whose life he had sworn to protect with his very own.

CHAPTER 18

IN REMO'S ABSENCE, CHAOS HAD DESCENDED on and around the Manhattan campus of Columbus University.

Remo had to abandon his rental car ten blocks away in what was technically not a parking space. It was technically the middle of the road filled with honking cars.

New Yorkers loved to blast their car horns at everything and nothing. The regular spontaneous rush hour performance was a gridlock symphony for everyone unable to get to Carnegie Hall. Remo figured that by leaving his car to tie up traffic for hours he was doing his small part to contribute to the fine arts.

The horn section blared at his back, accompanied by a few four-letter baritones, as he struck off on foot down the sidewalk.

Smith had been concerned about sending Remo back so soon. Remo had assured the CURE director that, while not one hundred percent, he was close enough to peak to be able to deal with whatever the vampire cult threw at him.

In fact, Remo was not as confident as he had led on to Smith. He was better, certainly. And it was true that he was well on his way to being fully recovered. But the difference between perfect and almost perfect in Sinanju was a gulf into which a Master of Remo's ancient art could fatally stumble. One fraction of an instant where his skills were uncertain and Remo could pay the ultimate price.

With every step along the Manhattan sidewalk, Remo fought the sluggishness that still lurked within his blood and organs. He was still feeling less than up to his full potential when he finally reached the university.

It seemed like every squad car and sawhorse in New York City had been deployed around the Columbus University campus.

Smith had told him that the school had been locked down since the previous day. No one was allowed in or out of the tight cordon, save government health officials.

He fished around in his pocket and found CDC identification, which he waved at every ring of manned sawhorses until he found himself in the ninth circle of hell.

There were open vans, large tents, and humming generators arranged on the sidewalk where the duties of the Columbus campus groundskeepers officially turned into the problem of New York's street sweepers. Medical personnel in hazmat suits, most of them without the hoods, moved around the area looking like the first settlers on the moon.

The only zone that appeared to require full hazmat gear, including hoods, was the campus itself. People coming and going on the trampled grass were fully decked out in suits and breathing apparatuses.

Remo began to bypass the last zone and head onto the campus when a voice called out behind him.

"Whoa, whoa, whoa!"

Remo looked around for the horse that somebody had apparently lost.

He didn't see Mr. Ed, but he did see an attractive woman running over to him waving her arms over her head. Even a formless, one-size-fits-all hazmat suit couldn't hide her perfect figure. If the cure for the common cold had been located in her chest, there would have been enough there to cure the planet's sniffles forever.

The woman bounced over to Remo's side and waved a stern finger in his face.

"You're not getting in here without proper protection, buddy."

"Is this a date?" Remo asked. "If it is, you could have phrased that a lot more romantically."

Remo read the tag on the jiggling chest of her white suit. It identified her as Dr. Connie Pelisse.

"Hey, my eyes are up here, buddy," Dr. Pelisse said.

"Yes, but your tits are down there. You can see my dilemma."

"Look, I don't know who you are, or what you think you're doing here —"

She was cut off by the I.D. card that Remo held out to her. According to the identification, he was Dr. Remo Barnard with the Centers for Disease Control in Atlanta. Connie Pelisse read each word of the card with growing skepticism.

"*You're* a doctor with the CDC?" she asked. *"You."*

"That's what it says on my card. I'm a molecular bi-whatsit."

"Biologist," Dr. Pelisse supplied.

"My specialty," Remo assured her with a wink.

He tried to step around her, but she bounced back in front of him. She held a palm to his chest, stopping him in his tracks.

"If we're grabbing each other's chests," Remo warned, "I'm going to have to call over a couple of other guys to help me out."

"*Doctor* Barnard," she said. "It's not just me saying this. No one gets in there without being suited up. This zone is blazing hot."

Remo looked around at the men and women in their protective gear. Dr. Pelisse was right. Remo would attract attention going in without a hazmat suit.

"Where can I get one of those Halloween costumes?" he asked. "I'd ask to borrow yours, but I imagine it would be udder chaos if you set those things loose."

She led him to the side of a tent where cases of suits similar to hers were piled. As Remo was pulling on a white hazmat outfit, he noticed someone giving a press conference a few yards away.

The man surrounded by microphones and cameras was under five feet but exuded the superciliousness of a man ten times his height. He managed to look down on the crowd while looking up at their knees.

"I respectfully disagree with the mayor," the little man was saying, his voice hoarse. "At this time it would be prudent for people to wear several surgical masks outside the outermost zone established around the school. I would recommend taping up windows and wrapping one's feet in cellophane if one has to go out. I would, however, chiefly recommend not going out at all for the foreseeable future. It could, frankly, be years before we find out what's happened here. The wisest course of action would be to stay inside for minimally the next five years."

The ordinarily combative New York press was reacting to the little man like teenage girls watching the Beatles land at JFK Airport.

"What's up with Dorf?" Remo asked.

"That's Dr. Frank Rossi, the Director of National Health from Washington," Connie said. "Whatever is going on at Columbus, it's not half as dangerous as getting between him and a news camera. He's the worst excuse for a doctor I've ever met. I suppose he's mostly harmless as long as he's never put in any position where anybody in power actually listens to him."

"I would recommend children be kept locked in their rooms," Dr. Rossi said into the array of microphones in response to a reporter's question. "They can be given board games like Parcheesi for the teenagers and Chutes and Ladders for the younger youngsters in order to keep them occupied, but by no means should one child interact with another child until there is absolutely no risk to their lives ever."

The reporters let out a collective shudder of such pure pleasure that afterwards Remo expected them to light up a cigarette.

"Quack," Connie muttered.

The press conference continued, but Connie turned away from it in disgust.

Remo was fully suited up. Connie had pulled on the rest of her own hazmat suit. As Remo headed for the campus, she fell in with him.

"You're coming with me?" Remo asked.

"Your ego is as big as Dr. Rossi's," Connie said. "I'm heading for the admissions office. I'm scheduled to take some samples there. You go wherever you like. Just turn on your oxygen before you do."

They were passing a rack on which sat a dozen oxygen tanks. She hefted a tank and tried to hand it to him. Remo refused it.

"Don't need it," Remo said. "I'll hold my breath."

Connie decided that she'd helped this rude stranger long enough.

The average person could hold his breath for thirty seconds to two minutes. Trained athletes could go longer, and world record-holders even longer still, but most people who went without fresh oxygen for more than a few minutes risked brain damage. And that was standing still, not walking around. If this Dr. Barnard from the CDC wanted to pass out after a minute on Columbus University's campus, that was his business.

The two of them headed away from the tents and vans, Dr. Rossi's press conference, and all the greatest buzz of activity outside the school. They threaded through the thinning crowd of health officials to a path that led into the college grounds.

Connie continued to cast glances at Remo, each time frowning more severely behind the clear plastic panel in her hood. It was well over two minutes after they'd donned their gear before she finally cracked.

"How are you doing that?" she asked.

"Doing what?" Remo replied.

"You've gone without oxygen for over two minutes, and you're strolling around like you're on the beach."

"I told you. I'm holding my breath."

"Dr. Barnard —" she began skeptically.

"Remo," he said.

"Fine, *Remo*. I'd like to know how you're walking and talking without an oxygen tank and without any apparent strain on your face."

"Do you have ten years to spare?" he asked wistfully.

"Not really, no," she said.

"Then sorry, doll, don't hold your breath that you'll ever find out. Besides, we're here."

Remo had allowed her to unwittingly lead him where he needed to go.

A sign for the admissions office was posted on the side of a building with a glass front. Remo held the door for her.

"You were heading here all along?" she asked.

"I'm looking for a student," Remo said, following her inside.

A wide, modern hallway ran off in either direction. The lights were off, but sunlight streamed in from the floor-to-ceiling windows that ran the length of the building.

"Good luck tracking down any student here," Connie said as they headed down the silent hallway. "This all started with a pair of murders early yesterday morning. It escalated to an entire dorm floor being killed. The police had barely started looking for the murderers when the first viral case broke out. Now the campus is on full lockdown, a thousand kids have already shown signs of this new virus, and the police are still trying to find a bunch of killers. It's been frying pan to fire for the past day here."

Smith had briefed Remo on the events that had taken place at Columbus after the two Sinanju Masters had been forced to return to Folcroft.

Apparently in the wake of the attack against Remo and Chiun, the vampire cult had released some new nightmare upon the school.

The CDC had first assumed that they were dealing with some new flesh-eating Ebola strain. They quickly discovered that it was something entirely new.

The infection caused the blood of its victims to congeal to Jell-O. The pressure caused blood to burst from every orifice. Some victims even had their eyes explode, although these appeared so far to be extreme cases. It was an excruciating death for the first two dozen victims before it was discovered that those infected could be treated with blood-thinning agents.

The first carriers had been a couple of exchange students from China. Remo couldn't question them. They had died the previous day. Smith extrapolated from the reports he'd read that they had been deliberately infected, then sent into crowded areas to spread the disease. Luckily this was after the police had instituted a campus lockdown, so the new virus had been contained to a single dormitory.

The two dead exchange students fit the description of *gyonshi*, but neither were the boy Chiun had seen outside the classroom where Remo had been infected.

Hop Yung, the student whose photo Chiun had identified, did not reside on campus, and Smith was unable to find his off-campus address. It was currently unknown if he was directing events at the university or if he was merely a foot soldier. What was known was that Hop Yung was a link. The CURE director had decided that the best place to find Yung's whereabouts was the admissions office.

"That's weird," Connie said when they reached the closed admissions office door. "I haven't seen any policemen in the building, have you?"

Remo had not. What he did sense was activity on the other side of the office door. A trio of low heartbeats thudded calmly inside the room.

Remo yanked off his hood and began stripping off the rest of his hazmat suit.

"What are you doing?" Connie demanded. "The virus could be airborne."

"Look, I humored you. Not to mention it kept my face off the six o'clock news. But I can't do my job from inside a garment bag."

"Remo, you could be contaminated already," she insisted.

"I was," he said. "I'm not now, and I won't let them get me again. Stay here."

He opened the door just wide enough to slip inside the office.

He found them feeding on the help desk a few yards in from the door. There were three of them. Their sallow-faced young leader was Chinese. The boy was dressed in black shirt and slacks. The other two — a girl and a boy — appeared to be ordinary Caucasian American students, but for the blood running from their mouths.

The three killers had the body of a middle-aged woman stretched out on the counter buffet style. Her stomach cavity had been slit wide open. The woman's harvested organs were currently residing in a trash can next to the counter.

When Remo entered the room, the trio were treating the woman's exposed belly like a punch bowl. The girl was just removing from the bloody cavity a mug that said, "You don't have to be crazy to work here, but we'll teach you!" Streaks of crimson dripped down the outside of the mug.

"The Red Cross definitely needs to do a much better job training its blood drive volunteers," Remo said to the group.

Three red-smeared faces snapped in his direction.

"If it's all the same to you guys, I'll just take my cookie and orange juice and go," Remo added.

The girl dropped her mug. It thudded to the floor and left a rolling blood splatter in an arc on the soft tile. The pair of American college students charged.

Remo could see that these were not full *gyonshi*. They did not possess the outward calm of true followers of the Creed.

The pair ran at him baring blood-smeared teeth and flashing their single pointed fingernails. Remo had fallen for that act once already. He would not do so again.

He appeared to them like a chained goat for slaughter, but the instant before their slashing nails could pierce his flesh Remo flexed his legs.

He was suddenly airborne.

It was an impossible move, more like that of a grasshopper than a human being. One second he was standing perfectly still, the next he was performing a flying somersault over the heads of his charging attackers.

His system was still on the fritz. He realized he was off nearly too late. The male's poisoned fingernail came perilously close to his bare ankle as he flipped overhead. He had to compensate in midair to avoid being scratched.

And then he was over. Not only the two students, but he'd also cleared the counter on which the trio had been feasting on their victim.

The main office area of the admissions office was an open space filled with desks, on the nearest of which a cup was loaded with mismatched pens. Remo scooped up a handful and let them fly.

Zip, zip, zip!

The pens were suddenly darts soaring back in the direction from which Remo had come.

His two attackers had wheeled back around and were racing around the blood-soaked counter. The flying pens thudded into their charging bodies in rapid succession. Two pens pierced thumping hearts. The remaining four were meant for the eyes. Three of this last quartet found their marks. The third missed the target entirely. The final pen soared back across the office and harpooned a bulletin board promotional flyer that advertised "The Third Annual All-Men-Are-Rapists Fun Run."

Remo was angry at himself for missing with one of the pens. He was still not at one hundred percent. The remaining toxin was still screwing with his system.

His error didn't matter with two charging *gyonshi*. The pair of pen pincushions were stopped dead in the tracks. They collapsed lifeless to the floor.

Remo had to concentrate to make certain his pores were shut down just in case the bodies produced some kind of fresh poison in death. Remo had not forgotten Smith's gruesome report about exploding eyeballs. But whatever had infected other victims did not seem to apply to these. The bodies of the boy and girl were still in death.

Two down, one to go.

The third vampire had hung back during the initial attack. Remo's Flying Wallendas routine and the subsequent brutal elimination of the pair of American vampires had happened so quickly that the young Chinese student had only now begun to react.

The college student's body began to shimmer, and very quickly a black cloud of impenetrable mist began to consume him.

Masters of Sinanju were able to control every part of their bodies, down to individual cells. Apparently whatever caused the mist to envelope the true servants of the ancient vampire Creed could be controlled by the *gyonshi*, as well.

The young man flashed a grin as he faded into the mist.

"You are too late again, Sinanju," he said.

The warping effect of the mist caused his voice to sound like it was coming from everywhere and nowhere.

"That's a pretty good trick," Remo said to the man who thought he had vanished utterly in the cloud. "Let's see if I can top it."

Remo reached into the mist and grabbed the vampire by the back of the neck.

"Peek-a-boo, I see you."

The vampire's eyes shot open wide. Not as precursor to the eyeballs exploding or even to the shock of being discovered in the cloud that should have confounded the senses of any opponent. He was shocked because he suddenly could not move a muscle.

Remo's grip paralyzed the man in place.

"What *is* all this?" a woman's stunned voice asked from across the room.

Dr. Connie Pelisse had gotten tired of waiting and had tiptoed into the admissions office. She reacted first in horror at the bodies on the floor that Remo had used as penholders, then at the amorphous black cloud into which she had just seen a man vanish, and in which Remo had just thrust his arm nearly up to the shoulder.

Remo found that the mist began to dissipate the instant he snagged the back of the young man's neck.

"Watch me pull a rabbit out of my hat," Remo called to Connie.

He lifted the *gyonshi* off his feet and drew him out of the cloud, which rapidly evaporated in the young man's absence from its center. To Connie, it was as if Remo had just pulled a body out of a parallel dimension.

"Where's Hop Yung?" Remo demanded.

Remo manipulated the upper spine, and the boy's voice returned.

"You may do to this shell as you will," the *gyonshi* said. "I do not fear death."

"I get that about you guys," Remo said. "The thing is, no matter how little someone fears death *everyone* hates pain."

Remo demonstrated what he meant to the young man.

It was like nothing his masters in the Manchurian forest had prepared him for. It was as if every nerve ending in his body had been exposed to burning, white-hot acid fire. He wanted to howl in pain, but the young Sinanju Master would not permit it. What was permitted by the man who held his spine and controlled the shockwaves of blinding pain was honesty. Complete and total honesty lessened the excruciating pain.

He answered everything. The number of *gyonshi* in America, the location of Hop Yung, the details of the Leader's return, the ultimate plan against the Masters of Sinanju, and the location of the City of the Dead.

When the young vampire had revealed everything he knew, Remo allowed him the merciful death he did not deserve.

The young man who had participated in the mass atrocity on the New York university campus felt and heard a simple crack, and then felt no more.

Remo let the body with the lolling head drop from his fingers.

He quickly hopped back over the counter and hurried to Dr. Connie Pelisse's side.

"We'd better get out of here. I need to breathe one of these days, and I don't know how well that suit will protect you if this one goes boom."

He grabbed her elbow and directed her out the door.

As soon as they were out in the hallway with the door shut behind them, Remo heard a loud pop from inside the admissions office. The wet residue did not reach as far as the door, but Remo's keen ears could hear soggy fragments of the exploding biological bomb sliding down the sides of distant desks.

"These bastards are full of disgusting surprises," he said. "Let's go."

Connie was numb with shock.

"But…you had a name to look up. A student."

"The human landmine in there told me where he is," Remo said. "And now that he's gone pop there's nobody to warn Hop Yung that the Grim Reaper he's wanted to meet all his life is about to pay him a house call."

He snatched up his discarded hazmat suit and quickly donned it. Once he was disguised once more from any prying TV cameras, he led the shaken Dr. Pelisse back toward the gleaming glass doors at the front of the building.

CHAPTER 19

THE MASTER OF SINANJU arranged the funeral pyre in the frigid wasteland a mile beyond the garbage heap at the edge of Sinanju.

A bitter wind whipped the wisps of white hair above his ears.

The kindling was driftwood from the rocky shore. On this was arranged wood harvested from the walls and floor of the dead washerwoman's shack. The woman herself was placed delicately on top of the pile. A strip of silk torn from one of Chiun's own kimonos was draped over her mangled eyes.

The woman could not be buried in the village cemetery. The risk of contamination was too great. Nor could the bodies of the Chinese vampires Chiun had killed be left anywhere near Sinanju, for the pollution of their bodies was a risk to the villagers. Chiun had piled the *gyonshi* in a small fishing boat and burned them in the bay.

The people of Sinanju had remained in their homes throughout the cleanup. The shame he felt from their fear cut the Master of Sinanju deeper than any knife, for it meant that the protector of the village had failed in his age-old mission.

Chiun twirled a twig rapidly in his fingers. A wisp of smoke flashed to flame. He used the fire to light the washerwoman's funeral pyre.

The flames roared high into the night sky, illuminating a circle of dancing orange on the barren plain.

Not so barren as it should have been.

A pair of gnarled, ancient trees had sprouted up on a plain that had not seen a tree grow on it in a thousand years.

Chiun knew well this ploy of Sinanju's old enemies. He poked at the raging fire with the end of a long stick. Flickering flame flashed in his hazel eyes.

"You have failed in your mission," the Master of Sinanju said to the ghosts in the night. "I live."

The eerie reply seemed to whisper from the trees.

"This will soon be remedied," a disembodied voice on the wind replied.

"Your kind hides in magic and vapor. Show yourselves, and I will visit upon you the death you desire."

The trees laughed and began to lose their shapes.

They were suddenly watercolor paintings left out in the rain. The hard bark of the trunks grew fuzzy. The branches evaporated to nothingness. The entirety of the squat trees churned first into clouds of black smoke, and then quickly took on the contours of men. In seconds, two pale figures dressed in black stood before Chiun, one tall, one short.

"You dare defile the home of the Masters of Sinanju?" Chiun said, his voice chilling for its lack of all emotion. He continued to tend the fire. "Masters who in ancient and recent times have sent many of your kind to their Final Deaths."

"We do not fear death, old one," the tall *gyonshi* replied.

Chiun had been leaning over the edge of the fire. He straightened up now, drawing himself up to his full five-foot height.

"You might not fear death, but you will fear me."

Without warning, Chiun lunged for the figure on the right. Before he could reach him, the tall *gyonshi* disappeared in smoke. Chiun passed through the edge of the cloud and out the other side, whirling around when he was once more in open space.

The Master of Sinanju did not break off the attack. The instant he missed his first target he was already pivoting for the second. He launched a flying kick at the chest of the *gyonshi* on the left. This assault ended as had the first. The short *gyonshi* turned to smoke and Chiun flew through the very edge and out the far side.

The clouds drew in tightly together and once more became men.

"*This* is the Master of Sinanju?" the taller *gyonshi* mocked. "You are nothing but a pathetic old man."

"I had strength enough to kill all your men in the village," Chiun said.

He barely managed to get the words out. The pair of failed attacks in rapid succession had left him winded. He stood panting in the glow of the funeral pyre, and braced his hands on his knees as he attempted to recover his breath.

"They were lesser members of the Creed," the tall one said. "Mere conscripts."

Chiun eyed the burning pile of wood. He suddenly lunged forward and grabbed one end of a piece of driftwood that had not yet fully caught fire. He yanked the branch from the pile. The far end burned like a torch as he flung it with what seemed like all his strength at the tall *gyonshi*. His face contorted with the effort.

The tall *gyonshi* easily sidestepped the hurled piece of wood. It skidded across the plain, sending out sparks, before settling under a bush that instantly whooshed aflame.

"He is nothing but a weak husk of a man," the short one said.

The Master of Sinanju's strength was utterly spent. He struggled for breath and shook his head helplessly at the sinister figures dressed in black.

"Why have you returned to the world, followers of a forgotten Creed?" Chiun pleaded. "The Leader is dead. I know it to be true. He was killed by my son."

"Your white lackey failed," the short one said. "The Leader's essence has returned to the City of the Dead. He has joined with one of the Creed, becoming flesh once more. He would not waste his time coming here. He sent five of his servants to your village, where we final two mock you in your infirmity."

Chiun straightened up. His breath had mysteriously returned. All at once his face did not look quite so aged in the dancing glow of the funeral pyre.

The Master of Sinanju had heard all that he needed to know.

"So, there were only three in my village, and you two here."

"Well…yes," the short one said.

"And the Leader is in Manchuria, in the fabled Forest of the Dead?" he demanded.

The tall one seemed to sense that something of great consequence had changed, but was not quite sure what it was.

"Yes, but it is of no matter to you where he is," the tall *gyonshi* said. "You will not live to see him. We were told that the Masters of Sinanju were formidable enemies. You are nothing but a weak old man."

The tall *gyonshi* laughed derisively. His short companion joined in the mirth.

They were still laughing when the pair of pebbles shot through their open mouths and burst through the backs of their heads, along the way severing their brain stems from their spinal columns. The pair had not the time to express shock at their sudden deaths before they were collapsing lifeless to the hard ground.

Of course the Master of Sinanju had seen them hiding in the shapes of trees. Their ability to do this was similar to the black smoke their Creed deployed as camouflage. Nothing more than the tricks of conjurors. Chiun had deliberately missed his targets during his attacks in order to fuel their overconfidence, then played the part of a tired old man when his blows failed to register. Although in truth this last part of his plan was a wise precaution. Touching the *gyonshi* even in death could prove fatal.

Chiun remained at a cautious distance, lest in death the bodies release some lethal poison. He addressed the corpses in the dancing light of the raging fire.

"Know you this, *gyonshi* dogs," the Master of Sinanju intoned. "Your Leader is dead, even if his twisted spirit knows it not. I will explain this truth to him and write the story of his end in his own blood. Your Creed is no more. Soon the Leader will find you in the realm of the dead, and your legends will join you in the dust of history."

The bodies did not make a sound, nor did they quiver as they lay on the ground. No poison emanated from the mouths or noses. The eyes remained intact, staring sightless at the million stars that were flung like jewels across the heavens.

Chiun would not defile the pyre of the washerwoman by tossing the bodies of the dead *gyonshi* into the fire with her.

The old Korean left the fire crackling behind him as he headed off into the night in search of another small boat and some more scraps of lumber.

CHAPTER 20

SMITH READ THE REPORTS FROM NEW YORK CITY with bloodshot eyes.

Every now and then he glanced at the blue contact phone. Each glance became longer, as if force of will could somehow make it ring.

The outbreak at Columbus University had started the previous morning after Remo and Chiun had returned to Folcroft. Smith was not a great believer in hunches. He preferred a world of cold, hard fact. But it was suspicious in the extreme that the outbreak had occurred after CURE's field agents had left the campus.

It reeked of a trap to lure them back in. Just as had the crisis that had drawn Chiun back to Sinanju.

Remo had said it. Divide and conquer. It was an age-old strategy, and one that a helpless Harold W. Smith very much hoped would not succeed.

The Centers for Disease Control had sent a containment unit up from Atlanta. The CDC was currently downplaying the seriousness of the epidemic, but Smith was privy to private reports coming out of Columbus U.

Things looked bleak, bordering on hopeless. A Dr. Connie Pelisse with the CDC had determined that the illness was some new virulent strain of airborne virus, related to polycythemia.

Most men would have had to look the disease up. Smith was unlike most men.

The CURE director was aware that polycythemia was a disease that caused blood to coagulate in the veins of the victim. It was generally treated with blood-thinning agents, which was the method currently being used by the CDC.

The success rate was poor. Cases were growing at an alarming rate.

There was no doubt this new threat was related to the Chinese vampire cult. Smith did not believe much concerning the mysticism Chiun attributed to the cult. The CURE director dealt in facts. And the facts were chilling enough.

The fact was that the *gyonshi* had already revealed themselves to be masters of poisons on two previous occasions. The first time CURE had dealt with them they had attempted to murder huge numbers of people with a deadly toxin hidden in beef. The next time it was poultry. Their evil Creed killed for religious purposes, a contradiction that the lapsed Protestant in Harold Smith could not reconcile.

Any religion that sanctioned wholesale murder was not a religion as far as Harold W. Smith was concerned.

If mass murder was still their goal, they had found a new deadly method that medical science was so far unable to combat.

Smith checked the time at the corner of his computer monitor. It was two minutes since the last time he'd checked.

Perhaps there was one thing he could check on while he was waiting for Remo.

Smith scooped up the phone and quickly punched in the number to Chiun's home in Sinanju. Chiun had not yet checked in. Given the unpredictability of the Master of Sinanju, it was possible that he would not. If the old Asian had eliminated whatever the threat to his village had been, Smith could make arrangements to get him back to the U.S. as fast as humanly possible to assist Remo in Manhattan.

He was deeply concerned to discover the phone in Chiun's house was not in service. It was an old-fashioned landline, but the North Korean government so feared the wrath of the Master of Sinanju that they maintained the pole and wire system with an efficiency unheard of anywhere else above the 38th parallel.

Chiun's home phone was dead. Smith hoped that it was not a portent.

The instant Smith replaced the phone to its cradle it jangled to life in his hand. He was startled for a moment before he snatched it back up.

"Report," he demanded.

"And a big old howdy-doody to you too," Remo said. "I'm not dead. Thanks for asking."

"Please, Remo," Smith said. "The situation at Columbus."

"Is under control, although you wouldn't know it to look around here."

"Explain."

Smith felt some of the tightness in his chest ease as Remo told him of his most recent confrontation with the Chinese vampires.

"Although is it racist to still call them Chinese vampires, Smitty?" Remo said. "I mean, they're Chinese and they come from China, but they're infecting all kinds of Americans here. I'd hate for the PC police to give me a ticket for being insensitive."

Smith noted that Remo was beginning to sound like his old self.

"I take it you are feeling better," the CURE director said dryly.

"Better, but not one hundred percent yet."

Smith heard a sudden cacophony of voices shouting what sounded like overlapping questions. He had to hold the receiver away from his ear until the noise died down.

"What was that racket?" Smith asked.

"Reporters," Remo said. "There's an unending press conference going on here with some midget government doctor. I wouldn't trust this guy to know which end to shove the tongue depressor in, Smitty. Why are my taxes going to some DMV worker with a medical degree and a Napoleon complex?"

"Need I remind you that you do not pay taxes?" Smith said.

Twenty miles south from where the CURE director sat behind his desk at Folcroft Sanitarium, Remo was sticking a finger in his free ear to block out the ongoing news conference. Dr. Rossi had been going on for at least an hour by Remo's best guess and, although hoarse, showed no sign of abandoning the gathered TV cameras.

"You ask an interesting question," Dr. Rossi rasped. "This crisis is unprecedented, and so until we know more I would recommend that no one leave their house for any reason for the foreseeable future. But if you meet a stranger online and he promises you he's clean, then unprotected anal sex is fine."

"God, he's an idiot," Dr. Connie Pelisse muttered.

Her face contorted in disgust, Connie yanked the rope on the inside of the tent in which Remo was using her borrowed cell phone to talk to Smith. The flap unrolled down across the entrance, blocking Dr. Rossi as well as the breathless throng of reporters who were hanging on the government doctor's every utterance.

"Who was that?" Smith demanded over the phone.

"Relax," Remo said. "She's a friend."

Remo had felt much better about Connie Pelisse ever since they'd returned from the university's administration building.

Connie had seen Remo in action, not to mention some of the Leader's minions. Watching a human being seemingly turn to smoke before one's eyes was something that caused the intellectually curious to question their preconceived ideas of the world, as had immediately been the case with the CDC doctor.

Connie had confessed that she now believed Remo had somehow managed to hold his breath for nearly forty-five minutes, yet she had no idea how. After he had hinted about what had happened to him the previous day, she also had a theory about Remo's blood.

Remo sat in a folding chair, Connie's cell phone pressed to his ear. She was loitering behind him, holding something down by her side.

"I've got a lead on the kid Hop Yung," Remo said into the phone. "He's supposedly got a place in Greenwich Village. The good news is that not only is he the one directing all the action stateside, he's the last of them that was sent here who's still alive. He and the guy I just took out were from the Creed, any others not from here were just Chinese exchange students who they infected. Once I track down Hop Yung and cash in his chips we end things here, completely and utterly. I'll be doing that as soon as I get off the phone, Smitty. That's why I'm calling. I want you to start arranging air travel for me to Sinanju."

"Yes, er, that might be a problem."

"It doesn't have to be to Pyongyang. I don't want to have to deal with that dipshit Kim with the sticking-up hair. Get me as far as Seoul. I'll figure it out from there."

"That is not the problem, Remo. Master Chiun is no longer in Korea."

Remo sat at attention at the edge of the folding chair.

"What the hell are you talking about?" he demanded.

"I have monitored his movements. He got out of the North on his own. He has taken a flight to Hong Kong."

"Shit," said Remo. "Shit, shit, and double-shit."

"What's wrong?"

"That's something else the exploding *gyonshi* here said. He said the Leader's plan was to separate us, so we were right with that. Kill us at first if possible, but separate. That's why they did Columbus U. and Sinanju at the same time. He wanted me to stay here to protect America's interests, while Chiun went to Sinanju to protect his. Divide and conquer. There was an attack waiting for Chiun in Sinanju."

"If there was, Master Chiun clearly survived it," Smith pointed out, "or else he would not have taken back off on the same plane in Hong Kong after it refueled."

"Survived it, but in what condition?" Remo said. "You saw the loop I got thrown for yesterday. The Leader could have him softened up. Now Chiun is walking straight into the outstretched arms of that blind psycho alone."

"The Leader," Smith repeated. "So you do believe he has returned."

"Keep up, Smitty," Remo said. "I don't understand it any more than you do, but this whole mess has his grubby undead fingerprints all over it."

Remo suddenly felt the pressure of a lunging body behind him. Connie Pelisse had selected that moment to make her move. The sharp object clutched in her hand jabbed at his exposed bicep. Remo caught her hand and set it to her side.

"Knock it off, Connie," he said.

There was no sense hiding it now. She raised the syringe she'd had hidden in her hand and held it out to him.

"Please, Remo," Connie begged.

"What is happening now?" Smith asked.

"Just another ghoul who wants to drain my blood," Remo said.

"I don't know who you are, Mr. Smith," Connie shouted at the phone. "But will you please tell him that his blood could hold a cure for this virus?"

Smith gasped at his name being mentioned by a stranger.

"We should break off this call," the CURE director said.

"Relax," Remo said. "She doesn't know who you are."

"No, I don't," Connie called. "What I do know is that I've seen this man perform some extraordinary things, and if what he's told me about beating one of these viruses in less than a day is true, his plasma could save many lives."

"Connie's got this thing for my sexy antibodies," Remo said.

"Connie?" Smith asked. "Is that Dr. Connie Pelisse?"

Remo could hear the CURE director typing over the phone.

"That's what it says on her hooters. But I'm not supposed to notice those, even though it's cold enough here that they're nearly poking my eyes out."

He could hear Smith finish typing with a flourish.

"Remo, Dr. Pelisse is one of the top infectious disease specialists in the country. She is correct about your immune system creating antibodies. You fought off the virus in record time. Not for you, obviously, but for the average human. Let her have some blood to test."

"What, you, too?"

Connie couldn't hear Smith's end of the conversation, but she knew an opportunity when she smelled one.

"We have isolated four distinct strains so far," she said. "But all of them are closely related. Your blood could hold the cure to this virus."

She didn't wait for permission. She pressed the tip of the needle to Remo's bicep. The skin seemed to dance away from the needle. She blinked. Remo smiled.

She tried again. This time when she tried to jab it in, the needle snapped.

"Are we finished?" Remo asked. Into the phone, he said, "I'll tell you, Smitty, what I told her. Whatever is in my system is still packing a wallop. I've got it contained. I don't know what poking a hole in me could do. I don't feel like scraping my popped eyeballs off the ceiling of this circus tent. Until I know it's dead, I'm not letting anybody in, for their sake as well as for mine. At the rate I've been kicking its ass, that should be roughly twelve to fourteen hours from now."

"Very well. I will begin making arrangements to get you as close to China as I possibly can, as quickly as possible. That's the best I will likely be able to do, Remo," Smith warned. "If you want to follow Master Chiun into China, you will be on your own. I am afraid I won't know where he's heading once he's there."

"That's okay," Remo said. "I do. While you're setting that up, I'll take care of this Hop Yung character."

Remo clicked the phone shut and tried handing it back to Connie.

She was over in the corner of the tent shoving items into a vinyl bag with a Velcro strip on the flap. She had already changed out of the white doctor's smock she had put on when they'd first entered the tent. She had put on a heavy parka and stocking hat. She had to battle her natural endowments to get the zipper even halfway up her torso.

"I'm ready," she announced.

"For what, a Canadian porno shoot?" Remo asked.

"I'm going with you."

She marched over and pulled her cell phone from his hand, shoving it into the pocket of her parka.

"I think I missed the part where you were invited," Remo said.

"I'm *coming*, Remo," she insisted. "You just told that Smitty fellow that it'll be twelve to fourteen hours before you're well enough to give a blood sample. When that happens, I intend to be standing there with a syringe. Lives depend on it."

She yanked up the flap on the tent.

"I've been consulting with New York state's top health officials," the hoarse voice of Dr. Rossi informed the crowd of spellbound reporters. "We have come up with a brilliant plan to place the sickest Columbus University students — those in the pre-eyeball-exploding stage and most likely to spread contamination — into nursing homes, cancer treatment centers, preschools, kindergartens, and Ronald McDonald Houses."

"That doesn't sound like a very good idea to me," said one reporter who was standing away from the rest of the crowd.

"Anti-science!" screeched an instantly recognizable woman who worked for a national network.

A nearby reporter with a Washington newspaper grabbed the heretical reporter's pad and flung it out into the street.

"Science deniers are a terrible threat to our society," Dr. Rossi said, nodding agreement with the mob.

The little man smiled deeply insincere sympathy at the only real reporter present, a man who was in the process of being shoved to the farthest reaches of the crowd.

"That dangerous glory hound wouldn't know what science was if it bit him on the ass," Dr. Connie Pelisse said, disgusted.

"The logistics would be difficult," Remo said. "He'd have to stand on a stepladder, otherwise science would have to get down on its hands and knees to reach it. Now shake a leg if you're coming along, Connie. My magic blood and I are hailing the first taxi out of this lunatic asylum."

Remo turned away from the press conference and began winding his way through the makeshift encampment of emergency personnel in the direction of where he'd last seen a glimpse of Broadway.

CHAPTER 21

NO ONE IN THE PEOPLE'S REPUBLIC OF CHINA wanted Premier Zhu Rongji to be unhappy. When the premier was angry, people sometimes disappeared.

Mysterious disappearances weren't a problem by themselves. After all, they had been going on since the birth of the People's Republic. Most famous of all in recent years had been the vanishings that had occurred immediately after the unpleasantness at Tiananmen Square. But no one cared if some lowly workers or dissidents vanished. The problem was that sometimes some who disappeared were actually important.

It would happen quietly, often in the dead of night. One day everyone was partners in the glorious Revolution, the next day, some of those partners would be gone.

One grew to accept the disappearances in silence, lest one become one of the disappeared.

The increased pressure for freedom in the wake of Tiananmen Square, coupled with the collapse of nearly every other communist regime on the planet, had created great pressure on the Chinese premier that sometimes exploded in unexpected directions.

General Yao Yilin prayed to his ancestors that he would not be in the path of such an explosion as he was ushered into the great office in the National Party Congress building in the ancient Chinese capital of Beijing.

Nervous sweat ran cold down the back of his stiff People's Army uniform. The perspiration gave him an involuntary shudder as he crossed the huge, drafty room.

Premier Zhu Rongji was reading from a thick pile of papers at a long desk before a high window. The premier looked up when General Yilin stopped before him.

"Ah, the latest intelligence briefing," the premier said. "So soon? Come. Sit down, general."

The premier waved the general to one of two seats before the desk.

"What news from the hot zone?" Zhu Rongji asked.

General Yilin was uncomfortably aware of the icy pool of sweat at his back.

"Guizhou remains under strict quarantine. Anyone who has attempted to leave has been shot."

The peasant village of Guizhou had been the center of some sort of viral outbreak. It had happened after the unauthorized visit to it by two female American workers several days before. The women had since gone missing in an adjacent forest. The People's Republic was preparing a formal expression of outrage for what appeared to be a biological attack on the poor emerging nation of China.

Premier Zhu put down the solid gold pen he'd been holding. He slowly turned it on the desk, aiming the nib like a miniature rocket launcher at his seated general. General Yilin stared at the tip of the pen as if it might go off.

"How did this outbreak begin, general?" the premier asked.

He had been asking the same question for days, with increasing impatience. There was nothing in this briefing that was going to make the premier happy. General Yilin was at least a tiny bit relieved to finally have an answer in this one small matter.

"There were two expeditions that entered the forest in search of the Americans," the general said. "Only one member of either group came back. Captain Gao Tiaphang. It appears that he is patient zero. He is the one who infected the villagers. Whatever he has, our virology experts believe he contracted it while in the forest."

"Has?" the premier asked. "You mean to tell me this man is not dead?"

"No, sir. He has confounded the People's experts. He has delivered death to many — inadvertently, it is believed — but he himself has not succumbed."

"Not yet," the premier said.

The Chinese leader made a note about this Captain Gao Tiaphang before returning to the business at hand. Premier Zhu finished writing then looked back up at the general.

"I presume the American women have not been discovered, or you would have told me that straight away," Zhu said.

General Yilin did his level best not to fidget in his chair.

"Actually, they finally were."

Premier Zhu waited for the rest. Unlike the past several days, there was finally information to report, yet he was having to draw it all out of the general.

"And what of the two Americans?" the premier demanded.

General Yilin took a deep breath and launched into the monologue he had hoped that he would somehow not have to deliver.

"They are dead," the general said. "They were discovered at dawn hanging from a tree at the edge of the forest that borders Guizhou. Their bodies had been desecrated, but we have made positive identifications of both. They were not hung there by the villagers. Apparently there is a group of peasants that live in the woods, unknown to us until now. They have been there as long as the locals can remember, and much longer in the local history. They are primitives, it sounds like. Cannibals. They keep to themselves in the forest, but it appears that our soldiers stumbled upon them in the search for the American women. It is believed that they...*ate* Captain Tiaphang's men."

"Preposterous," the premier insisted. "What does this Captain Tiaphang have to say about these forest people?"

General Yilin had prepared for this question. He knew precisely how to answer without bringing the word "vampire" into the conversation, the inclusion of which would likely lead to a bullet in the back of his head by day's end.

"He confirms the most outlandish stories of the locals," Yilin said.

This was the absolute, if incomplete, truth.

General Yilin had hoped that there would be no follow-up questions about this aspect of the briefing. He was not sure if he should be pleased that the next horrible news on the docket would almost certainly result in the premier forgetting all about the contaminated village, the Typhoid Mary captain, and the mysterious forest into which two companies of People's Republic soldiers had vanished.

"There is news separate from the situation in Guizhou that I fear needs to be brought to the premier's attention," the general said.

Yilin blurted this quickly, before the premier could direct questions that would inevitably lead to local Guizhou lore about the blood drinking cultists who supposedly haunted the neighboring forest.

"We have just received a report from our comrades in North Korea," General Yilin said. "The Master of Sinanju flew from Pyongyang to Hong Kong a few hours ago. His plane refueled there and took back off for Beijing."

As expected, all questions concerning the events currently playing out in Manchuria were forgotten. Premier Zhu Rongji's face blanched.

"The Master of Sinanju is coming *here*, to these shores?" China's leader demanded. "Why did not the idiots in Pyongyang tell us sooner?"

"It seems that someone there — a young soldier — did not know him," Yilin said. "He attempted to detain the old Master." The general shook his head. "I understand there were several deaths. Many are in the hospital. The North Koreans were too occupied dealing with the aftermath of his departure to inform us he was coming to us."

Sinanju and their deadly assassins were not known to the general public. Even some heads of state were unaware of the existence of the ancient martial artists. But a long history existed between China and the little fishing village on the West Korean Bay. In the past when things were good between Beijing and Sinanju, emperors of China hired the Sinanju Masters. More recent history had been more complicated.

It was never a good thing that the Master of Sinanju should come to any country when he had not been summoned. The premier's first thought was of what he might have done to earn a visit. The next was how fast he could get out of the country.

"How soon?" the premier demanded.

"He will be arriving in the hour," the general said.

The premier shot out of his chair and began edging around his desk.

"See that he is given the respectful greeting he deserves," Zhu Rongji commanded. "Be sure to give him my warmest wishes for long life and good health."

General Yilin stood, as well.

"You will not be here to greet him?" the general asked.

"Ah, lamentably, no," the premier said, nervously. He inched for a side door. "I will be out of the country. Soon. In fact, my plane will be leaving — When did you say the Master of Sinanju would be arriving?"

"This hour," the general replied.

"Ah, yes. A shame. I will be gone in less time than that. Our Nigerian partners have invited me to tour a new railway line our investments there have financed. Be certain to tell the Master of Sinanju this if he asks where I am. Tell him my trip was planned long ago and that, regrettably, it could not be cancelled." He held out his hands, palms up. "But do not mention my name if he does not first do so. Leave me out of it."

The premier was at the door, his hand on the handle.

"But this briefing," General Yilin said. "We have not finished."

"Hadn't we? Oh, well. When I get back. Is that the time? I must fly."

Premier Zhu Rongji ran from the room like it was on fire and slammed the door behind him.

General Yilin had feared when he entered the premier's office that his neck was on the chopping block. He would have liked to be relieved that it had been spared for another day, however now there was the unscheduled arrival of the Master of Sinanju to worry about. If the old Korean was in a foul mood, as rumor had it he always was, it could very well be that General Yilin's head had been given a reprieve of only one hour.

He checked his watch. Fifty-two minutes, to be precise.

The damp spot on his uniform shirt pressed against the base of his spine as he turned from the Chinese premier's desk, sending a chill throughout his entire body.

On his way from the room, General Yao Yilin reached back and pinched a clump of chilly fabric, pulling it away from where it had stuck to his flesh.

His sticky sweat reminded him of dripping blood, and his thoughts as he left the room briefly returned to photos of the pair of American women who had been discovered hanging like butchered livestock from a tree in a frozen forest in Manchuria.

CHAPTER 22

HAILING A CAB IN MANHATTAN at the height of a medical emergency proved to be the greatest challenge of the past challenging forty-eight hours.

Most of the cabs anywhere near the vicinity of Columbus University refused even to slow down. Remo was finally able to catch a slow-moving one, the back of which he held a foot in the air with a promise to the driver that he could have his rear tires back if the hack took them to Greenwich Village. The cabbie wholeheartedly agreed to the exchange.

"I've never seen anything like that," Dr. Connie Pelisse marveled as Remo dropped the back end of the cab back to the pavement.

"It only looks impressive," Remo said. "It really just comes down to a simple understanding of physics and Euclidian geometry. A child could do it."

"Really?" she asked.

"Sure. If you want a flat child. Get in."

He stuffed a hundred dollar bill through a hole in the partition that separated the back and front seats.

"That's for the ride," Remo said. "These —" He held up five more crisp hundred dollar bills. " —you get if you can keep your yap shut the whole ride."

"You got it, mac," the driver greedily vowed.

"That's one down," Remo said.

He opened the window a crack and let one of the hundreds flutter off into the wake of the speeding cab.

"Are you nuts?" the driver said.

"That's two," Remo said, giving a second bill its freedom.

The driver got the rules. After losing two hundred dollars in under twenty seconds, he screwed his mouth shut and set his angry eyes on the road ahead.

"That was remarkable what you did with the cab back there," Connie said. "You really are an amazing specimen."

"Aw, go on," Remo said. "You'll make me blush."

She slid closer to him so that her breasts, which were exploding from her half-zipped parka, rubbed against his upper arm. She leaned her face in close. He could feel her warm breath on his neck. The subtleness of her perfume was intoxicating. She pressed her lips to his ear.

"Let me have just a little blood."

"Geez, no, Count Dracula," Remo said, shoving away from her.

The cabbie was leering in the rearview mirror at the exposed décolletage of one of the world's premier virologists.

"I got somethin' a lot more fun than blood for you if youse want it, lady," the hack volunteered, flashing a lascivious grin.

"And there goes another one," Remo said, crumpling up another hundred and tossing it out the window.

"Shit," the cab driver said, a word which he instantly regretted and nearly repeated when Remo let the fourth of five bills fly out the back window.

Connie gave up trying to seduce a donation out of Remo. She sat back in the seat, tore open the Velcro on her bag, and began taking inventory of the contents.

"So you're sure there's only one of these guys left?" Connie said, suddenly all business.

"That's what the ghoul back at school said," Remo replied. "It gets a little tricky with them, though. They can enlist others to join them with this stuff they inject them with. They put it on that one sharp fingernail of theirs. That's how they inject all their poisons and viruses and whatevers. It's like a Swiss Army fingernail of toxins with these guys. So even though he's the last from China, this Hop

Yung bastard could have made more flying monkeys since the last time that other asshole saw him."

"That's remarkable."

She had witnessed his interrogation of the dead man back at the university, and had overheard Remo's half of his conversation with this Smith person. Remo had filled her in on some more of the details while he was trying to flag down a cab.

Dr. Connie Pelisse had become a doctor to help people. She had devoted her career to virology due to a natural aptitude as well as a fascination with the subject. When it came to mortality, human beings were conditioned to fear the big, the sudden, the understandable. Fatal car crashes were terrible, but people could wrap their brains around them. *Of course* large metal objects colliding into one another were deadly. One need only look at the twisted wreckage on the evening news to get that.

A heart attack was slightly more difficult since it was romantic hogwash that one wore one's heart on one's sleeve. The heart was hidden from view, thudding away in the chest cavity, yet people still understood that it was a large, mechanical object in continuous use. Things break. From toasters and dishwashers to human hearts.

It was the smaller things that people had the hardest time understanding. Bacteria, cancer, viruses. Infinitesimally small items which often wound up being the unexpected things that altered the course of a human being's entire life.

When she was eight years old Connie Pelisse had been fascinated to learn that her grandfather in Oklahoma had died as a result of an untreated wound.

Connie heard her mother discussing the death of her grandfather with a neighbor three weeks after the family had returned to New York from attending the services. Connie had not gone on the trip. She had only met Grandpa Ned a few times, and her parents had told her that she would find the wake and funeral frightening.

"Stepped on a nail," Mrs. Pelisse had informed the woman next door over coffee at the kitchen table while Connie played with her Barbie dolls on the living room rug. "Went right through his boot. Wouldn't have happened if mom was alive. You should have seen those boots. Worn down to nothing. Bob and I would have sent him a new pair for Christmas, but of course he told us he didn't need anything. Typical dad."

Connie pretended to be fascinated by the dolls in her little hands. Her mother could see her through the open door to the living room, and every once in a while she would cast a glance and lower her voice. Connie made sure she continued to bounce her Barbies around on the sofa cushions and to mutter occasional words into their mouths. But it was the conversation in the kitchen that interested her. The Barbie dolls would eventually go into a box for the Salvation Army, but that talk her mother had had in the kitchen with a neighbor had changed the course of Connie Pelisse's life.

Her mother had attributed her father's death to his worn-out boots, but in fact it was the result of something invisible living on the nail the old farmer had stepped on. *Clostridium tetani* was the technical name. It was a bacteria that thrived in an oxygen-free environment, which it had been introduced to via the rusty nail.

Grandpa Ned had suffered spasms, fever, and finally a fatal blood clot. Not only had he ignored the worsening symptoms until it was too late, he had failed to preemptively do the one thing that would have prevented him from getting sick in the first place. Grandpa Ned had never gotten a tetanus shot.

Even before Connie had enrolled in medical school she understood that it was a miracle her irascible farmer grandfather had lasted as long as he had.

Grandfather Ned used to boast that the last doctor he'd seen was the midwife who'd delivered him. He had gone from his first day as a squalling infant on the kitchen table of his parents' home, to his last day as a confused old man clutching his head on the bedroom floor of the same farmhouse, with a total lack of knowledge of the hundreds of invisible threats he had managed to dodge on every single intervening day.

Connie had vowed to help people like her grandfather, and so had devoted herself to the study of the invisible dangers that surrounded human beings every day.

She had excelled academically, burnished her credentials in the private sector, and eventually scored a position at the CDC, the place at which she felt her hard work and genius could help the greatest number of people.

Naturally she had been assigned to the crisis at Columbus University. The CDC would have been derelict had they not sent along one of the top infectious disease experts in the country to assist with a baffling viral outbreak of unknown origin.

Except the origin was no longer unknown.

According to a man she had only met a few hours ago there was an entire world of study that defied time and existed beyond known science. There were evil men who were specialists in ancient toxins and weaponized viruses, and their expertise long predated the Japanese dropping ceramic bombs filled with fleas infected with bubonic plague in World War Two or German weaponization of anthrax in World War One.

Of course she didn't believe this Remo Barnard was a doctor. Back at Columbus she had nudged the admissions office door open a crack before she'd entered the room. She saw him fly through the air from a standstill, then kill two of his attackers with a few hurled pens. She had seen him pull a third man out of a cloud and paralyze him while holding him off the floor one-handed. She watched him lift a taxicab barehanded.

Remo was obviously some kind of spy. But that didn't matter. This man had performed superhuman feats before her eyes.

Connie Pelisse was not some bimbo dimwit, outward appearance notwithstanding. She dealt in cold, hard reality. And the reality was that a man who could perform such miracles could have fought off sickness in a day, as he claimed to have done. If that was the case, his body contained within it something of incalculable value. The antibodies his immune system was producing could save the lives of hundreds today. Perhaps thousands or even millions tomorrow. Remo was a valuable scientific specimen, and for the sake of humanity Connie Pelisse would follow him to the ends of the earth.

She glanced over at him in the back seat of the taxi, wondering if Jonas Salk had felt the same monumental wonder and humility peering through his microscope.

Connie's potential medical breakthrough was saying something to her. She had been so distracted during the ride to Greenwich Village that she hadn't been listening.

"What?" Connie asked.

"I said we're here," Remo repeated. "Are those airbags on your chest blocking sound from reaching your ears?"

Of course, Dr. Connie Pelisse thought, Jonas Salk always had the option of flushing his experiments down the toilet.

Apparently Remo had thrown the last of the five hundred dollar bills out the window before they'd even left Morningside Heights, where Columbus University was located. Since then he had been keeping a running tally of every time the driver had opened his mouth to yell at another driver, pedestrian, or bike messenger. It had only been a fifteen minute drive to Greenwich Village.

From the sidewalk, Remo leaned in the front window of the cab.

"By my calculations you owe me twenty-seven hundred bucks," Remo informed the driver.

The cabbie paid him with a single finger and an accompanying phrase before peeling off down the road in a cloud of rubber.

Remo took a look up at the old, five-story brownstone. The vampire back at the Columbus University admissions office had told him that Hop Yung kept an apartment on the fifth floor.

Remo had felt the pressure waves from a pair of eyes from that floor following the cab to the curb. The sense of someone watching him fled when he stepped from the cab. He glanced up. Whoever had been watching was no longer at the window.

"Stay here," Remo told Connie.

"Oh, no. No way, buster," she said. "I've seen that a million times in movies. You said these people are like some kind of vampires? Well in the movies, the one who always 'stays here' always, but always winds up either a vampire or eaten by a vampire. I don't know what their deal really is, but vampires or not they murdered an entire floor of students at Columbus. A killer's a killer. I'm safer with you."

Her face was resolved. At least Remo assumed it was, given her tone. He wasn't certain because he had been distracted during her speech by her chests, which had been nodding 44D agreement with every word. They truly were mesmerizing.

He dragged his eyes to her face. He'd guessed correctly.

"Stay close," Remo warned. "I'm still not at the top of my game, and I don't know what we'll find in there."

Since they'd already been spotted there was no sense sneaking around to a back entrance. Remo had Connie stay behind him as they mounted the sandstone's front stairs.

CHAPTER 23

Hop Yung watched the taxi pull to a stop in front of his building.

He had flitted around the edges of the crowd of specialists and police at Columbus throughout most of the previous night, and so he recognized Connie Pelisse as one of the CDC people who'd been flown up to the university.

The surprise was the younger Sinanju Master.

The dose that had been given the white Master of Sinanju by Hop Yung's minion professor should have been lethal. At the very least the white man should have suffered brain damage and paralysis. At best he should have been an invalid for the rest of his life.

Yet there he was, stepping from the back of a taxicab looking perfectly healthy scarcely one day after receiving an injection of *gyonshi* poison.

The men from Sinanju had been feared by his sect going back a hundred generations. Hop Yung was beginning to understand why.

Yung was the oldest son of the most prestigious family from the Forest of the Dead. Few of their kind ever ventured out into the world. But Yung had shown an aptitude for experimentation with the Creed's old potions at a very young age. Because of his family's stature he had been permitted to attend schools outside of the forest.

Hop Yung had been a clever boy who had become a cleverer young man.

Unlike others placed in his position who would have forgotten the ancient ways, Yung had never turned his back on his sect. When word came from out of the Forest of the Dead that the one Leader had returned, Yung had happily returned to his homeland.

At this point Hop Yung was already an exchange student at Columbus University. In exchange for allowing him to leave China, he had been conscripted into service by the communist government in Beijing to be its eyes and ears in America. It was difficult to convince the government to allow him to make an unscheduled return.

Yung had been tempted to use some of the special formulas he had developed from the Creed's recipes. It was an easy enough matter to bend a man to the Creed's will. The problem was that once the weak-minded were bent, they never bent back.

A jolt of electricity had once worked to purge the most potent *gyonshi* toxin, which was a relative of nearly all the others. Hop Yung had seen to it that this no longer worked. Any attempt to cleanse a body of the poison now resulted in death.

Except in one man.

Hop Yung slipped forward and took another peek out the window.

The taxicab that had brought the white Master of Sinanju and the girl to Yung's apartment building had been stopped at the traffic light down the road. It was just turning the distant corner now. Its two passengers were nowhere to be seen.

They had entered the building.

An unaccustomed smile creased the sallow face of Hop Yung.

By some miracle the young Master of Sinanju had survived the attack at Columbus University. Not this time. There were five stories between him and Hop Yung. This time the white thing would fail. He would not make it as far as the second story landing. This time the young Sinanju Master would meet his Final Death.

CHAPTER 24

GENERAL YAO YILIN FOUND HIMSELF nearly alone on the tarmac of Beijing Capital International Airport.

It seemed that, like Premier Zhu Rongji, nearly all of China's highest ranking officials suddenly had other places to be when word got around that the Master of Sinanju was coming to town. Still, an official reception was necessary. No one wanted one of the two deadliest men on earth to feel slighted. So even as the Chinese leadership headed for the hills they delegated to their underlings the responsibility of greeting the ancient killer.

And so it was that General Yilin found himself at the airport in the company of a handful of younger party officials too unimportant to join the mass exodus.

General Yilin doubted any of the bland officials in their crisp business suits even knew who the Master of Sinanju was.

The existence of the Sinanju Masters was one of the best kept open secrets in the world. They might exist in history books on shelves in some dusty library, but they were part of man's forgotten past. Knowledge of their current existence was passed down from world leaders to their successors, and only in hushed tones.

Some in Beijing groused about the fact that the ancient house of mercenaries currently worked for the Americans. After all, in the old days China had been a frequent client of Sinanju. General Yilin was not one to complain. The Masters of Sinanju were notoriously unpredictable. The fear Yilin had of his own government was as nothing compared to the terror the old Korean could inspire in the hearts of the bravest men.

General Yilin felt his heart trip in his chest when he spotted the black dot of a plane in the white sky.

The aircraft was an Anatov An-148, built in Ukraine. It was a regional jet that was the personal plane of North Korean Premier Kim Jong Il.

The aircraft was technically not stolen, even though it had been borrowed without prior permission. As General Yilin understood it, Premier Kim had ordered the North Korean military to stand down as soon as he found out who it was that had commandeered the plane. According to China's top official in Pyongyang, Kim had been quite adamant about letting the Master of Sinanju get whatever he wanted.

"If that maniac wants my plane, he can have it with my blessing," Premier Kim was reported saying. "Hell, if he wants one of my kids he can have him, too. Take the second one. That little shit's so screwed up, his head is like a sack of cats."

The An-148 managed to land without any major parts dropping off. A minor miracle for a Ukrainian plane flown by pilots of Air Koryo, North Korea's national airline. The plane taxied to a stop in front of the small welcoming committee.

Some air stairs were hastily rolled to the side of the plane, and a red carpet was unfurled to the bottom step.

When the door opened, only one man emerged.

The wizened figure with the impassive face padded down the stairs.

"Welcome, O great Master of Sinanju, to the People's Republic of China," General Yilin announced, bowing at the waist. "It is our great honor that you have blessed our nation with this unexpected visit."

The ancient Master of Sinanju regarded the hastily assembled collection of marginal officials with disdain. When he spoke, he addressed General Yilin alone.

"I require immediate transportation to Manchuria," Chiun said.

General Yilin already did not like the sound of this.

"Would the Master of Sinanju permit his humble servant to ask where in Manchuria he wishes to be taken?" Yilin asked.

As the general feared, the place to which the Korean wanted to travel was the hot zone of Guizhou into which no one was permitted to go, and from which anyone who attempted to leave was shot dead. General Yilin had no idea what could possibly interest the Master of Sinanju in that region, but he now suspected there was something far greater happening there than a viral outbreak.

"If your lowly servant might be bold enough to ask another question of the great Master of Sinanju, does this matter that requires your august presence in Manchuria have to do with the missing American women?"

Yilin had no intention of telling the old Korean that the two women had been found, skinned and hanging from a tree. If the retrieval of the previously missing women on behalf of the Americans was the purpose of the Master of Sinanju's visit, General Yilin would let the old man learn the truth from an underling while General Yilin joined the rest of the Chinese leadership anywhere on the planet that was not China.

"What are you babbling about?" Chiun said. "It is bad enough that I have been forced to enter this nation of iniquity, not to mention that I had to do so on a craft that I thought would fall apart around me the entire terrifying way here. I have no time to answer the questions of some lowly airport worker." He clapped his hands. "Make haste, skycap. I require transportation. While you are at it, dismiss your fellow porters. I have no luggage for them to steal. Tell them the only tip I have for them is to be less Chinese, which is the most valuable gratuity they will ever receive."

General Yilin wasn't sure if the Master of Sinanju had truly mistaken his People's Army uniform for that of an airport luggage handler. He merely accepted the insult with gratitude that he could do so with his head still attached.

Yilin began shouting commands for a helicopter to be prepared at once to fly the old Korean to Manchuria. Some underlings who were waiting at attention in the nearby hanger began racing around to implement the orders.

"Hold!" the Master of Sinanju announced abruptly.

Yilin ordered everyone in the vicinity to freeze.

The old Korean tipped his head thoughtfully.

"I have changed my mind," Chiun said. "I would be taken to a hotel. I have traveled much and am weary. I require rest before I continue to Manchuria."

"Yes, Master of Sinanju," Yilin said.

"Five stars, no less," Chiun warned him.

"Of course, Master of Sinanju," General Yilin promised.

Yilin clapped his hands. A car was hastily driven forward, into the back of which slipped the ancient Korean.

General Yilin himself climbed in beside the driver, and the car sped off from beside the hanger and out of the sprawling Beijing Capital International Airport.

The small entourage that had awaited the arrival of the stranger from Korea began to break up. The minor party officials in suits whispered amongst themselves about the peculiar nature of the reception they had been ordered to attend, while soldiers rushed out of the hangar to roll up the red carpet and roll back the air stairs.

None in attendance noticed lurking in a corner of the large hangar a darker shadow amongst the shadows. It was like hot steam escaping from a vent, except there were no vents in the vicinity and steam was not black.

The swirling mist collapsed in on itself and rapidly congealed into the form of a young man with pale skin and sunken cheeks.

The man in the black business suit turned from the main door of the hanger and walked quickly to a side entrance.

CHAPTER 25

REMO NUDGED OPEN THE OLD FRONT DOOR of the apartment building.

Since he was entering a vampire's lair it was only appropriate that the door squeaked on hinges that hadn't seen a drop of oil since Prohibition.

Inside was a foyer with a marble floor. Many feet over many decades had worn a slight dip of a path from the front door of the building to a second set of doors on the far side of the front hall. Two dozen little silver mailbox doors on his right informed him that there were two dozen apartments, with likely more than one inhabitant in each.

The trip to the top floor was not likely to be easy.

"Suit up," Remo said.

Connie nodded and dropped her bag to the worn marble. She yanked a large item from the bag She pulled the respirator-gas mask down over her head, tugging the side straps tight. The mask covered her entire face, with a plastic shield over her eyes.

She gave Remo a confident thumbs-up.

"This is dumb," Remo said. "It would have been safer for you to stay outside."

"No way," Connie said, her voice muffled behind her mask. "Where your plasma goes, I go."

"You said that mask will only protect you against stuff that's airborne. I told you they can deliver their stuff through a scratch. That's how they got me."

Connie thought of her grandfather, contorting in pain alone on the floor of his farmhouse bedroom because of a rusty nail that had broken the skin of his foot. Then she thought of all the current victims at Columbus University, as well as the countless future victims if the outbreak there spread beyond the campus.

"That's where I'm counting on you to protect me," Connie said, firmly. "You'd better be as good as you claim. Besides, I've got this."

Connie reached down into the cavern between her breasts and produced a crucifix on a chain, which she held out before her.

"What the hell are you doing with that?" Remo asked.

"You said they were vampires," she said. She tipped her head to the cross in her hand. "Vampire repellent."

"Great," Remo muttered. "And you're supposed to be a scientist." He shook his head, and beckoned her forward. "Shake a leg, Buffy."

He pushed open the inner foyer door.

Remo was impressed that the woman immediately on the other side of the door had not made a sound. Even her heartbeat had been slowed to near-death.

She had been stationed in wait for Remo to enter, and the instant he stepped into the hallway she lunged.

"Aaaaarrrghhh!"

It was like being attacked by a gypsy from an old Universal horror movie. The woman was in her seventies, with a worn-out apron over her peasant skirt, a babushka wrapped around her blue-tinted hair, and more cheap costume jewelry than the Home Shopping Club. The rings on her fingers clicked as she swiped a claw at Remo.

Remo batted the hand away.

He'd barely deflected one hand before the other was slashing from the opposite direction, aimed for the soft flesh of his exposed neck.

In the dim light of the downstairs hallway he could see that every one of her fingernails had been sharpened to razor tips. Every one could have contained a different *gyonshi* poison.

She howled, she screamed, she bared yellow fangs.

Remo socked her in the side of the head and she dropped like a ton of bricks.

Connie had jumped back, slamming her spine against the wall as soon as the older woman had leapt out of the shadows. She was panting in shock, thin fog forming on the interior of her gas mask.

"What the hell, Remo?" Connie demanded.

She glanced up from the slumbering woman. Remo, on the other hand, kept his eyes locked on his babushka-wearing attacker, and so he was first to see the body begin to contort as if a thousand volts of electricity were suddenly shooting through it.

"Go!" he snapped.

He grabbed Connie by the arm and spirited her from the front doorway.

A door to his left sprang open. A fortyish man in a scruffy beard and a concert T-shirt sprang out. Remo sent the heel of a foot hard into the AC/DC logo just over the man's sternum. There was a crack of bone, and this new attacker folded in half and rocketed back into his apartment, crashing into a set of drums.

T-shirt man was dead before he landed, and his body was already bouncing like babushka woman's back at the front door. As he ran, Remo glanced back long enough to see the woman's eyeballs explode like a pair of tiny, viscous-filled water balloons.

Orange mist was seeping from the mouth and nose of the older woman, and presumably of the younger man lying in a heap amongst his drum set.

Remo made the same precautions as before to prevent the mist from entering his system, but the particles within the orange mist quickly became the least of their worries.

The downstairs hall abruptly erupted in bedlam as door after door popped open. Remo flew past them all, Connie in tow. The CDC scientist's mask had grown so foggy by this point that she was virtually blind as they ran for the stairs.

Hands lashed out at Remo and the girl, fingernails like miniature daggers.

Remo solved the problem by severing many of the grasping hands at the wrists. The infected men and women from the first floor weren't deterred. They continued to chase after Remo and

Connie, seemingly unaware that they had lost their hands. The residents remained determined to slash the intruders with the bleeding stumps of their wrists.

Remo and Connie reached the stairs.

"It gets trickier from here!" Remo yelled.

Connie could see nothing but vague shapes, a fact for which she was grateful when she felt herself suddenly weightless.

Remo flung the virologist over his shoulder and bounded up the stairs in two great strides. He launched his foot hard into the center of the top stair, then leaped for the railing when the subsequent crack and shock wave took out the entire first-floor flight.

The staircase collapsed, wiping out the six downstairs residents who had been chasing Remo and Connie upstairs.

"We're not out of the woods yet!" Remo shouted.

"What woods?" Connie snapped back. "I can't even see a damn tree!"

"Probably just as well," Remo said.

Connie's ears remained uncovered. She heard with crystal clarity what sounded like growls coming from a dozen vicious animals.

A welcoming committee was waiting on the second floor.

Remo bypassed them completely, bounding from balustrade to second-floor staircase, to third floor. The residents of the second floor didn't even have time to chase them up the stairs before this flight of stairs collapsed as well.

"What's all that smashing?" Connie asked.

"I'm working here," Remo snapped.

"It sounds like you're taking a wrecking ball to the place!"

"You know, you could have stayed back at that school."

"You know, I *could* have if you let me take a blood sample!"

Remo wished the gas mask did a better job muffling her mouth. It was taking all his concentration to keep both of them from being killed.

Years of training had made remarkable physical feats second nature to Remo, but he was finding now that his brush with *gyonshi* poison had made some things difficult that he had long accepted as second nature.

He nearly lost his footing running along the banister on the fourth floor, which would have been child's play even in his earliest days of training. It didn't help that he was out of balance carrying one hundred and thirty pounds of parka-clad scientist on his shoulder, or that a dozen extras from *Dawn of the Dead* were currently hot on his heels with snatching hands and snapping jaws.

He had hoped that some of the residents of the building weren't beyond saving, but it was clear from the first two attackers that they were too far gone. The people in the brownstone had been turned like none of the *gyonshi* he had ever encountered before. They seemed to be all animal, with the lone goal of murdering Remo programmed into them. All he could do was keep ahead of them or mow down any that got in his way.

The former he managed with the mob at his back when he reached the stairs to the fifth floor. The latter was forced upon him with four who were lying in wait ahead.

Exchange student Hop Yung had apparently drafted this last batch from Columbus University and not his apartment building.

The four college students were not feral like the specimens Remo had encountered on the lower floors. They had donned the black garb of the ancient Chinese vampire Creed, although three were white and one was black. They were arranged like a barbershop quartet in the hallway, the two farthest away standing closer together in the center of the hall while the closer pair were fanned out against the walls.

Remo half expected them to burst into a mournful dirge of *Sweet Adeline*.

He stopped dead at the top landing. Behind him, the final staircase collapsed on the snarling berserker horde below.

Remo set Connie down behind him. She could see next to nothing through her fogged gas mask.

"What's happening?" Connie whispered. She squinted up the hallway and saw a few vague black shapes blocking their path.

"He is expecting you," said a girl in the second staggered row before them, who looked as if a single ray of sunlight would have turned her to a pile of ash even before her transformation.

She was pasty and plain, with rings in her cheeks, nose, and one eyebrow. There were no rings on her fingers, although Remo did note one index finger possessed the gleaming guillotine shape of a *gyonshi* fingernail.

"I'm glad he's waiting, because I'm in kind of a rush," Remo said to the girl, who seemed to be the leader of the pack in the hall.

"Oh, *you* will not see him," the girl said, with absolute assurance. "We will bring you to him after you are dead. We will help him prepare your body according to the elder ways, and then he will take your corpse to the Leader."

"Carry-on or checked baggage? Either way is going to be difficult with me dripping blood all over the plane."

"The Leader told him you were smug," the girl said.

"The Leader," Remo mocked. "Did you ever meet him? Because I have. *Twice*. And I punched his ticket both times."

"Yet he lives," the girl said.

She took a step forward. So, too, did the other three figures in black.

"You're not really one of them," Remo said. "To them you're nothing but a bunch of poseurs. I doubt they'll keep you around after I'm dead. Hypothetically, of course, since you'll be dead before me."

He was very nearly wrong.

The girl had been right. He'd been too smug. That the opinion of the Leader had been filtered back to him through the mouth of some pierced gender studies major would have been the worst insult for him to take to the grave had the attack succeeded.

At the last instant, he felt the pressure waves of something rushing in from behind.

"Remo!" Connie shouted.

The fog on her gas mask shield had suddenly grown darker. She realized that the rushing black fog was not within the mask, but outside it.

Remo wheeled and dropped to one side. A charging-bull cloud of black mist flew past him.

His vision was still out of whack. He had nearly seen the shape within the cloud. It had nearly formed the outline of a man. But it was a disintegrating man with no features. The ghost of a deadly silhouette. It had been easier back at the college with the kid in the admissions office who had only begun his transformation to mist. This fully formed fog was nearly impossible for his eyes to penetrate.

The cloud stopped and swirled, then charged again. The faces of the quartet of black-clad college students grew eager with the anticipation of death.

Remo still could not see the man in the mist. It was damn frustrating. His eyes could not be trusted, and so he did the only thing he could do. He squeezed them shut.

He heard the roar of triumph. His attacker assumed Remo was giving up, at last surrendering to his inevitable fate at the hands of a member of the ancient Creed.

When the invisible figure was nearly upon him, Remo snapped out with both hands. He felt the pressure waves before the slashing hand with its sharpened nail. He snatched the unseen wrist and with a squeeze he pulverized the bones to dust. The useless hand dangled limp on the end of the shattered wrist.

At the same time Remo reached into the cloud with his other hand and grabbed the spot where his senses told him a throat would be.

He did not doubt himself. He was Sinanju; one with the forces that guided the hum of the universe.

The throat was where his training told him it would be. It collapsed under pressure even more easily than had the hand. The body grew limp in his hand, and when Remo opened his eyes he found himself looking at the shocked face of Hop Yung.

The photo that Smith had shown him back at Folcroft was the most accurate I.D. image Remo had ever seen in his life. The Chinese exchange student had looked like a corpse in his picture. The same was true for the man at the center of the dying fog in the fifth-floor hallway of the Greenwich Village brownstone.

Remo heaved Hop Yung's corpse at the four shocked *gyonshi* who had been bait for the failed ambush. As the body fell amongst them, so too did Remo.

The four recovered quickly from their shock. They attempted to put up a fight. But they were mere vassals of a dissipated gutter evil versus the distillation of five thousand years of a tradition that celebrated the magnificence of human creation.

Remo made short work of the remaining four.

When he was finished, five black-clad bodies lay at his feet, including that of Hop Yung whose features were growing more distinct as the cloud that had enveloped him in life slowly dissipated in death.

A timid voice called shakily from the far end of the hall near the stairs.

"Are you okay, Remo?" Dr. Connie Pelisse asked.

"Just a sec," Remo answered.

There were only three apartments on the top floor, plus some storage space. Remo took a quick inventory of all the rooms.

Hop Yung's apartment was a mad scientist's paradise. There were tables filled with beakers, Bunsen burners, and objects more suited to Dr. Frankenstein's lab than a Greenwich Village apartment. Many large fish tanks were stacked along the walls, in which dead rats, cats, and dogs were suspended in some kind of gelatinous goo.

The *gyonshi* exchange student clearly possessed chemistry skills far beyond Remo's knowledge. Remo could identify none of the mechanical devices in the apartment, with the exception of a dozen miniature dorm refrigerators. He wasn't even one hundred percent certain he was right about those until he opened one up.

The fridge was full of glass vials.

Connie Pelisse and the rest of the CDC would have a field day with whatever Hop Yung had been up to in here. One thing Remo was certain about: there were no more of the ancient Creed lurking in the shadows.

Remo headed back out into the hall.

Connie had felt her way as far as Hop Yung's door. She jumped when Remo stepped silently out in front of her. Through the fog on the shield of her gas mask, she thought she recognized a shape that she hoped was Remo.

"Coast is clear," Remo said. "Although the old vampire bastard still has some new tricks up his sleeve. They're like a beehive. The Leader is the queen bee, and the ones I've dealt with before were always worker bees. This new type downstairs is like the worker bees' lunatic meth head cousins."

He could still hear snarling coming from every floor below. He had recovered considerably since the previous day, but it had still been touch and go for a little while.

"So it's over?" Connie asked.

"This part is," Remo announced. "The worst is yet to come."

He'd located the fire escape against the back of the building in his search of the various apartments and storage rooms.

The feral growling from the lost souls Hop Yung had contaminated continued to echo up the stairwell. The exchange student's infected neighbors were apparently single-minded in their determination to follow Remo up the collapsed stairs, despite the fact that the stairs were no longer there.

Remo took Connie gently by the hand and led her away from the stairwell, down the hall to the rear of the building.

CHAPTER 26

THE MASTER OF SINANJU sat cross-legged on the carpet of his suite in the hotel St. Regis Beijing.

He had been locked up in his suite for nearly a full day, refusing everything offered by his Chinese government hosts save a single meal from room service.

He had barely touched the food. The plate with his cold rice and fish was sitting in the next room on the edge of the unused bed.

Chiun had also issued that which he considered a minor request, less important than even a mouthful of food. He had asked that the floor be emptied of all other guests, suggesting that their stomping, bathing, and rutting would disturb his slumber.

The accommodating Chinese general who had been assigned to see to the Master of Sinanju's every wish had readily agreed, as Chiun had given the soldier the impression that Chiun would throw the general off the balcony if he did not comply.

All the other rooms were empty. Chiun was alone, but for a young private who was left outside the suite just in case the Master required anything more during his stay.

The hotel supplied paper and pens to guests. Chiun had brought a pad from the desk and tore all the papers out of it, arranging them around him on the floor. The living room carpet of the suite looked like autumn in the paper supply store.

He would have preferred quill and parchment. The crude

implements of the modern age lacked permanence, like everything else in the world these days. But he had left America in haste, and the materials that he normally used to record the histories of Sinanju for posterity were packed away in a steamer trunk back at the condominium in Connecticut he shared with Remo.

It was for Remo that he had taken an ugly ballpoint pen in hand.

It was possible that Chiun would fail in his mission to stop the Leader. If so, Remo would wish to seek vengeance.

Remo was a good boy, which was why he would go after those who murdered his adopted father. But the continuation of the line of Masters of Sinanju was more important than any one Master. Should Chiun meet an untimely end at the hands of the *gyonshi* in the Forest of the Dead, he could not allow Remo's hotheadedness to risk the end of five thousand years of tradition.

Chiun made a few bold strokes on the sheet of paper before him. He held it up and examined what he had written.

He frowned at two of his own words.

Remo might not react positively to them, even though they were spoken with the utmost affection.

Chiun put the paper back down between his knees and crossed out the words "idiot" and "stupid."

The text lost some of its oomph, but at least Remo wouldn't stop reading and throw it in the trash. As good a boy as he was, he could also be overly sensitive.

Chiun resumed writing. His bald head bobbed over the hotel stationary, and the wisps of hair at his ears and chin floated with the gentle disturbance of the air.

So engrossed in his work was he that he appeared not to notice the sound of the man being brutally murdered in the hallway just outside his door.

Two vampire men pinned the soldier's arms behind his back while their leader drew his razor-sharp *gyonshi* fingernail across the young Chinese army private's throat.

The soldier who had been stationed outside the door of the

Master of Sinanju's hotel suite attempted to struggle. He tried to yell. The hand clamped over his mouth prevented sound from escaping from between his lips. Blood from his severed carotids sprayed the wall across the hall, decorating the wallpaper with splashes of crimson.

The fight drained abruptly from the soldier. His eyes fluttered shut and he slumped, dead. The men who had held him during his murder laid him out quietly on the floor. They removed a key card from his pocket.

A nod was exchanged amongst the trio of cult members. As if a switch had been flipped, black mist began to swirl up around them, concealing them from prying eyes.

Before they had vanished completely, a hand from out one cloud slipped the key card in the door. The door opened silently into the room.

The *gyonshi* mist formed a single impenetrable cloud as it slowly seeped into the room of the Master of Sinanju, silent as death.

CHAPTER 27

GENERAL YAO YILIN BEGAN HIS DAY as he had ended the previous one: worrying about the Master of Sinanju.

As if the Chinese People's Army general did not already have enough to worry about with containing the viral outbreak of unknown origin in Manchuria, that original crisis had now expanded to include babysitting the Korean assassin.

Yilin still did not know what interest the Master of Sinanju had in the village where the outbreak had originated. He was no longer certain that it had anything to do with the two previously missing American women who had been found dead there.

General Yilin was pondering what new problems this day would deliver him as he rode the elevator from the lobby of the hotel St. Regis Beijing to the floor that the elderly Korean had forced the general to clear of other guests the previous day.

Yilin was alerted to yet another crisis the instant the elevator doors pinged open.

A body lay on the floor, surrounded by congealed blood. General Yilin had left one soldier to report on the Master of Sinanju's activities were he to leave the hotel.

Two People's soldiers had accompanied Yilin up in the lift. With a nod, he ordered the men to draw their sidearms and advance up the hall.

The old Korean's hotel room door was ajar.

Yilin feared the scene he would find inside. The reputation of the white American Master of Sinanju was known among certain circles. Some who had encountered him had found him more terrifying than the old Master.

Yilin feared the hell that the young Master of Sinanju would unleash on any he deemed responsible for the death of his aged teacher.

The two soldiers crept up the hall. General Yilin trailed them.

They tiptoed past the body and very carefully nudged the hotel room door open.

A mummified corpse sat in the middle of the carpet, a stack of papers before it.

The old master did not appear to breathe. He did not move.

General Yilin held his breath.

At last, the wisps of hair on the aged head shuddered. A face like wrinkled parchment turned in the direction of the men at the door.

"It is about time room service arrived," the Master of Sinanju complained. "Someone made a mess in the bathroom."

General Yilin heaved a sigh of relief and ordered his men to have the body in the hallway removed. The two soldiers hustled from the suite.

The bathroom door was closed, but the glass wall it shared with the bedroom made the entire small room visible even with the door shut. General Yilin saw three bodies in the room. It appeared as if an attempt had been made to flush one of them down the toilet. His head was down the commode and water had spilled around the floor. There was a toilet plunger sticking to the back of his head like a misplaced unicorn horn. The other two dead men were a jumble of arms and legs dumped in the bathtub.

Unbeknownst to General Yilin, Chiun had spotted the man whose head was currently soiling the toilet lurking in the hangar near where he'd deplaned at Beijing Capital International Airport. The Leader had anticipated the arrival of the Master of Sinanju and had sent more of his minions to waylay the Creed's oldest enemy, likely with the hope of further weakening the Master of Sinanju.

The trial ahead of him was difficult enough on its own, Chiun had not wanted to deal with more of these creatures attacking from behind while en route to Manchuria. And so he had been forced to wait until his pursuers made their move.

But the delay did give the Master of Sinanju time to take care of some important business.

Chiun rose from the floor of the living room like a puff of steam.

"I assume you are a bellman, given that foolish uniform you are strutting around in," the Master of Sinanju said. "I have a very important task for you."

He held aloft a sealed envelope.

"This is to be delivered to my son in one week's time," Chiun said gravely. "I am entrusting you with this great task. I will be leaving for Manchuria as soon as arrangements are made, but do not use that as an excuse to goldbrick. Woe be unto you if you fail in this task."

He handed the envelope to General Yilin.

"Also, charge your tip to the room," the Master of Sinanju added. "The thieves who run this miserable nation can afford it. Come, bellman!"

In a swirl of kimono hems, the old Korean swept from the hotel room. Clutching the letter in his hand, General Yao Yilin hustled after the old man out into the hall.

CHAPTER 28

THE LEADER STROLLED PAST THE ROCK-HEWN ALTAR in the belly of the Temple of the Dead. His sightless eyes could not take in the awesome spectacle of the room, yet he walked the rock floor with the confident memory of a long-ago youth.

The building was cold. No fires were permitted within its great stone walls. Only at the end of times would a final, cleansing fire be permitted to burn.

His ancestors had designed the temple to symbolize human sacrifice, which was sacrosanct to the ancient Creed.

The open main hall represented the hollow chest cavity of the victim. At one point all the rock surfaces were dyed red, but the color of blood had faded over time. Curving stone benches were arranged in two rows, symbolizing the ribcage.

The stone altar was positioned where the human heart would go.

Many sacrifices had taken place in that room, abandoned now for centuries.

His people were dead. It had taken strength beyond his own death for him to return to the land of his ancestors, only to find nearly none left alive.

He had learned that it had been twenty years since a child had been born to the sect. The last child of the old line, Hop Yung, had left the Forest of the Dead to pursue an education. In *America*, of all places. Twice the land of the Leader's disgrace.

But young Hop Yung had proven to be an unexpected boon. The child was fanatically devoted to the old ways, and had been delighted to learn that the Leader had returned. The Leader, who had left the forest city decades before Hop Yung was even born, and at his return had been raised to mythical stature in the eyes of Hop Yung.

The boy had been more than happy to deploy his knowledge and cunning in America in service to the Leader.

The ancient master of the Temple of the Dead only wished that he was in communication with the boy. He had been aware of the new telephone devices that could be carried on one's person when he had inhabited the body of the American woman. It was technology with which he would need to familiarize himself in this new world if he was going to become master of it. And rule it he would, from the Throne of Skulls.

The Leader had a younger body now, although that seemed not to be working out quite as he expected it would. The eyes of the shell in which he walked had been lost to him immediately. His new hair soon began to come out in clumps. At the same time his new teeth dropped out one by one. The body of the young man he had inhabited had decided to conform to the memory of that which the Leader had been. So be it. Thanks to the ancient secrets of the Creed he lived again, which soon would be more than could be said about his great enemies.

The last report from Hop Yung had the white Master of Sinanju poisoned. The old Master had been forced to carry his limp body from the university. The Leader took particular delight in knowing that the arrogant cur was most likely dead by now.

The old Master of Sinanju would be despairing at either the illness or the loss of his pupil. Before he could process the emotion of so personal an attack the Leader had arranged for a second assault, this one in Sinanju itself.

Ancient enemies had always stayed away from that filthy Korean village of worthless fisherman. The wrath of the Master of Sinanju was too great to risk venturing into the place of his birth. The mystique surrounding the discipline of the Masters of Sinanju was sufficient to keep terrified foes from setting foot there.

The Leader had broken a thousand-year tradition when he sent his minions to that little village on the West Korean Bay.

A thrust into the heart of the Master of Sinanju.

First the loss of his adopted son. Then an incursion into his village, followed by the death of one of the people he had sworn to protect.

The Master of Sinanju was old. The Leader knew better than most how fragile were the hearts of men, for he had held many human hearts in his hand in his long life. The strain of it all would weaken his adversary. He might already be dead, for the Leader had dispatched yet more agents to waylay him when he reached Beijing. If the Master of Sinanju survived that attack as well, when he at last came to the Forest of the Dead he would be a shattered man. He might even beg the Leader to end his torment.

The Leader had no doubt that the old one would come, assuming he even survived each step of the trial. The infection of the village of Guizhou was the final piece of the puzzle. It was a sign that the ancient vampire sect was moving out of the forest and back into the world. A previous Sinanju Master had restricted the *gyonshi* to the boundaries of the Forest of the Dead. Even in his despair, the current Master of Sinanju could not ignore this final offense.

As he stood before the altar that he was unable to see, the Leader heard the sound of footsteps running up the distant steps and into the great hall.

The Leader turned just as the breathless man stopped behind him.

"The Master of Sinanju has entered the forest," the herald said.

The Leader nodded calm acceptance of that which he had predicted.

"He is alone," the Leader said.

It was not spoken as a question. When his minion gave confirmation, the Leader offered the man a toothless smile.

"See to it that our guest is given the greeting he deserves," the Leader said.

When the man turned to go, the Leader stopped him.

"Hold!"

The man was standing before him. The Leader slowly circled his acolyte. He could hear the man's heart pumping. His mind's eyes sketched an outline of the entire body simply from the smell of the blood coursing through every artery and vein.

The Leader's hand suddenly flashed out, pinching a spot near where the man's neck met his shoulder. His hand snapped back.

The Leader held out for inspection a mosquito that had been interrupted mid-feast.

"Now go," the old man in the young man's body commanded.

He heard the beating heart hurry away more than he did the man's footsteps.

The Leader brought the buzzing mosquito up to his lips and licked the drop of blood that hung from six needlelike stylets that jutted from the insect's mouth.

After, he crushed the insect between his thumb and forefinger, smiling with the confident knowledge that the mosquito would not be the only nuisance bug whose life would this day be snuffed out in the Forest of the Dead.

CHAPTER 29

REMO WATCHED THE PAVED RUNWAYS and terminal buildings of Beijing Capital International Airport rush up to meet the belly of his borrowed Gulfstream III.

He had to hand it to Smith.

The CURE director could not involve the U.S. military on this leg of Remo's journey as he had for the Master of Sinanju's emergency trip East. The risk to security if Remo arrived in China's capital in an American warplane was unacceptable.

Thanks to the viral outbreak in Manchuria, however, which was just beginning to leak out into the news, medical experts from around the world were starting to fly in to China. The astronomically expensive jet Smith had wrangled belonged to the World Health Organization, since fretting over malaria in Ethiopia or dengue fever in the Philippines was best accomplished at 40,000 feet with a gym, sauna, private dining room, big-screen screening room, and fully stocked bar close at hand.

It helped the ruse that Dr. Connie Pelisse was a card-carrying WHO member, although she told him that she had never flown to hot zones in such luxury. There was no champagne and caviar in the back of the decrepit twin-props she'd flown in.

Remo had tried to ditch the virologist back in the U.S. but she was adamant in her commitment to go wherever Remo's blood went, no matter the personal risk.

"I hope this is safe," Connie asked as the jet screamed onto the ground and began decelerating down the runway.

She was sitting next to Remo and looking out the window as the scenery flew by.

"Of course it's not safe," Remo replied. "If you wanted safe you could have stayed in New York."

"I was safe with you there," she said. "Let's hope your luck holds out."

She took his hand in hers and gave a squeeze to go along with her confident nod and smile.

Remo liked the feel of her hand in his. He squeezed back.

"It's not luck, sweetheart," he said. "It's unplanned strategizing."

Several luxury WHO planes had landed around the same time, and all had been instructed to taxi to the same location. Passengers were told to remain in their aircraft and await release from captivity by Chinese officials. The wait, they were informed, could be many hours.

Remo didn't have time to wait. He popped the door, hopped down the stairs and flagged down the first uniform he saw.

The Chinese officer was angry at first at the break in protocol. The soldiers accompanying him quickly leveled rifles at Remo as he approached.

"Everybody who wants a rifle barrel jammed up his ass, keep pointing one at me," Remo said.

General Yao Yilin grew furious at the young white man's words, until the American uttered the ultimate get-out-of-jail-free card.

"Sinanju."

It was not possible. It simply could not be. Not two times in as many days.

"Weapons down! Weapons down!" General Yilin commanded.

The soldiers instantly did as they were ordered.

"Smart move, skycap," Remo said, unknowingly repeating the insult delivered by the Master of Sinanju twenty-four hours before. "The fact that you already know about us means I don't have to start harvesting ears until somebody listens. Where is —"

Before Remo could get out the question, General Yilin blurted out, "Manchuria. He left not an hour ago."

"An hour?" Remo said. "He got here yesterday."

"The Master of Sinanju had...*business* to take care of in Beijing. I can arrange to have you sent to his current location."

Remo was still absorbing this latest information. He'd thought he was a full day behind Chiun, but he had only missed him by an hour. There was still time. The elderly Korean would not have to leap into the lion's den alone.

General Yilin jumped when the young Master of Sinanju — a man some said was even more dangerous than the old one — grabbed him by the wrists.

Remo inspected the soldier's fingernails. They were normal. He returned the general's hands to him.

"You're coming along. It helps to have someone aboard the team who can get the army not to shoot at me. It especially helps anybody who would otherwise have tried to shoot at me, because they get to keep breathing."

"Remo?" a voice called from behind him.

Connie Pelisse had apparently gotten nervous that Remo's plasma might forget about her. The CDC doctor had climbed down from their Gulfstream and was cautiously crossing the tarmac, her nylon bag in hand.

The young soldiers accompanying General Yilin immediately snapped their rifles at Connie, who promptly raised her hands high above her head. The move caused her breasts to tumble out from the confines of her white parka. She smiled nervously.

"Oh, yeah," Remo said to General Yilin. "I brought a date."

CHAPTER 30

CHIUN PADDED ACROSS THE DEAD ZONE adjacent to the ruined village of Guizhou and entered the Forest of the Dead.

The trees grew high and closed in thick around him. The sky quickly became a memory. All sound of the outside world soon faded as he walked farther back into the ancient mists that existed even before the first Master of Sinanju.

He passed several Chinese military vehicles caught up on rocks or stuck between trees. Trucks and jeeps were anachronisms thrown back in time to the ancient forest. Chiun saw none of the soldiers to whom the vehicles belonged, nor did he expect to.

He was certain that the enemy would not wait to come to him, and his instinct was almost immediately rewarded by a rush of cold, putrid air.

Up ahead, four distinct clouds flitted amongst the trees. One moment they were there, the next they were gone. But always they moved closer.

When he rounded a bend in the nearly invisible path he suddenly found his way blocked by a quartet of figures, all dressed in the black robes of the vampire cult.

"Begone, wretches," Chiun said. "Woe be to he who would interrupt the passage of the Master of Sinanju."

One of the men smiled. His face was bony and pale.

"There is no passage for you, ancient one. You have come to the place of the ages, where in days long past uncounted numbers of travelers met their doom. You are the latest, not the last. The Leader has foreseen it."

The one man remained on the path, while the others glided off in both directions, slowly circling Chiun, methodically hemming him in.

"Your Leader has cheated death," Chiun said to the one ahead, ignoring the other three. "I am here to remind him of its sting."

"It is you who will not live to see this day end," the vampire said. "We will crack your bones and feast on your marrow."

"You dare, unholy offspring of a wicked Creed?" Chiun demanded. "I am the Master of Sinanju, not some ignorant traveler to be waylaid by *gyonshi* vermin."

"The Masters of Sinanju are no more," the man said. The broad smile that cracked his face lacked mirth. "This day sees the end of your line, old one."

The words were no sooner delivered than the man lashed out.

Chiun was surprised by the swiftness of the attack. The first man's finger darted forward in a flash, the sharp nail stabbing at Chiun's belly like the tip of a spear.

It was a flawless move that would have scored a killing laceration in the stomach of a lesser man. But the Master of Sinanju was no lesser man.

Before the vampire's blow could register he was shocked to find his target abruptly vanish into a nothingness more complete than the mere trick of *gyonshi* mist. It was as if the old man had been vaporized where he stood, only to reappear two feet to the left, the swirling hem of his kimono settling around his ankles the only proof of movement.

The vampire felt a sudden thud against his wrist, followed by a horrid tearing sensation. It happened faster than an eye could blink.

The Master of Sinanju's own deadly fingernails — hardened by diet and honed sharper than any knife blade — sliced straight through the man's wrist.

The vampire looked down at the bleeding stump at the end of his arm. On the frozen earth at his feet twitched his detached hand with his own once-deadly nail still extended, now nothing more than an impotent digit on a dead appendage.

He tried to scream, but before he had even opened his mouth the nail of Chiun's index finger pierced his forehead, burying deep in brain.

In, snap, out. Chiun's hand was back at his side.

The aborted shriek in the man's throat became a gurgle, and the collapsing vampire joined his severed hand on the ground.

Even as the first body was falling the remaining three attacked.

Another *gyonshi* fingernail attempted the move that had failed for the first man. Chiun grabbed his arm and directed the lunging man's hand forward. The fingernail tore into a belly that was not Chiun's. Organs, blood and viscera spilled onto the ground.

With a twirling kick Chiun finished the man with the steaming belly wound. The *gyonshi*'s head twisted one hundred and eighty degrees on his cracking spine and he joined the first in death on the forest floor.

The Master of Sinanju continued the pivot, and his flying heel came to rest in the temple of the man whose hand he had redirected.

And now a third had joined the others in mortal slumber.

The last was a woman who attempted to cloud herself in mesmerizing mist. The cloud seeped up from out of her pores and quickly concealed her.

Thinking she was hidden, she took a step to the right.

The Master of Sinanju was suddenly standing before her.

She held her breath and turned for the left.

Again the old Korean somehow blocked her path.

She realized just before her end that the Leader might have been wrong about the weakened state the Master of Sinanju would be in when finally he reached the Forest of the Dead. This was a man in full control of his powers, whose keen vision was somehow able to pierce the cloud into which no other mortal man could see.

Chiun's hazel eyes locked on hers. A hint of lethal mirth danced in their depths.

And then the thin black of the mist that surrounded her turned the color of weeping blood, and the Forest of the Dead where she had lived her entire life became the forest of her own unexpected demise.

Chiun let the limp body of the woman fall from his hand.

These four had been but vassals. The wellspring of this wickedness still waited in the heart of the forest.

Chiun continued along the narrow path, leaving the forest to reclaim the rotting carcasses he had discarded in his wake.

The helicopter carrying Remo, Connie, and General Yao Yilin landed on the widest levee in the network of rice paddies adjacent to the village of Guizhou.

The autumn rice had recently been harvested. Brackish water formed puddles in the upper terraces. Here and there a few malformed stalks jutted from the water.

Remo had seen as the helicopter swooped over the village that this year's rice crop would be the last for the people of Guizhou.

The Chinese government had set up a makeshift encampment of tents and vehicles surrounding Guizhou. It resembled the one with which the U.S. government had contained the outbreak at Columbus University. But for the bodies.

The village was a graveyard.

The dead lay in the open in the narrow lanes between huts. More were sprawled in the open areas outside the village, shot while trying to flee. Not a single soul was left alive in the village that neighbored the Forest of the Dead.

"My God, what have you done?" Connie Pelisse said to General Yilin upon viewing the atrocity, and only once she was finally able to find her voice.

"Only that which was necessary," Yilin stiffly replied.

"They weren't *all* beyond hope," Connie snapped, the blood rising in her cheeks. "Some of them might have been saved."

Remo did not tell her that she did not know that. He didn't let her know that she did not know exactly what strain of virus had afflicted the citizens of Guizhou. Nor did he remind her of the people he had killed in self-defense in the past day; people who might have differed from those of Guizhou only in the severity of their cases.

Connie was an intelligent woman. She'd figure it out on her own. For now he let her anger rise, then crash. Connie withdrew, weeping a few quiet tears for all the innocents she had been unable to save.

They hurried down the path from the rice paddies to the encampment outside the village. A wide strip of dead weeds bordered the primeval forest that loomed beyond.

General Yilin located the colonel who was in command.

"The old man," Yilin barked at his subordinate. "The Korean. How long ago did he pass into the forest?"

"Ten minutes," the colonel said.

He would have pointed with his right hand, but that arm had been recently broken and was in a makeshift sling. The colonel's face had soured at the mention of the elderly foreigner to whom he had been ordered to extend every courtesy, but to which command he had clearly not strictly adhered.

"Where's that doohickey?" Remo demanded of Yilin.

The general hurried over to an area directly beside the collection of tents and scientists to the platoon of soldiers that awaited orders among many idle People's Army tanks, jeeps, and trucks. He returned from the military camp with a small silver device that resembled a fat, squat pen. There was a red button on one end locked in place with a silver pin. Yilin handed the device to Remo.

"Pull the pin and press the button," the general said.

Remo nodded and stuck the object in his chinos pocket.

"I'm off," he announced. "Stay here," he told Connie.

The CDC virologist was still wiping her eyes.

"What do you mean?" she said. "I'm coming with you."

"Not this time," Remo said. He put an index finger an inch from General Yilin's nose. "Keep her safe, or else. And remember what we discussed in the helicopter. Don't screw up or you'll have more to worry about than a busted wing like your pal here."

The colonel with his arm in a sling had been observing the scene with quiet disdain, and bridled at Remo's words. General Yilin nodded.

The general held Connie's arms to prevent her from running

with Remo into the cordoned hot zone beyond the Chinese military and government encampment.

Remo flew through the very edge of Guizhou where there were fewer bullet-riddled bodies littering the landscape. He noted a woman and two children lying face-up near what looked to be the site of some kind of flea market. The eyes of the dead victims had burst. Sockets smeared with blood stared at the vast abyss.

In past encounters, the Leader had mostly wanted to rack up a body count to feed his bloodthirsty ancestors in the afterlife. Revenge had been a secondary motive. This time was different. All of this carnage was because of one man's twisted plot of revenge.

Remo ran on, charting a direct course for his ultimate destination.

The village inside the government cordon had been declared the epicenter of the outbreak. Remo knew the true source. He flew out of the village outskirts, across the gulf of dead weeds where nothing seemed to live, and into the dense forest.

The sounds from the Chinese camp, as well as the hum of all human life from the outside world slipped away behind him until the only noises that could be detected even by his Sinanju-trained ears were those that originated within the Forest of the Dead.

He was a gazelle, leaping over rocks and fallen limbs. His speed did not diminish as he sprinted deeper into the woods. Trees flew by at lightning speed, as well as a handful of Chinese Army vehicles that had foolishly ventured into the cursed woods.

His senses were tuned to their utmost, and so he was aware of the two figures loitering amongst the trees even before they were alerted to his presence.

The figures in black were slipping like ghosts through a graveyard. Their cadaverous faces registered shock when Remo suddenly leaped out before them.

"You are he!" one of the men gasped. "But you are dead. So the Leader has prophesied."

"Looks like Old Cataract Eyes' tea leaves are on the fritz," Remo said.

The men rapidly pulled themselves together. They slashed at

Remo's throat and chest with their guillotine fingernails, like crazed gang members in a PCP stiletto fight.

Remo dodged, spun, and somehow sprouted up directly between the two men.

"See," Remo said. "That's the problem with you guys."

He clamped onto their wrists and yanked his arms crisscross. The spear tip of each man's fingernail impaled the Adam's apple of the other.

Their bloodshot eyes sprang wide and their mouths popped open, spraying the landscape with blood.

Remo had already jumped from between them. He was safely out of range as the two men dropped to the ground.

"You've only got one move," Remo informed them. "Probably works for the tourists, but I've seen your hackneyed show one time too many."

He spun from the corpses and took off through the forest.

Remo had avoided a rudimentary path he'd seen at the edge of the trees and trusted the compass in his nose to lead him directly to the heart of the forest. His direct route as well as the winding path to the east both intersected at a clearing.

He sensed the wide opening in the woods up ahead even before he ran into it. So too did he detect the sounds of a battle taking place.

Remo emerged from the thicket at a full sprint.

The wide clearing looked as if it had been home to many people for many years. The tumbledown huts and open-air fire pits had been recently abandoned.

The small village that was the place the ancient vampire Creed had called home for the past hundred years was currently the site of a conflict which would by hour's end determine the ultimate fate of the Chinese blood drinkers.

Clouds of black *gyonshi* smoke swirled around shacks. Still more amorphous mist billowed into the glade from the surrounding forest.

The Chinese vampires were converging on a single source.

Remo spotted the wizened figure in the center of the maelstrom the instant he emerged from the forest.

The Master of Sinanju was tearing through the *gyonshi* lines as fast as the men and women could attack. Many already lay dead amongst the ruined village.

A sunken-eyed man had given up on his sharpened fingernail. He was charging the Master of Sinanju with a long knife he'd grabbed from a nearby communal fire pit.

"Aiiiiieee!" Chiun cried.

The old Korean plucked the knife from the man's hand and swirled from his path. The instant the man charged past, Chiun let the knife fly from the tips of his long fingers. The blade soared straight through the back of the man's head and emerged from between his eyes. Not content to kill one bird with a single stone, the knife continued into the heart of a *gyonshi* shadow and buried itself into the heart of the man hidden at its center.

Two figures emerged from two more clouds of mist and raced around the pair of falling bodies. They were met not by the Master of Sinanju who they'd been attacking, but by a new figure that sprang up between them and the old Korean.

"Is this a private party, or is anybody invited?" Remo asked Chiun.

As he spoke, he grabbed the two startled men by the necks and yanked, tearing out the throats of both attackers. The men fell, and Remo flung onto their backs their own bloody throats, trailing dripping gore.

"It is about time you showed up," the Master of Sinanju sniffed.

He became a feral cat, hands moving in a blur impossible to follow, long fingernails becoming violent dealers of death. A shredded chest erupted in yawning chasms of blood. Another enemy dropped in his tracks.

"You seem to be doing okay," Remo commented. "It looks like you're reenacting the Battle of Hastings with dust devils."

Swirls of black were all around them, closing in through the field already drenched with the blood of many fallen comrades.

"You see them?" Chiun demanded sharply.

Remo knew what the old man meant. The Master of Sinanju referred not to the shadows, which the eyes of ordinary men could perceive, but of the ghoulish figures that dwelt within them. The dwindling numbers of Chinese blood drinkers were as apparent to Remo within their camouflage as if they were clad in neon.

"Clear as a bell, Little Father," Remo replied.

The two Masters of Sinanju were back-to-back. Mirrored image thrusts from both men collapsed to jelly the foreheads of the nearest *gyonshi*.

"You have purged then your system of the poison?" Chiun asked.

"A hundred percent," Remo said. "I look good, I feel good. How's the monster mash been going for you?"

"Bah! These things are like weeds," Chiun said, irritated. "I no sooner pluck one up when another one springs up in its place."

A swirling black mist resolved into a demented human shape directly in the Master of Sinanju's path. Chiun sent his heel against the man's chest and the *gyonshi* flew back as if he were jet-propelled against the trunk of an ancient tree. Bones and tree splintered into a thousand pulpy fragments.

"You see? You see?" the Master of Sinanju complained. "I'm glad you finally elected to get out of bed. I thought I would be stuck pulling up weeds all day."

"Hey, give me a break," Remo said. "I could have died."

"Nonsense. You would never humiliate me so grievously. Behind you."

Remo did a little spin that turned into a buzz saw blade. The *gyonshi* woman who had been charging him from the rear continued racing forward, despite the fact that her head remained where the side of Remo's flashing hand had sliced through her neck.

The pores of both Masters of Sinanju were locked tight, and neither allowed a single breath to enter their lungs. The precautions proved unnecessary. It seemed the Leader and his minion in New York had infected nearly exclusively non-cult members with the newer *gyonshi* virus. For the men and women in the Forest of the Dead there were no seizures after death, no exploding eyeballs, no clouds of poison slipping from mouths and noses. When mortality claimed the true descendants of the ancient vampire cult, they slipped quietly into the void as did all other men.

It seemed to Remo as the diminishing waves of assailants rolled in that the battle in the clearing of the Forest of the Dead was a modern Battle of Little Bighorn, with the Chinese vampires cast in the roles of Colonel George Armstrong Custer's men.

The inhabitants of the forest fought to the last, a fight as much against the eons that had ravaged their once powerful cult as it was against the two Masters of Sinanju who had become the focus of centuries of impotent rage.

When it was over only two men stood at the center of the carnage.

The last body slipped from Chiun's hand to join the rest of their bloody comrades in eternal slumber.

The old Korean clicked his tongue.

"There is no punishment sufficient for he who unleashed this evil on the world," the Master of Sinanju intoned.

"It could be worse," Remo observed. "At least we're out in the sunshine."

He found that he was speaking only to the dead.

The Master of Sinanju had already bounded from the clearing and was heading for the distant path that led to the City of the Dead.

Remo looked around at the dozens of bodies clad in black. He quietly agreed with the old Korean's grim assessment. Death might be too good for the architect of this scheme, but it was nonetheless the punishment he would receive.

Remo sprang over the nearest cluster of corpses and raced after the resolute form of the Master of Sinanju.

CHAPTER 31

THE LEADER STOOD ON TIPTOE on the hidden stone balcony in the great Temple of the Dead. He held his nose to the air.

The elders of the ancient Creed were like sharks that could detect a drop of blood in an ocean of water. Those who fully embraced the tenets of the cult of death had for untold years possessed the ability to smell the sweet aroma on the wind.

The scent of death had always been fragrant to the Leader. Today it carried with it the foul stench of defeat.

The last of his kind had encountered the hated Masters of Sinanju on a field of blood, and the Creed had surrendered its last drop to the enemy.

Nearly the last. The Leader lived, as did the ashen figure in black who stood in the stone door at his back and watched the head of his dark sect sniff the wind.

"They have failed me," the Leader intoned.

In the doorway, the ancient soul's much younger acolyte frowned.

There was no "me" in the Creed. There was only the Creed, only the sacrifice, only death. The goal of the last of their line should have been to feed all who had gone before them in the afterlife. The final great blood feast. The Final Death.

The Leader turned his head slightly to one side, sipping chill air in through his right nostril. He tasted the breeze on his tongue, like a connoisseur of fine wine.

"Hop Yung in America has failed me, as well," the Leader announced. "The young one lives. He is here."

The fine particles in the air told him that it was not only the elderly Master of Sinanju who was dealing death in the squalid village in the forest clearing. There were two. Both Masters, at the height of their abilities.

This new body the Leader inhabited had returned to him some of the senses of his long-ago youth, but the gift was bittersweet. At this moment ignorance would be preferable to knowing that which was en route to the ancient city.

The Leader turned his nose from the forest. He directed his milky white eyes at the man waiting in the stone archway.

"All is not yet lost," the Leader said. "Today I may surrender the final breath in this wretched body, but I will drag my hated enemy to the grave with me. Go! It is time to draw the Last Shroud over the place of the ancients."

The sickly figure in black nodded, though the blind man could not see the gesture, and ran into the temple.

The Leader turned his face back to the wind.

"The curtain draws at last on our ancient Creed," he said. "But so too will the shroud close up and suffocate the last Masters of Sinanju."

He flashed a wicked, toothless grin before turning from the forest and shuffling with quiet confidence into the Temple of the Dead.

Remo spotted the curl of smoke rising above the trees even before he and Chiun burst through the forest's edge into the ancient city.

The place was a marvel from a bygone age. Great stone shapes slouched off into the surrounding forest. Most of the buildings had surrendered to the march of time, collapsing into piles of rubble, but a surprising number of them still stood, including the large stone temple that rose up like a squat Egyptian pyramid amongst the encroaching trees in the center of the dead city.

The smoke he had glimpsed from the forest was coming from the temple. Huge billowing clouds were emanating from a dozen vents built into the rock sides.

"What fresh hell is this?" Remo said as they ran through the outskirts of the old city toward the central temple.

The smoke was not like that which was produced by ordinary fire. Something mixed in it was preventing it from rising into the air and dissipating on the breeze. This was a smoke too dense for the eye to penetrate, and also far heavier. It slipped from the cracks in the temple and down the sides, spreading out across the ruined city.

"Another of the vile fiend's tricks," Chiun snapped over his shoulder.

The smoke crept down the stairs like a lava flow. The Master of Sinanju was in the lead, running straight into the breach.

"Hold on!" Remo yelled, grabbing the old man by the arm.

"What now?" Chiun impatiently demanded.

"I'm calling in the Chinese cavalry."

Remo pulled from his pocket the silver device given him by General Yilin.

It was a homing signal. He needed only to pull the silver pin and press the red button and the general would be alerted and come running. Remo had warned Yilin that if he failed to come with his troops when Remo signaled there was no place on earth where he could run to avoid Remo's wrath.

Remo pulled the silver pin and pressed the red button. The little light that was supposed to go on under the button failed to come on. Remo was lousy with gadgets, but this was different. This was only a single button. This had to be the fault of the device.

Remo pressed again, very carefully increasing pressure. The light blinked red for an instant before the pressure he was exerting crushed the plastic cap, extinguished the tiny bulb inside, and shattered the squat silver tube. He was left with a palmful of plastic.

"Are you quite finished?" Chiun asked.

"Made in goddamn China," Remo groused.

He flung away the shards of the worthless homing device and the two men ran across the last open space that separated them from the temple steps.

They flew up the stairs side-by-side.

Remo could feel the cloying brush of the smoke against his skin. It deposited droplets which he was certain would have been lethal had he allowed them to be absorbed into his system. Instead, as he ran he shuddered his skin. Like a dog shedding water the drops flew off in every direction.

A distant sound seemed to brush the very edges of his hearing. It was a feeling of sound more than it was actual sound. It was almost as if all the victims of the vampire cult throughout all the many centuries were crying out for vengeance.

Remo and Chiun reached the top of the stairs and flew past the stone throne whose occupants in ages past had sat in judgment over all below.

The interior of the temple was largely free of the thick smoke that now flooded the city behind them. They ran through vine-choked corridors made damp from weeping water and into the heart of the ancient stone edifice.

They found their quarry seated calmly on a rock bench behind a granite altar.

This was not the Leader they had encountered twice before.

The man before them was younger than the ancient figure they knew, although the body appeared to be in the midst of some kind of metamorphosis. Only a few strands of black hair clung to a scalp that had recently gone drastically bald. As he ran the tip of his tongue across his bare gums Remo could see the sockets only recently occupied by teeth. He was attempting to sit upright, but was hampered by an uncooperative spine that seemed intent to bend him into a shoehorn-shape.

It was the eyes that convinced Remo. There was an ancient malevolence that emanated from the depths of his milky white orbs that proved beyond all doubt that, no matter his current form, Remo was looking into the eyes of his old enemy.

"Prepare, evil one," Chiun announced, "for your long life of wicked deeds has at last come to an end."

"I might end today, but Sinanju will die with me," the Leader announced with a confident smile. "The cloud that consumes this city will make it uninhabitable for a thousand years. Even now the poison that you traveled through to get to me is flooding through you both. It will soon liquefy your organs. They will bleed through your skin. And I, the last Leader of my ancient Creed, will stand over your oozing bodies and hear you gasp your final breath."

The look of triumph on his face changed to one of disbelief when Remo marched up to the altar and dropped his fist in its dead center.

The great granite slab split into two massive halves, which thundered in either direction to the temple floor.

"Your tricks only work if we let them in, Bela Lugosi," Remo said. "And you, asshole, are absolutely not welcome."

Remo took one step through the rubble of the altar.

The vibrations from the shattered altar had rumbled down to the foundation of the temple. All at once, it seemed as if those echoing tremors returned back to the room in which Remo and Chiun stood before the leader of the ancient cult.

These vibrations came up from the ground with even more force than those that had rolled away from the granite slabs, and it was only at the last instant that Remo became aware of the whistling sound that came from outside the temple.

"Incoming!" he hollered at the Master of Sinanju.

Remo and Chiun both managed to leap behind the nearest shattered slab of altar and were thus protected when the first shell detonated against the side of the temple.

The wall of the main room exploded inward, collapsing part of the roof above. The tons of rock that did not cascade directly into the room skidded down the side of the temple to the forest floor far below.

Remo hopped back to his feet. Through the new opening in the wall he saw a wash of white sky above. Below the pale sky the trees were swaying. As Remo watched, the trunks began to split apart then fall to the ground, crushed beneath the treads of rumbling tanks.

More shells came whistling in, exploding against the lower wall of the temple. Others blasted apart other buildings that had remained intact for thousands of years. The Chinese Army was reducing the City of the Dead to rubble.

"That idiot Yilin is driving his men straight into the poison!" Remo yelled to Chiun as another shell whistled past the gap in the wall and exploded somewhere far too near for comfort. "I've got to warn him back. You get the Leader."

He glanced to where the blind man had been sitting.

The Leader was gone.

"Well isn't that a spoonful of shit on the shit sundae," Remo groused.

He jumped over the ruins of the altar to the bench behind it. He flipped the stone seat over. In the floor underneath was a pitch black hole just large enough for a man to fit through.

Remo started to jump in the hole. Chiun grabbed his arm.

"No, my son," Chiun said. "We do not know what awaits us down there. Come. This place of evil will not stand much longer."

The Master of Sinanju was right. The number of shells being lobbed into the ancient city was increasing as the Chinese army closed in. The temple was the most visible landmark, and so was recipient of a relentless barrage.

The floor was beginning to buckle beneath their feet. More of the ceiling began to give way, collapsing great chunks of stone that thundered down all around.

Remo abandoned the hole through which the Leader had escaped. He and Chiun raced back the way they had come.

Walls fell around them, belching clouds of dust. The stairs rocked beneath their feet as they raced down to the ruins of the city.

Poisoned smoke still poured from the holes that had not yet collapsed in the sides of the temple. When they hit the ground the two Masters of Sinanju found themselves in a dense fog which was nearly impossible for even their keen eyes to see through.

They ran back the way they had come, and soon emerged from the leading edge of the cloud. They found they were racing into an advancing army.

Tanks led the way, followed by trucks and a smattering of jeeps.

General Yilin was standing atop the lead tank. He waved to Remo.

"I did not get your signal, but I saw the smoke," the Chinese general proudly announced.

"Great," Remo hollered up at him. "Now turn everybody around and get them the hell out of here, unless you want even more bodies on your hands."

In a past life Remo had been a beat cop. He never imagined back then that he'd be called on to be a traffic cop in a forest in Manchuria. By tweaking enough ears of drivers, plus the delivery of a few well-aimed rocks, he managed to turn back the Chinese army before any of the men succumbed to the smoke pouring from the ruined temple.

Remo herded the caravan of military vehicles back through the forest and to the tent village that had sprung up outside of Guizhou.

Dr. Connie Pelisse had been waiting anxiously with the Chinese civilian medical experts. Her face lit up when she spotted Remo walking with Chiun next to General Yilin's tank. She ran over and threw her arms around his neck.

"Remo! You're okay!"

"Down to the last corpuscle," he said. "You can have your sample now."

When she planted a kiss on his lips he wasn't sure at first if it had more to do with his blood than it did with him, but after it went on for a few long seconds he didn't care.

A throat cleared behind him. He would have severed the vocal cords of whoever was responsible for the interruption, but it wound up it was General Yilin and Remo didn't feel like causing an international incident.

"I was instructed to deliver this to you in a week," General Yilin said, his tone questioning. "But I am not sure under the circumstances if now…"

The general held out the letter Chiun had entrusted to him in the hotel in Beijing. Yilin glanced, confused, from Remo to the Master of Sinanju, who stood a few feet away.

Chiun's eyes grew wide. He leapt for the letter. Remo was faster.

Remo tore open the envelope and held the note written on hotel St. Regis Beijing stationary out of reach of Chiun's grabbing hands.

He only read a few lines before the Master of Sinanju managed to snatch the letter from his fingers. The old Korean's slashing fingernails quickly reduced the sheet of paper to confetti.

"I feel the same way about you, Little Father," Remo said, grinning. "Of course, with a few less 'dimwits,' but otherwise we're on the same page."

The Master of Sinanju glanced at Yilin and the rest of the nearby soldiers. Chiun's cheeks flushed red.

"Please, Remo," the old Korean said. "You are embarrassing me in front of the Chinamen."

Before his pupil could make him even more uncomfortable, the wizened figure turned and quickly marched away.

Remo was still grinning as his elderly teacher ducked for cover behind a rolling Chinese tank.

CHAPTER 32

As the Leader stumbled through the Forest of the Dead, he cursed the crippled leg of this new body.

The tunnel down which he had fled led a mile outside the ancient city. It would have been an easy escape had not a chunk of falling granite crushed the bones in his lower right leg. As it was he had barely managed to crawl up into open air.

The pall of poisonous smoke was to his back, as was the village of Guizhou, the Chinese army, and the hated Masters of Sinanju.

But he was alive.

As long as he survived, the Creed lived.

And he was not alone.

His young acolyte from the temple held the struggling Leader up under the armpits. The two of them picked their way over the ruts and rocks on the forest floor, the Leader dragging his crushed leg behind him.

Vengeance would still be his. His only error was not taking more lives when he had the chance. He should not have focused solely on revenge against the men from Sinanju. He could have slaughtered many more at that school in New York. Next time. For there would always be a next time for the Leader.

He bumped his broken leg against a log. The pain was excruciating. For a moment he pressed his eyes shut and waited for the blinding pain to pass.

The instant he closed his eyes, the young man who had been propping him up abruptly released his grip. The Leader stumbled and fell against a tree trunk.

"Fool," the Leader snapped. "Help me up."

He opened his eyes.

He found that the young temple acolyte could not have helped him even if he wanted to. He could not see, but he could smell the fresh blood. It would have been impossible for the younger man to assist the Leader now that his arms had been detached and flung into a nearby bush. The young man was lying on the ground, a bubbling crimson declivity in the center of his pale forehead.

Two figures appeared before the Leader. He felt the warmth of their bodies and could sense the hot blood coursing through their veins. It was just as well that he could not see that one was young and smiling, the other was old and irritated.

"How's it hanging, Count Chocula?" Remo said. "We flipped a coin to decide what to do with you. Tough luck. Heads you lose."

Remo's hand sliced through the air from the left, Chiun's from the right. The hands traveled through opposite sides of the Leader's neck. They met in the middle, and when they did the leader of the ancient cult's severed head toppled from his neck and thudded to the ground.

Chiun did not wait for the body to join the decapitated head. He spun around and marched back through the forest.

Remo looked down at the twisted, headless remains of his old enemy.

"It was an honor to have killed you," Remo said. "Again."

He waited until the animating orange mist seeped from both open ends of the severed neck. It rose into the air and dissipated on the breeze. The Leader was gone.

Remo turned to follow the departing Master of Sinanju, leaving the corpse of the last of the Chinese vampires to rot in the dense heart of the forgotten forest.

EPILOGUE

"WE DO NOT KNOW THE SOURCE of the viral outbreak in Guizhou," Dr. Lin Chaing said. "If the military is aware, they have not been forthcoming. We only know that which we have been told, and we were assured that this was the only survivor."

Chaing and his two companions were walking down a long, antiseptic corridor. Even though the corridor had been sealed behind them to prevent the escape of anything microscopic, the three doctors were wearing only white lab coats over their civilian clothes. The two men wore suits, the lone female in their small group wore a white blouse and black skirt.

Hazmat suits were necessary in many rooms throughout the complex, but the halls connecting them were safe unless there was an incident with containment.

"An entire village was infected," Chiang said. "Apparently he was the cause. He had entered some nearby woods with a company of soldiers. He was the only one to come out. Whatever he encountered, he brought to Guizhou."

"A team should be dispatched to investigate the source in the woods," the female scientist said.

"I suggested the same thing, Dr. Fan," Chiang said. "They are off-limits. In fact, Guizhou has been removed from all official maps. A team that was onsite was recalled. WHO teams that arrived to offer assistance were detained in Beijing, and ultimately sent away. The only source of information available to us is here, in the institute."

They had reached a window at the end of the hall. A brightly-lit room lay beyond the thick, sealed glass. Men in full hazmat suits worked around a figure that was strapped to a table in the center of the room.

"His name is Captain Gao Tiaphang, and he was with the Chinese People's Liberation Army," Dr. Chiang said. "Captain Tiaphang is a remarkable specimen. It is not scientific to say, but his blood is basically poison. He simply should not be alive."

"What is wrong with his hair?" Dr. Fan asked.

"We do not yet know. We assume a side effect of whatever he was exposed to in that forest. His hair has been falling out in clumps the past few days. His teeth as well. He has developed an inexplicable case of kyphosis. Experts we have consulted say that they have never seen a spine become so curved so quickly. It is something seen in much older patients. But he seems otherwise healthy."

It was as if the man lying on the table could hear what was being said about him, despite the thickness of the protective glass that separated him from the three doctors out in the hallway. He very slowly turned his face in their direction.

Dr. Fan gasped.

"Ah, I should have mentioned his eyes," said Dr. Chiang. "We cannot figure out the source of his sudden blindness either. He could see perfectly well until a few days ago. That tissue formed rapidly. Whatever it is, it is far thicker than normal cataracts."

The man who had until recently been Captain Gao Tiaphang smiled a mouthful of bloody sockets at the spectators at the window.

Dr. Fan shuddered. So, too, did Dr. Lin Chiang, although he hid it better than his female subordinate. It would not do as director of the institute for him to openly display revulsion at one of his test subjects, especially one whose unique system might be able to unlock the secrets to dozens of viruses currently plaguing the world.

"Come, I will show you the data we have collected thus far."

Dr. Lin Chiang, director of the Wuhan Institute of Virology, shepherded his two subordinate scientists back down the sterile corridor.

READ MORE

If you enjoyed *Blood Brotherhood*, no one's gonna stop you from clicking back to whatever online merchant sold it to you and leaving a nice review. Maybe with some stars attached. Do the man a solid, hey? That's the nature of the ebook biz, sweetheart.

Maybe you'll like some of the others in the *Destroyer* series, too. There's a lot to like, and the odds are this isn't the first one you picked up, anyway, so you know what you're in for. Get the straight skinny from Warren Murphy et Fils at destroyerbooks.com.

Dark Horse
Destroyer #89

His name was Remo, and he had a dilemma.

Should he do the hit before, or after, the target was baptized?

It was, Remo had to admit, a first.

Remo had done hits many times. Too many to count. Big shots. Small fish. This particular fish was big. And ugly. There would be no mistaking him amid the small army of Federal marshals, FBI agents, press, and invited observers that, according to Upstairs, were due at any moment.

It couldn't be too soon for Remo Williams.

He was crouched in a thicket on a spongy isle in the heart of the Florida Everglades. It was hot. The air steamed. Love bugs danced in the heat. Remo showed barely a trace of sweat on his cruel face and bare arms. Still, that did not mean he was comfortable—only that he was the master of his own body.

For twenty years he had not felt cold, or heat, or pain or any ordinary discomfort that he was not able to will his body to ignore. For twenty years he had breathed not merely with his lungs, but through his entire body: nose, mouth, unclogged pores. For two decades he had been Sinanju. A Master of Sinanju. The latest Master of Sinanju in an unbroken line that stretched back to the dawn of recorded history. A line that had begun in a ramshackle fishing village on the West Korea Bay where men hired themselves out as assassins and bodyguards in order to feed the village, and now continued in Remo Williams, the first white Master of Sinanju, who served the newest empire on earth, the United States of America, as its secret assassin.

On a nearby hump, a heron flew up.

Remo had heard it unfold its wings preparatory to flight. The sudden upflinging of colorful feathers did not take him by surprise —although it startled an alligator into slithering into the water.

Why would anyone pick the Florida Everglades to be baptized in? Remo wondered, not exactly for the first time.

It was probably the least of the questions hanging in the humid Florida air.

Remo had been assigned the job of eliminating General Emmanuel Alejandro Nogeira, the deposed dictator of the Central American nation of Bananama. Snuffing out General Nogeira was something the Medellin drug cartel, assorted political enemies, and even the U.S. Rangers had attempted over the years.

Ever since he had risen up from rent-a-colonel in the Bananamian version of the CIA, to the day he was seized by U.S. forces as they liberated the country he had bankrupted through greed and corruption, Emmanuel Nogeira had proven immune to assassination.

The former general and self-proclaimed Maximum Chief had grinningly attributed his longevity to Voodoo–specifically to the red underwear he wore to ward off the Evil Eye. He ascribed his continual survival to a wide array of charms, friendly spirits, and ritual sacrifices—usually involving beheaded chickens. In actual fact, he had simply found the perfect—if somewhat inconvenient— sanctuary from his numerous enemies.

A United States federal prison.

The U.S. government had proclaimed a great victory on the day they captured General Nogeira. American servicemen had lost their lives in the effort to bring him to justice. He had been spirited into the U.S. and charged with violating American law through a pattern of drug-smuggling activities. The evidence against him was overwhelming.

Then General Nogeira proceeded to turn the tables on his captors, making a mockery of the American judicial system. He demanded—and got—prisoner-of-war status, a private cell, and privileges usually reserved for criminals serving time in corrupt Mexican jails. Not to mention the unfreezing of his assets.

Despite this, Nogeira had been convicted of drug trafficking, and sentenced to life without parole. But no sooner had that happened than the appeals began. It was estimated that the appeals process would not be entirely exhausted until the year 2093.

Since he had time to kill, General Nogeira announced that he had given up Voodoo, and was now a born-again Baptist. Or would be, once, as he put it, the "gringos" allowed him to be baptized.

Naturally, the prison authorities to whom he had put this unusual request had denied his petition, citing security risks.

Dipping into his seemingly limitless legal fund—the product of his voracious drug dealings, which he had managed to safeguard from confiscation by claiming it represented his income from the days when he was a CIA informer—General Nogeira enlisted the American Civil Rights Collective in his attempts to embrace his newfound religion.

It had taken nearly a year, but the ACRC had taken the issue all the way to the Florida Supreme Court. The Justice Department had caved in at that point. Not on principle, but because the appeals process was threatening to devour their entire operating budget.

General Emmanuel Nogeira had won—once again.

This time he publicly thanked Jesus Christ, whom he had claimed as his personal savior.

General Nogeira asked to be baptized in the Florida Everglades, claiming that it was the environment most like that of his native country, which he missed very much.

For the first time in nearly two years, General Emmanuel Alejandro Nogeira would be outside the walls of the maximum-security federal prison in Miami.

There were rumors that the Medellin Cartel would hit him then. There was other intelligence that they actually planned to liberate Nogeira and reinstall him in Bananama, which he had single-handedly turned into the major coke transshipping point between Colombia and the United States.

That was when Upstairs had ordered the hit on Nogeira.

"Not that I mind," Remo had said at the time, "but why? He's going to rot in prison until the next century. Why not let him rot?"

"Because," he was told, "the man is costing this country thousands of dollars a day in legal fees. He's a common criminal, yet he has been declared a prisoner of war, entitled to wear his uniform and to an allowance of seventy-five Swiss Francs a day. He has his own private cell, and two adjoining ones for his shredding machine and a safe that contains classified U.S. documents the CIA was compelled to surrender to him in the name of a fair trial." Upstairs thinned already thin lips. It was clear that Remo's superior was offended by all this. Deeply offended.

Remo had to admit that Upstairs had a point. He didn't care if there were hit teams sent out to interrupt the baptism. He just wanted to get the hit over with and get out of the Everglades.

So the question remained: Before the baptism, or after?

It was a serious dilemma. If he hit Nogeira before he was baptized, then the general would probably go straight to hell. After, and maybe the guy had a chance to do penance. Spend a few centuries in Purgatory. Remo wasn't sure about that part. He had been raised Catholic. The Baptists might as well have been Jains for all he knew of their theological rules. Did they even have confession?

Crouching on the spongy isle, Remo frowned. The frown made his cruel face harden into angular lines. He was neither handsome nor ugly. Certainly not as ugly as Emmanuel Nogeira, who looked like a comic-book depiction of the Incredible Toad Man.

Remo's eyes were set deep into his skull, and his cheekbones pronounced. His body was lean, almost skinny, and unremarkable, except for his wrists. They were as thick as door posts, as if some mad surgeon had implanted steel rods where his ulna and radius connected with his metacarpals.

Except that the wrists were Remo's own. The two decades of training in the discipline that was Sinanju, the sun-source of the martial arts, had produced this freakish side effect.

Remo tried to imagine what his mentor, the Reigning Master of Sinanju, would say about his dilemma.

He could hear the squeaky voice in his mind's ear after only a moment's reflection.

"Do the House of Sinanju proud. Leave no trace."

Not much help there. Remo thought back to his orphanage days, and Sister Mary Margaret.

Remo wasn't quite sure what Sister Mary Margaret would have said, but it probably would have entailed calling off the hit. Not an option for America's secret assassin.

Finally, Remo considered the counsel of his superior, Dr. Harold W. Smith.

It was easy to figure out Smith's hypothetical advice. "Just do it quietly," Smith would say.

That went without saying. Smith, who ran the supersecret government organization for which Remo worked, had a mania for secrecy. And with good reason. The agency officially did not exist. It was known only as CURE. CURE was no acronym. The letters had no individual meaning. CURE was the symbolic name for the agency's function. That is, a prescription for American society, which criminals such as Emmanuel Nogeira had made sick by twisting constitutional guarantees to serve their own criminal purposes.

Remo had dealt with a great many people who made a mockery of the Constitution, but few did so as blatantly as General Nogeira, who wasn't even a U.S. citizen. This, perhaps more than anything, Remo decided, had offended the proper Smith.

The more Remo thought about it, the more it offended him, too.

He made his decision.

"Screw the baptism," he murmured. "Let him burn forever."

Just then the sound of approaching air-boats sent birds fleeing, and brought on a spasm of splashing in the cypress roots. Remo counted eight splashes. The identical number of alligator heartbeats his sensitive ears had detected pumping in syncopation with reptilian lungs.

Maybe, Remo thought with a fierce grin, the gators will enjoy a nice Bananamanian snack.

Remo parted a thicket of yellow-green leaves that felt like cardboard cutouts, and got a good look at the noisy procession.

There were six air-boats in all. The lead boat was choked with Federal marshals, and a few others in blue windbreakers emblazoned with the stenciled letters FBI. They brandished machine pistols.

The occupants of the second boat were too well dressed to be law-enforcement officials. Unless gold Rolexes and hand-tooled leather briefcases had become standard-issue. Remo decided that they were Nogeira's lawyers. He counted twenty. The rest must have had the day off.

There was no mistaking General Emmanuel Alejandro Nogeira, as the first two air-boats rounded a twisted oak dressed in Spanish moss, and the third came into view.

The general wore his fawn-colored military uniform, with its row of three bronze stars on black shoulder boards. His uniform was impeccable–no doubt dry-cleaned at U.S. taxpayer expense.

The general stood in the blunt bow of the air-boat, unfettered, because the ACRC insisted that it was unconstitutional to manacle an individual while he practiced his religion. The Florida Supreme Court had agreed to that–by a narrow margin.

He was, Remo saw, even uglier in person than on TV.

The general was short and squat, like a repulsive frog. Remo recalled reading that in his native country he was called El Sapo— the Toad—because of his bestial brown face and heavy-lidded serpent's eyes. He was also sometimes called Cara Piña, or "Pineapple Face." He had more acne scars than Tom Hayden.

Remo decided right then and there that the alligators probably would not touch the man. Unless alligators practiced cannibalism.

The first air-boat turned, and Remo saw that the three boats trailing in the rear were filled with reporters. There were a lot of reporters, burdened with minicams and camera equipment. They were busy interviewing a man and a woman. The man was dressed in minister's black. The woman he couldn't see clearly.

This presented Remo with a fresh dilemma. Since officially he no longer existed, he would have to figure out a way to take out Nogeira without getting his latest face on nationwide TV. Every time that happened, Upstairs insisted he go under the knife. Remo had had so much plastic surgery over the years the only change Upstairs hadn't made was to turn his face inside out.

There was a big hump of dry isle nearby, and one by one the airboats throttled down and glided up to this. Their prows beached with gritty hissing sounds.

General Emmanuel Nogeira stepped off the air-boat like Napoleon onto Saint Helena.

He lifted his hands into the air, fists clenched—a gesture that would have been familiar to anyone who had watched television in the months before the U.S. intervention that had turned Nogeira into a prisoner of war. His thick, blubbery lips peeled back into a dazzling smile. It was the only thing about General Nogeira that was not inherently repulsive. The smile was dazzling. It belonged on someone else's face.

The baptist minister stepped forward, open prayer book in hand.

"Shall we begin?" he inquired.

A throaty female voice cut in. "Not until the speech."

This brought a glower from one of the Federal marshals, who said, "We are here to allow the prisoner to exercise his freedom of religion, not to give a speech."

"Not him," the throaty voice snapped. "Me."

"No time," the marshal said.

"If I am not allowed to exercise my constitutional right to free speech," the voice growled, "then I fully intend to sue you, your superiors, and the entire United States government."

The Federal marshal turned red. An FBI agent stepped forward. They conferred briefly.

Finally the Federal marshal said, "Make it short." He did not sound happy about the delay.

The woman came into view. Remo recognized her then. Rona Ripper. The ACRC lawyer who had single-handedly spearheaded the legal drive to get General Nogeira baptized. She looked like Elvira, plus forty pounds.

Rona Ripper stepped up to General Nogeira and put her arm around his shoulder. The general's smile gained an inch at either side of his mouth as he placed his arm under hers. His hand came to rest at the small of her back, above the belt line.

"This man," she said loudly, "stands before you a victim of U.S. imperialism!"

Camera flashbulbs popped. Microphones rose. Pencils scribbled furiously in lined note pads.

"This man, this patriot in his country, was exercising his right to rule his nation as he saw fit, when murderous U.S. killer-soldiers descended from the skies and virtually kidnapped him out of his lawful seat of power!"

Remo wondered if Rona Ripper was talking about the same General Nogeira who had nullified an election, and had his goons stone the duly-elected president and vice-president of Bananama in full view of television cameras.

From his vantage point, Remo had an excellent view as the general's hand slipped down over the woman's right buttock. He gave her a playful squeeze. Rona Ripper went on as if she hadn't noticed.

"They accuse this man of all kinds of barbarism!" she thundered. "None of it true!"

General Nogeira pinched experimentally.

"This man is neither a criminal nor a torturer nor a murderer. He is kind, gentle, and loving. Children write him letters, and he answers every one of them."

General Nogeira took a fistful of buttock and gave Rona Ripper a hard squeeze.

Rona Ripper turned bright red. It was impossible to tell if the coloring was the result of blushing, or the passion aroused in her by her speech. She plowed on.

"He is a great man, a man who—"

General Nogeira's straying hand went up to the top of Rona's skirt and slipped down inside it.

This produced an immediate reaction. Rona Ripper shoved him away and simultaneously slapped him in his pocked face.

Remo took this as his cue.

He withdrew into the water. It smelled. Remo drew in a deep breath and his head went under. He struck out in the general direction of the isle where the baptism was to take place.

Even though it smelled, the water conducted sound perfectly. It brought to Remo's alert ears the slither and splash of an alligator entering the water.

Remo changed direction. He scarcely had to turn his head in the direction he wanted to go, and his body followed. That was Sinanju, which unified every cell in the body into a single responsive organic engine.

The alligator was long and greenish-black, like a mutant glob of snot, and it had hooded eyes that reminded Remo very much of General Nogeira's. Sleepy, yet as creepy.

The gator was working in his direction by kicking and pawing the water with its feet. Its mouth yawned open, disclosing rows of yellowed needle teeth

Remo knew little enough about alligators. He did know they could grab hold of a man's arm and literally saw off the limb. He got that from a Leave it to Beaver episode. Their muscular tails could lash out and stun a man senseless, perhaps kill him. Remo wasn't sure where he'd picked up that morsel of information. He might actually have read it somewhere, but the "where" escaped him, and there was no time to think about it because the alligator had suddenly shot forward, his jaws distending.

For a wild moment, Remo wondered if it was going to attempt to swallow his head. Did alligators do that?

Remo made a half fist that left his lower palm exposed and drove the hard heel of his right hand into the alligator's snout

Limp-legged, the reptile shot back as if equipped with reverse thrusters. And why not? It had just been struck by a blow that carried as much force behind it as a steam-powered pile driver.

Remo shot ahead, catching up to the reptile.

He took hold of its jaws and closed them like a crude suitcase.

Then, twisting, he took hold of the creature's forelegs, aligning his body with that of the reptile's.

Remo allowed himself to float upward. The feel of the alligator's knobby stomach against his back was like a pebbled beach. Although he was certain the creature had been stunned, he reached up and gave the slick stomach a tickle. He had heard that that made alligators go to sleep. He didn't believe it, but what could it hurt?

When the alligator's ridged back and protuberant eyes popped above the water's surface, there was no sign of Remo Williams.

The alligator started moving forward, looking for all the world like any ordinary alligator swimming through the Everglades—except that this one's legs did not kick and his long tail, instead of trailing behind, drooped forlornly in the brackish water.

Because he wanted the reptile to look as natural as possible, Remo made more splashings with his feet than he needed to pilot the alligator to his destination.

Remo's plan was simple. He was going to push the alligator along like a horny torpedo, toward the baptismal site, then slip away.

While everyone—and more importantly, every camera—was focused on the reptile, he would slip out of the water, deal with the target, and slip back. A single heartstopping blow would make it look like Nogeira had suffered a heart attack.

The unexpected crackle of gunfire made Remo abandon the plan, and the alligator. At first Remo thought they had spotted the gator too soon, and had opened up on it.

He pushed against the beast, seeking the water bottom. His idea was to get as deep as possible. Most bullets lost force and direction upon entering the water.

As soon as Remo touched bottom, he realized the gunfire was not directed toward him or the gator. There were almost no sounds of bullets plunking into water.

Remo took a chance. He thrust his head above the waterline.

He saw pandemonium.

The phalanx of beached air-boats was coming apart in a storm of automatic weapons fire. The protective steel cages over the pusher propellers seemed to be melting, the firing was so fierce.

The Federal marshals and FBI agents drew weapons and dived for cover. The media, however, simply stood their ground busily recording every bullet strike and sound as if they had papal dispensations to protect them from harm.

The sources of the firing were the approaching airboats and cigarette boats. Brown-skinned gunmen lined the rails. Assorted Uzis, Mac-10s, Tec-9s and other vicious weapons were pouring out concentrated hell.

Everyone seemed to have a role to play in the sudden drama—except General Emmanuel Nogeira. He stood frozen, bestial face going from the converging attackers to the federal agents digging in for cover. His wide mouth hung open like a greedy frog's.

It was clear the general didn't know whether he was being attacked or rescued.

In the act of pulling the general's groping hand from her skirt, Rona Ripper went white as a sheet.

General Nogeira grabbed her and wrestled her around and in front of him. Bullets chopped moss off cypress tree branches and made plinking sounds in the water.

Remo submerged.

The attacking boats were not far from his position. He laid his palms on his thighs and gave a great double kick.

Remo became a human arrow. As he passed under a pair of boats, he poked holes in the careening hulls. If any of the cameras had been underwater, they would have recorded a casual tapping. Remo used one finger. It was enough.

Perfectly round finger-sized holes perforated the hulls. Water surged in. Then the crafts began to wallow and slow down.

Remo veered toward an air-boat. Its flat bottom surged over him.

He took hold of the dangling rudder and made a fist. The fist went through the aluminum hull as if the fist were aluminum and the hull mere flesh.

Kicking back, Remo got out of the way.

The air-boat, being shallow, simply dropped. Mud began stirring up when the great spinning fan dropped below the water line.

Remo moved among the floundering passengers, pulling them down by their legs and breaking their spines at the neck like a farmer harvesting chickens.

Through the nicely sound-conducting water, Remo caught the shrill scream of panic.

"Gators! Look out! Gators!"

Remo grinned, letting a solitary air bubble escape through his teeth. If they thought he was an alligator, so much the better. He continued with his work.

He got a glimpse of brown faces as he pulled the attackers down. Bananamian or Colombian? He couldn't tell. It didn't matter. They were bad guys. Dealing with bad guys was his job.

Remo quickly brought most of the boats down. He didn't come up for air once. He didn't need to. If necessary he could hold his breath for hours, releasing only a little carbon dioxide at a time.

Keeping submerged, Remo swam around to the other side of the isle, away from the tumult.

When he stuck his head back up, he saw that the press had retreated for cover. All except one man, who lay screaming, clutching his minicam with one hand and his bleeding leg with the other. He was crying, "Medic! Medic!" and the look on his face was one of disbelief.

The FBI and Federal marshals had staked out firing positions. They were returning fire in a steady, methodical way, not wasting ammunition or firing recklessly.

A shrill voice carried over the concatenation, crying, "I'll sue! I'm suing everyone for violating my civil rights."

It was Rona Ripper. She was crawling on her stomach for shelter.

An FBI agent in a blue windbreaker started out to assist her. His head disappeared in a fine crimson mist as a dozen machine pistols sought his head.

Rona Ripper instantly started crawling backward, crying, "I surrender! I surrender!" Her face dragged in the sand because she was trying to crawl with her hands raised.

"Damn!" Remo growled, seeing no sign of General Nogeira.

A surviving cigarette boat veered off from the rest of the attacking flotilla and rounded the isle on the opposite side.

Remo figured it had gone after Nogeira. He jackknifed under and began swimming at high speed.

His ears picked up a clumsy splashing and he popped out of the water like a dolphin.

General Nogeira was stumbling out of the back side of the island. His pocked face was a picture of ugly fear.

He saw the churning boat, and his expression became ludicrous. He doubled back.

The cigarette boat piled up on the isle, and its passengers jumped off and gave chase. Some of them wore fawn-colored uniforms not much different from General Nogeira's. One, wounded, had to be helped along.

They all disappeared into the thick foliage.

Hanging back in the water, Remo wondered if he shouldn't let nature take its course. The way he saw it, the Bananamanian armed forces had dibs on the man who had ruined their country.

The decision was made for him. A scream rose up in the close, humid air.

A few seconds later, a man came stumbling back into the water. He ran blindly, his hands clutching his eyes. His fingers and lower face were slick with blood. The blood was coming from his eyes. The five bronze stars on his shoulder boards more than identified him.

The general was screaming in Spanish, a language Remo didn't understand. But the horrible tones told him all he had to know.

The man had been blinded. Probably by a knife across his eyeballs.

He proved this by stumbling over a twisted cypress root and falling face-first into the water.

Remo was wondering if he should put the suffering brute out of his misery when an alligator came charging out of the thicket.

"Charging" was the only word for it. The reptile erupted into view and ran like an absurd, clumsy dog for the water's edge. Its jaws snapped open and shut with every clumsy step.

The alligator plunged into the water and snapped up the general by one flailing arm. It wasted no time. It dragged the screaming man, pounding against its greenish hide, below the water.

After that, Remo decided to tread water and count bubbles.

When the bubbles stopped, Remo had counted forty-two. The water had become a diffuse color resembling pink lemonade.

Remo climbed onto shore with the intention of taking care of the assailants. They must be pretty dumb, he thought, to let the general get away from them like that. Or maybe not so dumb—since he hadn't actually gotten away.

The gunfire had died down.

It started up again, more ferocious than before.

Remo went through the saw grass like a lawnmower through hay. He got to the high hump and looked down.

The FBI and Federal marshals were pinned down in a crossfire. The withering fire was coming up, from the surviving boats, and down, from a line of fawn-uniformed attackers not a dozen yards below Remo's position.

Maybe he was wrong. Maybe this was a Colombian hit team, after all.

Remo slipped down to the line and began relieving the assailants of their weapons. He did this in a novel way. He literally disarmed them.

The first man to be disarmed was down on one knee hosing the low ground with his Uzi when it happened.

Remo slipped up behind him, took him by the hard balls of his shoulder bones, and separated his hands. He seemed to exert casual effort. But five thousand years of accumulated knowledge were behind the gesture.

The shoulder joints went pop!

The man's arms came away in Remo hands. He threw them in two directions.

The man jumped up and, squirting blood from each shoulder like a human lawn sprinkler, began to dance and caper until blood loss had turned him into a squirming pile on the ground.

By that time, Remo was flinging arms in all directions with joyous abandon.

This spectacle didn't exactly go unnoticed. Gunmen scattered, firing to cover their retreat. Remo was forced to waste time evading the crossfire. He could dodge bullets as if they were spring rain, but this was a slashing rain.

Remo was forced to drop to his stomach and let the storm pass over him.

When the firing finally had died down, Remo stood up in time to see the remaining attackers pile into the water under a hail of FBI return fire. The attackers were stubborn. They did not desert their comrades. A few died in the attempt to rescue the others who had fallen.

This forced Remo to revise his opinion yet again. No drug-killer worked this way. This was a military operation.

Then, under harassing fire, they waded up on a single air-boat and blasted away at the grassy isle that had been chosen for a baptism but instead had become a baptism of fire for a number of federal agents.

Hearing the FBI getting itself organized, Remo faded back to the back end of the isle and the water.

He swam past the bloated body in the fawn-colored uniform. The alligator had hold of it by the head and was vigorously attempting to crack open its skull.

As Remo, swimming underwater to avoid detection, left it behind, his ears were rewarded by an ugly crack of a sound.

He hoped Upstairs would be satisfied with the way things had turned out. The target had been taken out, even if Remo had had help. As for the attackers—whoever they turned out to be—they would have a hard time getting out of the country once the FBI had alerted Washington.

The last thing Remo heard as he put the day's work behind him was the throaty voice of Rona Ripper, threatening to sue everyone from the FBI to the President of the United States.

It annoyed him—but the thought of General Emmanuel Alejandro Nogeira, roasting in Hell, unbaptized, more than made up for that.

ABOUT THE AUTHORS

JAMES MULLANEY is a Shamus Award-nominated author of nearly 50 books, as well as comics, short stories, novellas, and screenplays. His work has been published by New American Library, Gold Eagle/Harlequin, Marvel Comics, Tor, Moonstone Books, and Bold Venture Press. He was ghostwriter and later credited writer of 28 novels in *The Destroyer* series, and wrote the series companion guide *The Assassin's Handbook 2*. He is currently the author of *The Red Menace* action series as well as the comic-fantasy *Crag Banyon Mysteries* detective series.

He was born in Taxachusetts and wishes he were an only child, save one.

WARREN MURPHY was born in Jersey City, where he worked in journalism and politics until launching the *Destroyer* series with Richard Sapir in 1971. A screenwriter (*Lethal Weapon II*, *The Eiger Sanction*) as well as a novelist, Murphy's work won a dozen national awards, including multiple Edgars and Shamuses. He lectured at many colleges and universities, and offered writing lessons at his website, warrenmurphy.com. A Korean War veteran, some of Murphy's hobbies included golf, mathematics, opera, and investing. He served on the board of the Mystery Writers of America, and was

ABOUT THE AUTHORS

a member of the Screenwriters Guild, the Private Eye Writers of America, the International Association of Crime Writers, and the American Crime Writers League. He has five children: Deirdre, Megan, Brian, Ardath, and Devin.

> "He has served as a mentor and teacher to a whole generation of crime and thriller writers."
>
> – *Prentice Hall's Encyclopedia Mysteriosa*

RICHARD BEN SAPIR was a New York native who worked as an editor and in public relations before creating the *Destroyer* series with Warren Murphy. Before his untimely death in 1987, Sapir had also penned a number of thriller and historical mainstream novels, best known of which were *The Far Arena*, *Quest* and *The Body*, the last of which was made into a film. The book review section of the *New York Times* called him "a brilliant professional."